Dead Blind

Rebecca Bradley

Do you want to claim your FREE copy of Three Weeks Dead, the prequel novella to Shallow Waters, Made to be Broken and Fighting Monsters? I'd love it if you joined my readers' club and joined the many others who have enjoyed the book that starts the DI Hannah Robbins series.

The great thing about Three Weeks Dead is that it can be read before or after Shallow Waters.

Claim it on Rebecca's website at rebeccabradleycrime.com

Prologue

St Andrew's Church, climbing out of the ground towards the oppressive granite sky overhead, passed by on his left much faster than DI Ray Patrick would have liked.

Rain lashed down, slamming into the windshield, the wipers working hard to clear the way. Visibility close to non-existent.

The orange needle of the speedometer nosed around the clock and touched close to double the legal speed limit for the road.

'This bastard is crazy,' said DS Elaine Hart from the passenger seat.

'You didn't pick that up from behind the locked door?' Ray asked.

'Well ...' She laughed.

The glow from the street lights turned the evening darkness into a sepia-toned jumble of shapes which were fractured by the blue strobes emitted from the grille of the unmarked police car.

The road wasn't particularly wide, and though it was late a trickle of traffic still crawled through the barrage of rain, as it always did, no matter what borough of London you were in, and Stoke Newington was no different. There were few pedestrians about, umbrellas pushed up against the onslaught, heads pulled down as far into collars as they'd go, but they stopped and stared as the two cars flew past them.

Ray needed all his senses about him. He was glad to have Elaine with him to update the control room and provide the running commentary. They could hear the location of their backup through their radios, so they knew an intercept was on the cards.

The Fabia they were following swerved and completed a wide overtake of the driver in front of him, who panicked as he heard the two-tone siren and saw the blues flash in his rear-view mirror. He stopped dead in the middle of the road. Ray swore. It was an all too common response. The sound and lights crashed into a driver's brain, causing them to freeze up.

But Ray was ready; he pulled around the stationary car and kept his forward momentum.

'Left left left onto West Bank,' commentated Elaine as the blue Fabia skidded hard in that direction, its tyres squealing as the driver made the manoeuvre. She braced herself, one hand on the dashboard, for what she knew would come.

Ray slowed as much as he could and took the turn, feeling the back end of the car give from under them slightly. The late-summer day had ended in a massive downpour and conditions were poor for the sharp turn.

'Shit.' Elaine pushed her glasses back up the bridge of her nose. West Bank was filled with cars parked on both sides, and it was so narrow that it was only possible for one car to drive down at once. Terraced houses lined the left-hand side of the street and thick evergreen shrubs and trees lined the right.

The problem was the parked cars. A bead of sweat slid down Ray's spine, pricking at his skin as it did so.

They'd been after this guy for the last six months and he'd finally slipped up. After he'd murdered his third victim it appeared that he might have got sloppy, or overconfident, or overexcited. A partial print had been found on the latest woman's belt buckle. It wasn't enough for a conviction as it could reasonably have belonged to someone she'd met before her murder. He could have had a plausible explanation, but the fact that they were now in a high-speed chase with him gave Ray reason enough to believe they had their man. All they needed to do was prove it once they had him locked up. As they chased him down, Ray knew the full forensic team was tearing his house apart, and he was confident they would find evidence of the crimes.

But, fucking hell, he drove like a bastard. He wanted him locked up and answering for what he'd done, not wrapped around a lamp-post or tree.

You would never have guessed there was a problem when he answered the door. You would have considered him the lover – but really, what does a killer look like? This guy looked like a stereotypical teacher. Late twenties, thick bouncy hair, dark-framed glasses and a V-neck Argyle jumper with open-neck shirt underneath. He looked smart, together in himself. He'd invited them in and put the kettle on. They were only there for a chat, after all. But before Ray knew it, the guy was out of the front door, having locked it behind him, and was away in his car.

They'd been locked in the flat. Inside! Now that was a new one. One he and Elaine would never live down. The rest of the team would give them hell about it. They'd had to break down a door – to get out.

Son of a bitch.

Now he was leading them a merry dance, and Ray didn't like it. He didn't like it one bit. His driving was reckless for the time of day and conditions. The rain was coming down in sheets, the windscreen wipers sliding at full speed. Ray lifted his foot off the gas slightly, gave him some room. 'We're not going to kill this guy tonight,' he said to Elaine as the headlights splintered in the water through his windshield.

The car in front weaved through tight spots, cars parked too close together on opposite sides of the road. A wing mirror flew off, rose upwards before it crashed to the road.

'Sounds good to me. Too much paperwork involved in that.' She held on to the edge of her seat with one hand as she updated the control room as to their whereabouts and speed on a continual basis with the other.

The Fabia was pulling away, picking up speed. It started to swerve on the narrow road.

'What the hell's he trying to do?'

'I don't think he wants to talk to us,' she answered.

'Really? But we're such nice people. I don't see his problem.' Ray dropped his speed again, 35 mph – the conditions were getting worse. Elaine updated control. Other cars were close by and would intercept shortly, all Ray had to do was keep his eyes on him.

Where the road became Holmdale Terrace the parked cars diminished and the road widened. The Fabia weaved about even more.

'You think he watches too much television and thinks we're going to ram him?' asked Elaine.

'What, 1970s television?'

'Well, he'd get further if he stayed in a straight line.'

He was on the wrong side of the road again and a sharp left-hand bend was approaching.

'Shit, is he going to pull back across?' Ray dropped his speed a little more while the driver in front stayed on the wrong side of the road as he travelled the bend.

There was a burst of horns.

A squeal of tyres.

Metal scraped against metal.

Rain continued to slash down.

Then, directly in front of them, on the bend, another car, another driver, head turned to look at the lunatic he'd managed to avoid, the crazy driver who'd made this other guy correct to the wrong side of the road to avoid a head-on collision – and this second car was headed straight for them.

There was no time. Ray saw the hint of anger and frustration on the driver's face, the relief that he wasn't dead, as Elaine's scream perforated his brain. The word brake flashed into his head with the scream.

But; time.

Time was both stretched and over. Ray didn't have the time to get the brake signal from his brain to his leg. The other driver barely had time to turn back and look in the direction his car was moving, moving on the wrong side of the road after it had swerved and missed one collision.

Elaine didn't have the time to think of her children, but the image was seared into her pupils.

The sound of smashing, crushing, twisting metal could be heard through the driving rain by the approaching officers who were there to back up Ray and Elaine.

1

Walking through the secure doors into Stoke Newington police station held a sense of familiarity. A sense of coming home. There was the everyday smell of shredded paper, printer ink, cleaning fluids from the cleaners' trolleys and the odours from all the bodies that passed through the corridors: masculine aftershaves, feminine perfumes and the very particular whiff of those who didn't bother with either.

This hadn't changed in the six months Ray had been on sick leave recuperating from his injuries. Recuperating – that was the line HR believed, and he had let them. There was no reason for them to suspect anything was wrong with him other than broken bones. His signed sick-notes had all been for his physical injuries, his fractured ribs, his arm, the more serious compound fracture in his femur, which had required surgery to place a metal rod in his leg, and which had then become infected. The punctured lung was not a big issue. It had been a small pneumothorax, taking only a couple of weeks to heal. He'd been lucky. So yes, it was the breaks that had slowed his return to work, and these were the ones he'd had to prove his recovery from. The rest, he wasn't checked for. The rest, he wasn't owning up to.

For Ray, the time away had been time to get his head around the change in his life. His bones and physical body were the easy transitions. Rest, physio and exercise to get back into shape and take him to the point where he could return; a simple enough plan.

But the other problem, that took some adjustment. When he looked back at the time he woke at the hospital to find his ex-wife, Helen, and their children in the room, it broke his heart. Remembering the look his children gave him as tears streaked their faces. Eyes flooded like broken riverbanks as pain tore down their cheeks in tidal surges. Knowing he had been responsible, with his denial that their mother was his ex-wife, his denial that he even knew her. It had been an excruciating time. Helen had been there in the first place because of the children. Because she wanted them to continue to have a well-rounded family unit, even if they were separated. Even if they were still trying to find their footing to make that work.

It was because of the hours he'd put in at this place that his marriage had broken down. Helen hadn't appreciated coming second to the job. Not many wives and husbands did – it was why there were so many break-ups. Cops were human and they sought out human warmth and understanding where it was easiest. Not that Ray had; their breakdown was lack of time together and he gave her the divorce without a fight. He couldn't argue with her, he couldn't promise to be at home more. The job made demands and he submitted. Simple as that. And he didn't deny her at the hospital because of any frictions they may have been harbouring, he denied her because he simply didn't recognise her.

The station, though: he could remember every corridor and every office, including who it belonged to – which boss or unit – and every stationery cupboard and toilet.

Ray pushed his hands into his pockets, took a deep breath and started his ascent of the stairs to his office and the incident room where his colleagues would gather in the next couple of hours or so. An early start would give him a chance to settle before the arduous task of pretence started.

Catching the villains, the chase, was what it was all about. For Ray, though, paperwork and email would be his sanctuary today. He'd seek solace behind his desk, because at least he remembered where his desk was.

Those first steps into the station after six months sick weren't the issue; the ability to recognise his colleagues – now that would be a problem.

His leg ached in the background as he walked up the stairs towards his office, old memories flooding his senses with each step. Then Ray heard footsteps headed down towards him.

A single set. Alone.

His fist clenched in his pocket. Otherwise he kept his relaxed pose in place and one foot moving in front of the other.

'Sir!' A young officer in uniform. 'It's good to see you back. First day?'

'Morning.' Ray smiled at the young lad. Dark hair, dark eyes, and, in that familiar uniform, looked pretty much like everyone else. There was no use in looking for 'identifiers' as his nurse, Elizabeth, had taught him, as he had only prepared for his team. He tried for relaxed, but felt tight. 'Yes, first day, expecting to be crushed under the weight of the paper on my desk.'

The young officer laughed and carried on down the stairs. 'We'll expect a tasking for a search party later then, sir.' And he was out of sight.

Ray breathed. No idea who he had spoken with.

It was all quiet as he had hoped when he reached the incident room and his office. The perks of being a DI meant that he had his own space to hide out in, and because he knew the routine of the team he knew what time they'd be in, even if there was a job on. He had had the foresight to call his boss and good friend, Detective Superintendent Prabhat Jain, who had said they did have a job, but it wasn't one where the unit would need to be in early, so he would have some time to himself if he wanted to acclimatise before they came in. Prabhat said he would also come in earlier than usual to meet up with him, so Ray knew they'd be able to sit and chat, but he also knew he wouldn't disclose the facts he didn't have to. He had passed his fitness to work. All his injuries were healed; he hadn't lied about any of his physical injuries.

After six months off, his office looked bedraggled. Cops had obviously used it as a spare room when they needed the space and had then tried to clear it out again when they knew of his return. Chairs were shoved to the sides against walls, and there were stacks of opened letters on his desk. Prabhat had warned him that he had opened them in case any needed urgent action. The ones left here were ones for him to deal with now.

Ray slipped off his coat and hung it up. It felt like coming home. Home after teenagers had partied in the house, but home nonetheless. He fired up the laptop on his desk and started to work his way through the hundreds of emails that waited for him.

'Well, if it isn't Humpty Dumpty himself.'

Ray recognised the voice in his doorway as that of Jain and looked at the time on the screen; an hour had passed.

'But this good egg doesn't stay –' He looked up, he had expected it, but the shock still stopped his flow. He needed to do better.

'What's that, mate?' the Asian guy in the smart suit asked as he walked into the office with a big smile on his face.

Ray needed to act as though this was normal. He forced his legs to move, stood to meet him and walked around his desk. '– doesn't stay down.' He grasped Jain's hand, and he used both hands in return, shaking vigorously.

'It's a good job, mate.' He let go of Ray's hand and pulled a chair over. 'Can you imagine the outrage if we'd have had to do a second collection for your funeral flowers after we'd already done a collection for the hospital gift, with this bunch of tight-arses?'

Ray turned back to his desk, closed his eyes. The voice was the same. He knew who he was. He now had to keep this up all day and try to figure it out for every single member of staff who walked through the door.

2

'So.' Ray walked back into his office with two mugs, warm coffee wafting under his nose. He handed one to Jain. 'What is the job we have on?' He sat behind his desk, creating distance between them. He had expected this, and had come in early so he could take it at his own pace, but still it had taken him by surprise and now there was no escape. He was locked in a room with his guv, his mate – and he needed to do this with Prabhat. If he could do this with him, then there was half a chance he could keep it up with an office full of staff. This was the big test. So much more than the MRI and CT he'd had at the hospital after failing to recognise Helen and the kids. Tests that had come back normal. The hospital cited retrograde amnesia for a while; that was until they had the real answer.

He felt his shirt start to cling to him as his body reacted to the stress. He sucked in a breath, held it, looked at the ceiling and let it go.

Jain watched him. 'You sure you're okay?'

'Yes. Fine. It's been a while since I was here. The usual worries that I might have slipped from my game, that's all.'

'Not you, Ray. I give you a couple of hours. At the outside. And you'll feel as though you've never been away.'

The voice was so familiar. The mellow tone, so soothing.

'You're right. So –' he straightened himself '– the job that we have?'

18

'It's an interesting one.' Jain crossed one leg over the other, settled himself in. 'It'll get your juices going. We've only had one charged in the UK before and not the people at the top of an operation like this. This is a unique chance to get the people behind the curtain.'

'Okay, you've piqued my interest.'

Prabhat put his mug on Ray's desk and leaned forward on his knees, an intense look on his face. 'Trading in human organs.'

'What? Seriously? In the UK? How?'

'Yes, that is what I said, yes, yes, and – that's a long story.'

'Well, I'll have to hear it.'

'I know, but we have an op running that you've come back just in time for, so I need to know you're okay to take over supervision of a case of this magnitude?'

Ray paused, looked at the Asian skin tone and the dark black hair, worn so neatly, of his friend and guv. It was the only way he knew it was Jain, and the only way he would be able to differentiate him from his DSs and DCs below him.

Prosopagnosia. That's what they had called it when one doctor had figured it out after he'd walked out of the room and then back in again. Or in layman's terms, face blindness. He was face blind. He couldn't recognise a single goddamn person. Cop, witness or offender.

It appeared that the head injury from the car accident had damaged his fusiform gyrus, which was a part of his brain located behind his right ear, though this damage wouldn't specifically show up on an MRI scan.

And there was no cure. It was a diagnosis he would have to learn to live with.

Other than his problem with faces, everything else was fine, he was healthy, fit, his mental agility was great. He could do this. He'd proved it in his life for the past five months. That was why he had made the decision to return to work, even with the problem. He had learned to compensate for his lack of facial recognition by using the tips and skills that his nurse, Elizabeth, had taught him. It worked in the main. It was only if he was in a situation when he didn't expect to see someone that a problem arose. But in this role, mostly office-based as a supervisor, working with the same people day in, day out, only going to crime scenes after the offence had been committed and long after any offender had been there, he didn't foresee a time when it would cause the force a problem. He'd spent many a day considering his options, seriously thinking about whether he ought to jack in his job because of the hand life had dealt him. But, with practice, he knew he could cope. And the job wouldn't suffer for it. After all, he wasn't what they called frontline policing. If he had been, then the diagnosis would be a problem and he would have no choice but to medically retire, leave the job. But no, he was dealing with crimes and people after the fact. There wouldn't be a problem.

So he would continue to deceive, to pull the wool over the eyes of his friends. He'd made the decision and he knew he couldn't own up. The job was too risk-averse. Christ, they had gone through a phase where you had to have training to climb a ladder when doing a search! Luckily someone had seen sense on that one, but that was the way things were going and Ray didn't want to be a casualty of the health and safety squad. He knew he could do the job and that he still had a hell of a lot to offer.

'I'm good to go,' he said. And he meant it.

3

They trickled in. Carrying handbags, cups of takeaway coffee, newspapers and bacon sandwiches. The morning unfurled before him like a flower under the glare of the sun. Steady at first and then all at once, at which point Ray felt as though he was drowning.

He'd made two lists in the week before he came back to work. Well, one was a list, the other was more of a drawing, a seating plan of the office and where everyone sat. The list was of all the people he worked with and all the ways in which he could identify them. Idiosyncrasies he could pick up on, identifiable hairstyles, heights, weights, walks, speech patterns and accents, though that one would be difficult if they didn't talk. He tried to list a marker for everyone he knew he would encounter, including the civilian staff. But, there were too many staff here, he wasn't sure he had managed to memorise it all or whether he had thought of an identifier for everyone or had chosen well for each of them. He had two detective sergeants, eight detective constables and a couple of civvies in the office full time. That was a hell of a lot of people to memorise. It was a work in progress.

Tamsin was in first. One of his two DSs; he remembered how she liked to get in before her DCs. She was eager, dedicated, focused on the job and little else. Ray didn't know if she had much of a home life. She'd dated some but they'd never seemed to stick. He remembered her hair was a bundle of curls and this made Tamsin's identification one of the easier ones.

'Guv! Great to see you back.' She refused to call him Ray. A stickler for protocol.

'Good to be back, Tamsin. I trust you've managed without me.'

She smiled. 'Only just. We need you to keep everyone in check. It hasn't been the same without you.'

'Ah, Will and Paula?'

'How did you guess?' Another smile as she flicked on her computer terminal.

He was glad she'd kept her hair the same. He started to walk back to his office. This would be a long day and he needed time to breathe, to process between each conversation, as much as he could anyway.

'Never fear, normality has resumed, Tamsin.'

The guy knocked on his office door. Ray scanned him, looked for tells, tried to figure out who this was. He scratched his head. Couldn't do it. He'd have to wing it.

'Hey, come on in.'

He was smartly dressed, not a cheap suit. An expensive-looking watch on his wrist. Not a single hair on his head. 'DI Patrick, I'm DI Joe Lang, I covered for you while you were recuperating. I'm glad you're fit enough to be back.' He held a hand out across the desk. Ray stood and took it. That was why he didn't recognise him: he didn't know him. Thank Christ.

He indicated with his hand for Joe to take a seat. 'Thanks for running the ship, Joe, I appreciate it. I hope they behaved while I was gone.'

'It was my pleasure. You've a great team here. Work well together. All I've done is keep it ticking over. I've made no changes. I'm headed back to my stomping ground today so I thought I'd show my face and welcome you back. Let you know who's been sitting in your chair and all that.'

'Appreciate it. Where is your ground?'

'South of the river, at Brixton. I'm sure there's a ton-load of work waiting for me.'

'It never stops, does it?'

'They don't know how to take a day off to let us catch up.'

'It'd be nice.'

'I know the Super arranged a briefing for your first day back to catch you up and for you to meet Billy, I'm sure you'll be up to speed in no time, but if I can do anything to help, give me a shout.'

'Thanks. Trading in human organs – sounds a fascinating one.'

Lang rubbed his already shined head. 'That's the one. Definitely an interesting job you got there. I'm quite sad to leave at this point, but as it's because you're back to full health, I'm good with it.' He stood. 'Cheers, mate.'

'Would you stay for the briefing?' asked Ray, 'You've been here from the start and I've had a call from reception to say that Billy is here. I'm new to him, it'd help if you were here to hand over.'

'Absolutely. Let's get this show on the road.'

4

The kids decided that this morning would be the day they would do everything in their power to make Elaine late for work. Paul had already left. Without fail he was out the door at seven a.m. for his drive to school. That left Elaine to get the kids out of bed, breakfasted, dressed and dropped off at the childminder so she could take them to school, so that Elaine could make it in time for her job.

But today – today she stood and watched as Halle flicked soggy cornflakes at her brother, who was turning a darker shade of red as the seconds ticked by.

Had someone drip fed Halle E numbers in the night? Elaine wondered as she took in the scene as if from a distance, watching but not quite connecting. This couldn't happen, today of all days, so if she didn't engage with it, then maybe it wasn't.

Eventually Hayden reared up, roared, split the air in the kitchen diner and broke through the fog that had been protecting Elaine. His cereal bowl flew as his hand moved upwards and caught the rim of the bowl.

Elaine shouted one word at the two children in front of her. 'NO.'

They froze. Looked at their mother. Silenced.

The bowl ended its journey upside down in Halle's lap.

Elaine ran her hands through her hair. Looked at her watch.

'Get upstairs. Get changed and get straight back down here.' The two children were mesmerised by the anger in their mother's face. 'Now.' They scuttled off.

It was his first day back at work and she'd wanted to get in early. Kids seemed to have a sensor for things like this. If ever she needed to get somewhere early they threw a spanner in the works.

Sod's law, the drive to the childminder's house was more congested than usual. An inconsequential bump between two drivers half an hour earlier had caused traffic to concertina to a crawl past the two cars as the drivers exchanged details and the younger driver waited for a parent to come along and soothe stressed nerves.

Elaine practically threw the children at Priya, and drove as quickly as the traffic allowed to get into the office. Past the new White Hart Lane ground, which had proved a challenge for a long time in her efforts to get to work but was now back to pre-construction traffic levels, south into Stoke Newington, she managed to make the thirty-minute journey in just short of twenty-five minutes. It would probably be wise to approach the post in a morning with some level of caution for the next two weeks in case there were any red lights she may have had a close call with.

She hadn't seen Ray since the hospital. She felt that he'd avoided her. He had only picked the phone up in response to her calls on one occasion. (Though, in fairness, he'd pretty much avoided everyone, if what they'd all said was right.) But Elaine had felt an undercurrent when they met at the hospital. A distance that wasn't usually there. Yes, circumstances were well outside their usual parameters in that they were both recovering from a serious car accident, but still, she hadn't expected the reserve she'd experienced from him.

She took her right hand off the steering wheel and traced the outline of the scar that trailed from the side of her right eye down and around under it. Caused by the narrow metal of the glasses she'd worn on the day of the smash, she'd now taken to wearing contacts. Something about the feel of spectacles on her face made her uncomfortable, claustrophobic almost. The skin was smoothing, feeling less rough under her fingers, but it was still visible and would be for some time. The doctors had told her she would always have it; it would fade, but the scar would stay. It didn't bother her. She had a strong marriage and she was confident in herself. It was a small section of her face and it didn't bother her. It couldn't have been avoided so there was no point in feeling angry about it, but as she felt the slightly puckered skin under her fingers, Elaine wondered if the reason for Ray's distance was this very scar on her face.

She pushed her foot down on the gas pedal and cursed the car in front when they didn't do the same. The clock on the dashboard mocked her. With every minute that passed it reminded her that she had failed this morning. Her plan to be in early, to have a quiet word, all gone to shit.

Everyone was in by the time she rushed up the stairs. It was cool outside but the stress of the morning, trying to find a spot to park in the cramped yard out back and then the run up the stairs, had only served to heat Elaine up and she felt warm, sticky, uncomfortable.

Dumping her bag on her chair, she looked around for the guv, found him in his office with the stand-in DI, cursed under her breath again and pulled the hair-elastic from her wrist and wrapped it around her hair, tying it up and away from her now damp neck.

'You okay?' asked Tamsin as she looked at the dishevelled mess Elaine knew she must look.

'Yeah.' She threw her bag on the floor and dropped into the now vacant seat. 'I wanted to see the guv before the day got started properly. You spoke to him? How is he?'

'He seems okay.' With a look from Elaine, she clarified. 'Really.' Tamsin tapped her pen on the desk a couple of times before speaking again. 'What about you?'

'Me?'

'Yes, you. You okay? You look a little … stressed.'

'The kids.'

Tamsin waited a beat. 'You know, if you need to chat … now he's back …'

Elaine tightened the band that held her hair in its ponytail and looked at Ray's office again.

5

The incident room was packed, and Ray's nerves were shot. His early morning, when he could take his return to work in his own stride, had been and gone, and now his senses were under assault as he attempted to assimilate all the people around him into the information he knew about his work colleagues.

He'd said a good morning and identified Paula and Will, two DCs on the team who worked together, travelled in together and were pretty much like a comedy double-act. And who rarely took any subject seriously. Paula had a gentle, lilting Scottish accent. Ray recalled a conversation with her when she told him she'd moved down from Edinburgh and he'd looked shocked. Her accent was too soft. She'd laughed at him and said that she wasn't originally from the city, she had been brought up by her grandmother in the Highlands, but at the earliest opportunity had moved to the bright lights. As for visual cues, she wore a large, white gold ring on her right thumb. He hoped she never decided to take it off or he'd be screwed until she opened her mouth. Relying on speech wasn't a sensible way to work identification.

Will, meanwhile, was short for a guy, but what he lacked in height he more than made up in girth. And, as Ray remembered (there was nothing wrong with his memory), he was one of the best interviewers on the team. Patient, calm and tenacious.

Standing at the front of the room with Joe, Ray felt he was about to complete the biggest bluff of his career.

'Settle down, guys.' He banged on the desk he was perched on with an empty mug that he'd found abandoned there. (A thin layer of what was probably coffee sat at the bottom, but was now growing antibiotics. They were a disgusting lot. Never ones to clear up after themselves.) The room fell silent. All eyes on him.

He could see the eyes, only he couldn't recognise a single pair.

'I've spoken to a few of you as you've come in today. It's good to be back. Thank you for your support over the past few months.' He meant it. They'd visited – even on the days he'd refused visitors, he'd been told who had been in. They'd sent cards and alcohol – though the hospital had refused to allow him to drink it. His team knew he'd prefer it to a bunch of flowers.

A cheer went up from the room.

'You managed to get out your house okay this morning I see, guv?'

Ray ran his eyes over the desks, the layout of the room, ran names through his head as he did it. Will. He furrowed his brow at the comment.

'Didn't lock yourself in.'

Ah. There was a roar of laughter around the room. Joe gave him a puzzled look; he shook his head.

'I made sure I left the key where I could find it. Doors are a troublesome issue if you're not careful.'

Will stood; he held something in his hand. 'We got you a little gift for your return, guv.' And held out his hand.

Ray walked over to him, picked up the item Will held in his palm and held it up for all to see. It was a length of wool. At one end was a child's mitten and at the other end, where the other mitten should be, was knotted on a key.

'Your office door key, in case you … you know, get locked in.'

There were guffaws all round now.

Ray held it up in a cheers pose and placed it on the desk to one side. 'Good to know I have it. Thank you.' He'd forgotten the door incident in the last six months. If there was a piss-take to be had though, cops had good memories. 'I'm grateful to have you lot to take care of me.' He smiled at them. 'But now, we have to get back to work. I understand we have an unusual job in the office and an op that we're about to run. Operation Amphibious. As I haven't been here for the start of it, I'll let Joe run the briefing, give me a chance to catch up.'

Joe stepped forward.

'Before I start, I also want to thank you for being a great team and allowing me to do my job while I've been here. You could have been a bunch of twats, but … oh, wait, you were.'

The room roared with laughter.

'Seriously, though, you bloody were.' He laughed. 'And on to the job at hand.'

6

Billy didn't know the new guy. How could he know if he could trust him? In all the time he'd been talking to the cops, he'd dealt with Joe and occasionally one of the others. The team were nice enough but Joe was great. Treated him like a human being. Listened to him. Understood what he'd done, or seemed to, anyway. Told him he'd put himself in danger, but also told him he could see why he'd thought he needed to do it. In Billy's eyes, he may as well have told him he'd done the right thing.

But this new guy in front of him, the slim guy with greying hair, he didn't know him from Adam.

He could see the guy eyeing him up, too. Giving him the once over. Appraising him, like.

Well, two could play at that game. It wasn't him putting his life in anyone's hands, was it. It was Billy who had come to them. Trusted them with information and trusted them not to fuck it up and get him killed.

The guy's dark eyes were penetrating. Billy felt the weight of his stare. He wanted to tell him to do one, but he couldn't. Not here. Not on the guy's own turf. It felt like he was committing everything about Billy to memory. Billy stood there, rigid, trying to stay calm, and took it.

Eventually the scrutiny was over and the meeting started. It was weird.

'You all know Billy –' Joe looked across at the new guy, did some weird movement with his arm '– Collier.' The new guy lifted his chin at him in acknowledgement.

Billy thought Joe would lead the meeting but as it progressed the new guy took over. Spiders skittered about in Billy's stomach. He wasn't happy about the sudden change, although apparently the new guy, Ray Patrick, had been off for a while but this was his team and Joe had only been a temporary fix.

Tamsin handed him a can of Coke. He popped the ring-pull and supped. Having something to do with his hands was a distraction. The team talked around him. Talked about him coming in and giving up the organisation. Talked about his Mama. Updating Patrick.

'Billy came to us a couple of weeks ago because he wants a gang he's infiltrated bringing down by the police.'

'Let me get this straight, Billy,' Patrick interjected as he looked him in the eye. 'You infiltrated the gang. As in, joined with the purpose of ratting them out?'

Billy gave a slow, purposeful nod.

Joe explained for him. 'A couple of years ago Billy's brother, Jamie, took over the care of Billy after their mum got banged up for a pretty nasty GBH. She used a guy's face as a weapon against a glass bottle in a bar fight. It took the hospital eight hours to put him back together that night and he's had five more ops since then.'

'Ouch.'

Joe looked at him then. 'Billy, do you want to explain what happened?'

He moved the Coke can up to his mouth, took a deep breath and drank. Wiped his mouth on the back of his hand. He knew these people. He'd been here before, but this story had only been given to Joe in private. Now he had to say it out loud to a room full of feds. He ground his teeth. Spun the cool Coke can between his hands. The room stayed silent.

Waited for him.

'Yeah. Anyway,' he started, 'Jamie, he were only three years older than me but you'd have thought he were ten years older, the way he looked after me. Though I told him he was bossy. Gave him a hard time. He took it. Worked in the local twenty-four-hour supermarket, pulled in double shifts where he could, to pay the rent. It meant I spent a lot of time on my own but he always made me answer to him. Wanted to know who I hung about with, what I did at school, shouted at me if I di'nt do me homework.'

He finished the Coke.

'Want another one of those, Billy?' Tamsin offered. He shook his head, but kept the can in his hands.

'He wanted me to do well. Said he didn't want me to end up in a place like him. So, to get him off me back I told him about the drama stuff I were doing at school. I weren't no good at studies but I were good at drama. Really good, like.'

He put the can to his mouth. Tipped it right up. The smallest dribble slipped onto his tongue. It was still empty. Tamsin got up and quietly left the room.

'Jamie was thrilled. He told me he was scared that if I didn't follow my dream I'd end up either in a dead-end job like his, a

34

gang, in prison, or dead. So he found a theatre school, but it were expensive, like. It were ridiculous to think someone like me could go to somewhere like there.' He was angry now. His voice rising. Tamsin handed him another can from the vending machine. He put the empty on the desk with a quiet clang, then flicked at the pull on the new can but didn't open it, his mind now elsewhere. 'One day Jamie told me he could get the money and then another day he had it, but he was also sick. I pleaded with him to tell me what he'd done. He made me promise to use the money to go to theatre school. No matter what happened.'

Billy dropped his head. 'I promised him.' A whisper. 'He told me he'd trawled the dark web and sold his kidney. He died two days later.'

7

'Jesus Christ.' Ray looked at the skinny black kid with the shaved head and three circular gold rings through a pierced eyebrow, who now refused to make eye contact.

'He made it his mission to bring the group down.' Joe spoke again. Giving Billy time to gather himself. 'He located them, earned their trust. He has worked his way up the group until he's at a place where he knows enough information to be able to come to us.' Joe clapped his hands together. 'And that's where we are.'

Ray softened his voice. 'It must have difficult for you this past couple of years, Billy.'

A quiet 'yes'. If he was this nervous in here, Ray didn't understand how he'd managed to infiltrate such a dark and vicious gang. Maybe it was his apparent vulnerability that had made them trust him.

'And, while we don't advocate doing what you've done, we do appreciate the information you are now able to provide. I don't think we have ever been able to get close to a group like this before. What you're doing in talking to us is incredibly helpful and incredibly brave.' This time he caught the boy's eye. 'Thank you.'

Billy looked uncomfortable.

'Billy is going to meet the man behind it all and ID him for us.'

Ray paced a couple of steps. 'You want to send Billy in? To meet the head guy?' He looked so vulnerable. He wasn't sure how this had happened.

'How else could we run this? And ID someone?' asked Joe.

'What about the website on the dark net? Surely we have eCrime working on it?'

Joe sighed. 'I spoke to them, yes. They've agreed to have a look, but they said the ability to identify anyone behind the site is slim to zero. That's why people go and set up on there. Our best bet is Billy; if it doesn't work then we'll have to place our eggs in the electronic trail basket.'

Ray wracked his brains. He'd only been brought in on this job this morning. Everyone else had had time to consider the options. He was playing catch-up. He hated being back-footed. His hand went up to his head and rubbed through his hair. 'I take it we've been in contact with the coroner, attempted to identify other potential victims.'

'We did and we are. Nothing has come up. But we are keeping an eye on that strand of the investigation. Any sudden death that comes in looking like it might be related to organ donation and it will come straight to us. And with the help of NHS England, hospitals have been made aware of the issue and will get in touch if a patient comes in ill having donated an organ.'

It was a shame there were no leads from this line of inquiry yet. There may well have been other deaths in the country. Having the hospitals on alert now helped though.

Ray paced back. 'These are dangerous people. They already killed his brother and you want to send him in alone? How old are you, Billy?'

Billy looked at Joe, then at Ray, lifted his chin. 'Eighteen now. Old enough to make my own decisions.'

'Jesus.'

Joe jumped in: 'Look, he's been in alone for the last two years without us knowing about it, what's one more day? And they didn't hands-on kill his brother …' He looked to Billy and clarified. 'Yes, they did kill him, Billy, but what I'm saying to DI Patrick is, in terms of their level of danger, they didn't physically assault with the intent to hurt.' He pulled a face at the difficulty of trying to explain what he meant when every sentence that might explain his meaning could easily be twisted to fit what had actually happened. Ray looked at him with a raised eyebrow.

'Okay, but you know what I'm saying.'

'And how exactly are we to pull this feat off?' asked Ray.

'We're going to arrest their web guy and Billy has the tech knowhow to be perfectly placed to step into his shoes,' replied Joe.

'Just like that? Any particular reason for the arrest or are we to make it up as we go along?'

Joe gave him a look. The office was quiet. Ray knew he needed to shut up and listen. The op had run for long enough while he'd been away. He couldn't come back and trample all over it. He at least needed to hear them out.

'He has a sideline in selling drugs on the dark net, but he also likes to smoke his product. We pull him over in a random stop, smell the weed in the car because he can't resist smoking in his car, which provides us grounds to search it, and I'm reliably informed there will be a stash in there that will make your local street dealer proud.'

'And this has been signed off?' Ray ran his hands through his hair.

'All of it, yes. Billy is registered as a CHIS and has a handler,' replied Joe, 'and though we don't normally attend the meet-up between CHIS and target, everyone feels that these are unusual circumstances. If we don't go to the meet then there would be no way for us to know who the guy was. He walks away after it and could disappear. So we go as well, and that keeps Billy safe. We'll need him to give us a signal that the top man is there, and we swoop in.' Joe made it sound so simple.

Billy watched the exchange, more concerned the longer the two detectives talked. Ray looked at him.

'You're okay with this, Billy?'

He looked to Joe. 'I'm okay.'

His second DS, Elaine Hart, then took Billy out. Billy didn't need to know the specifics of the police side of the op, he was here to provide the info that would get them there, and the information he'd given them was like gold. Shiny and worthwhile.

'He okay?' Ray asked when Elaine returned after breaking away from the staffing conversation. Ray hated that he had to identify her by the scar on her face. He had been the one in the driver's seat. Felt guilty every time he looked at her.

'Yeah. He'll let us know when the big boss-man asks to meet him after we've made the arrest. The guy is cautious so Billy thinks he will screw everyone around for a few weeks, keep them on their toes first. Gives us time to plan it out, get all the support in place we need. But it all depends on how well the website is running without the need for tech support.'

'Can't believe he's been doing this for the past two years already, to be honest. We need to get the Central Criminal Court Trials Unit involved and make sure the kid walks away from this. I'm not sure he realises he's been committing offences for the past couple of years.'

8

Vova Rusnac clenched his fists, but kept them down at his side. A muscle in his jaw flickered as he clamped his teeth together. His eyes glittered. He looked from the man talking in front of him to his friend Ion Borta sitting to the side of them. Borta would recognise Rusnac's impatience with this sliver of a man in front of them. If the man didn't shut up soon he would find out what happened to men who disrespected him.

Rusnac and Borta had come to England together from their home country of Moldova. Along with Mihai Popa. Rusnac knew a jealousy simmered underneath Borta's solid exterior because he, Rusnac, had managed to get to Romania before they'd left, and he'd secured a Romanian passport. At the time, the Romanian President had been handing out hundreds of thousands of Romanian passports to Moldovan nationals in an attempt to increase his own country's citizenship, in a belief he was providing some kind of resistance to the Russophile elements in the Moldovan government. To all intents and purposes, then, Vova Rusnac was now in the UK legally. Whereas Borta had failed to organise himself and make the journey. It was his own lazy fault.

The man Rusnac was facing off with, a small man, petite of frame, bald, with the brightest green eyes, stopped speaking. Looked at Rusnac. Held his eye. Borta turned his attention back to the television that was in the room. A makeshift office space in a temporary office building. Some put-it-together-like-Lego thing.

Then the man spoke again. 'If you insist on pushing this man through, I can't guarantee he will survive.'

Rusnac took a deep intake of breath, a whisper heard beneath the clatter of the television.

The male stopped. Waited.

Borta kept his eyes on the screen but his concentration was on the conversation. If it was going to turn from talking to something else, he didn't want to miss the first hit.

'I don't care if he survives. He is paying and he knows the risk. He is signing the paperwork to say as much.'

Rusnac watched the man's face as it contorted, desperate to release more words. To say his piece. He wouldn't allow such a confrontation. 'You need to remember who pays your fees. Or should that be, who pays for your very expensive gambling habit.' His words were slow. Deliberate. He wanted them to sink in.

The man's face twisted some more. 'I'm more than happy to work for you …'

Rusnac had no patience with the word but. 'You'd rather go to your debtors and let them know you don't have the –' he stared hard at him '– how much was it?' He knew, but that wasn't the point.

The man scrubbed at his face, a flash of despair visible before he covered it with his palms. He turned away from Rusnac. A sound, maybe a whimper, came from behind his hands.

'That will be a no, then.'

He felt nothing for the man who had everything. Rusnac wasn't wealthy by anyone's standards. In fact, most of the money he made

42

was sent back home to his Mama and back to the Russians who had sent him to England, who made it all possible for him to be here, to operate here, to send the money to his Mama and for her to have the drugs she needed to live. He didn't care that he had little left for himself. He lived in a small dingy flat in a rundown area of Upton Park in London, where it felt like the walls pushed in on him and which stank of rainwater that had been left to stand for three months.

But he was a free man, living in a free country, where the streetlights were always on in the winter. He'd been used to the lights being off, to the world being pitched into a soulless darkness you were afraid to enter. Here he was in a country where water ran out of taps instead of being collected from rain-filled wooden barrels, and where heat wasn't derived from baked potatoes in your pocket.

So when he was confronted by the whimpers of a man who had squandered so much and took so much for granted, there were no feelings other than disdain and a desire to bend the man to his will. They had a job to do, this man and him. Along with Borta and Popa and the others he had recruited. All he needed was for them to do what they were supposed to do, without any drama.

The man pulled himself straight. Rusnac smiled to himself: he didn't have the height for this to be much of a statement. 'Yes, I will do this. Because that is what I have signed up for. And because he understands the risks himself. But, make no mistake about it, I will be outlining the risks to him.'

'Outline away.' Rusnac was done now. 'Because there is one thing stronger in this world than guarantees.'

'What's that?' asked the man.

'Hope,' replied Rusnac. 'We are giving him hope.'

9

Celeste was parked in the bay across the road from the police station, in front of the solicitor's. Ray took a deep breath, reminded himself he wouldn't recognise her and that he'd need to accept it, and opened the passenger door, sliding in beside her.

She looked just as beautiful as she always did. She'd come straight from the office, her hair was tied up and she wore a fitted black skirt suit with a cream blouse and heels. There was something about the cut of her clothes, even though they were similar to those worn by the women at work, that made her stand out. He imagined it would be something to do with the price tag.

'Hey, how was your first day back at work?' She leaned across the centre console for a kiss. He closed his eyes and kissed her lightly. The scent of her perfume reminded him of who she was as it tickled his senses in the closed confines of the car.

'It was full on.' He leaned back in his seat. 'They've thrown me straight in the deep end, certainly no gentle return to work.'

Celeste indicated, checked her mirrors and nosed her way out, not waiting for a break in the traffic – she was going and she was making them let her out. That was her way. She was a determined woman, and predictably, with the nose of her car stuck out, the car behind waved her through. 'How do you feel about that?'

Ray sighed. It really had been a long day. 'I don't know. On the one hand, I could have done with a steady day to reacquaint myself with work and to catch up on all the paperwork that has accumulated in my office, but on the other hand, it's one way to feel as though you've never been away.' He looked at her profile. Something about it was easier to recognise than her face. 'There's something to be said for being thrown in like that and not worrying that you've lost what you had.'

She turned to him and he looked out of the passenger window. 'You would never lose your work game, Ray. You're too passionate about it.' She went back to driving. 'So where do you fancy going to celebrate this throwing into the deep end?'

'You choose.' He smiled. 'I think I'm too tired, trying to swim up from the deep end.'

Celeste laughed. He loved the sound of her voice, the scent of her in the car, the clothes she wore. All the familiar things that were part of who she was.

'Well, I fancy Thai, then.'

YumYum's was warm and welcoming; the dark wood and discreet lighting always made Ray feel comfortable there, and the food was delicious. He sat back and rubbed his face.

'You look tired,' Celeste observed.

He was tired. It was hard work with Celeste. Facing her this way. Not recognising her. It had been difficult since his release from the hospital, but he had worked on it. They had had time to work on it. But he was tired and a little frazzled from having to push himself so hard to identify everyone throughout the day. The map of the office he had drawn and the list he had made up constantly scrolling through his head, as well as the everyday work he had be getting on with. This was an added complication and he wasn't sure he could continue to juggle it all.

'I am tired. I'm sorry.'

'We'll get the bill and I'll take you home. It's been a long day.'

He rubbed his face again, frustration needling him. 'I don't want to cut short your evening. We can stay, have another drink. Maybe dessert?'

'Ray.' She waited until he looked at her.

Reluctantly he dragged his eyes over. He wished he could tell her the truth but he was afraid that having something wrong with his head would break them apart.

'Stop it. I understand you're tired. It's not a problem. You've been off work six months. You've had a busy day. Let's get you home where you can get some rest.'

10

'What the hell do you mean we're doing it this afternoon?' Ray yelled at Jain, who in turn raised his eyebrows, an expression intended to remind Ray of his higher rank.

Ray sank into the chair behind his desk. A sigh escaped as he bent over to his knees.

'We're not ready,' he said, still doubled over, his voice subdued now, buried in his lap. 'We only made the arrest the night before last, we expected him to play Billy a bit longer before agreeing to meet him.'

'Billy has said the guy has brought it forward specifically so that no sting can be organised in time.'

'The guy would be correct then, wouldn't he? We only spoke about this with Billy at the briefing three days ago, how are we supposed to organise an operation like this in two hours, Prabhat?' He looked up and stared into the unrecognisable face of his friend.

'You can do it because we have to. This is our one shot. We can't screw it up.'

'God dammit, Prabhat.' He was right about that at least. 'But we're nowhere near organiscd for this. I take it you'll write the policy book for Billy being in there, because I'm damn well not signing off on it.'

'I'll speak to source handling and let them know it's on. He's signed up as an official CHIS. It shouldn't be a problem.'

Ray scrubbed at his hair as his mind whirled. This wasn't a situation he particularly wanted to put himself or his team in. Not with his diagnosis. There was no fighting Prabhat on it though. He wasn't budging. If he thought about it sensibly, it shouldn't prove to be an issue. He was to travel to the meet with the team he already knew, and it was Billy who was responsible for the identification. His team would be doing the leg-work. His role, as always now, was supervisory. They'd control Billy and the offender once Billy indicated the one they were after. His own inability to recognise a face should not cause this particular operation a problem.

As far as that went, he was good. As far as them not having enough time – he still wasn't happy.

The door to the office opened.

A female. Bundle of curls. 'Tamsin, you know what we're doing?' Ray asked.

She looked at Prabhat. He gave a barely perceptible nod. She'd known before Ray. Prabhat had clearly wanted her on side because he knew Ray wouldn't be.

'I do. It's a tough call, but these people are killing civilians desperate for new lives. We need to take them out.'

'And Billy?'

'Billy's been in with them for two years. No need for them to suspect him now. We scoop him up with the rest of them, all's good.' She smiled. Made it sound so simple.

Only things were never as simple as they sounded.

11

It was tight, but Ray was happy everyone was in place. Billy had texted him the location. The gas holders at Beckton. An unusual place to meet, but Ray could see the appeal. It was open land. Wide open and flat. Home to the gasworks, and across Amanda Way was the shopping outlet with a steady stream of civilians, and in the other direction the DLR depot. From their vantage point they would be able to see any surveillance teams easily. Ray had a full team, but had managed to secrete them from view. There were some trees that offered some shielding and he had made use of the shopping outlet's car park. It was further back from the actual meet than he'd have liked, but they'd had enough time to attach some discreet microphones and cameras to the first rung of the gas holder. They had eyes and ears and they would also be able to get to Billy within a few seconds when the time came.

Today the sky was a bright blue, littered with white clouds skipping their way gently across. Below, the gas holders and gasworks offered a dreary grey contrast. A grim scene of bland, industrialised land.

Ray hadn't been happy about the speed with which they'd had to organise this. He would rather be prepared than for the op to go wrong, but they'd managed to do it and now they had an hour before Billy was to meet more of the key players, including the head of the organisation.

How the hell Billy had managed to make himself so indispensable Ray didn't even want to think. The kid had been through enough, but it was a subject they'd have to pick apart when this was all over.

Who would have thought this was happening in the UK? In their own backyard. Yes, he knew people were desperate enough to go abroad for organs, but he hadn't heard about an organisation that conducted the surgeries here.

'You okay, guv?' The scar on her face. His stomach clenched. Would this happen every time he saw her?

'Yes, just thinking about what Billy has been through.'

'Can't have been easy. Pretty isolating for him, in fact.' She looked Ray in the eye. All he could focus on was the scar that ran down the side of her eye. 'People are resilient though. I hope the good he does today will go in his favour.'

Ray knew he looked fine now. Fit and well. He could never tell her what he struggled with every day, no matter what they had gone through together. He had to keep this between him, his doctors and Helen, otherwise he risked it leaking out and him losing control of the situation. Nor could he tell her how strung-out he felt about having to remember all the little identifiers about people. How he hated that the way he remembered her was by her scar. The scar he was responsible for.

'Guv?'

'Yes, sorry. I would think this will indicate his real intent, don't you?' He checked his phone. 'The show will be on the road soon.'

It was then that his phone beeped with an incoming text alert:

Location changed. They want to make sure no one involved with cops. River Road, Barking, half an hour.

What the hell? They might get there in time, but they certainly couldn't get electronic surveillance coverage set up, they couldn't get microphones in place, or cameras. Again it was a wide open space. They would be hard pressed to get any officer close enough to see or hear anything. He called Billy but there was no reply. He sent a text message.

Abort.

Billy responded.

No. This is your chance. Be there.

Shit. He was being led around by the nose by a kid who was in too deep, and there was no way to stop it.

This was falling apart faster than a sandcastle in the incoming tide.

12

The knuckles on Ray's hands glowed white as he gripped the steering wheel. He imagined that, in contrast, his face was some shade of red; he felt as though someone had inflated a balloon in his head and it was about to burst at any minute.

'Damn stupid kid. He'll get himself killed.' Elaine was in the car beside him, which didn't help his stress levels. It was the first time he'd driven with her as a passenger since the accident. He felt as though he was driving a piece of valuable china about and one wrong move would smash it into small pieces that would never be able to be put back together again.

'He's been okay until now. If he pushes against the instructions he's been given, it's more likely to appear suspicious,' Elaine said.

Ray grunted. It didn't help that he hadn't been in control of the job from the start. It was always much easier if you knew the job inside out, if it was yours from the get-go. Walking in like this, halfway through, was probably what was setting his teeth on edge.

'We'll never set up in this warehouse in time. Not with the surveillance equipment.'

'We'll have to do it the old-fashioned way then.' A sensible response every time. 'And at least with a warehouse we'll be able to get closer to them.'

She had a point. He sneaked a glance at her. Saw the scar sliding down her face and stared back at the road.

The call to the source handler to try to get him to change Billy's mind had been in vain. Joe had a better relationship with Billy than anyone, as he had been the person involved from the very start, but he was no longer involved. And they didn't have time to pull him in now. It had most definitely turned to shit.

Will and Paula were in the car behind him, and Tamsin and others in the cars behind them. Ray turned left and watched in his rear-view as they continued on the road they'd been on.

'Where are we going?' asked Elaine, a puzzled tone to her voice.

Shit. He had no idea. He had thought it was this way but now he'd taken the turn he didn't recognise where he was and he knew he'd got it wrong. As well as his failure to recognise faces, it seemed he had also lost his sense of direction. He'd been warned that this could happen.

'Dammit.' He slammed his hand down on the steering wheel. 'Dammit Elaine – I'm sorry. I'm exhausted. I didn't sleep well last night. Some residual pain.' Shit, he was a bastard. He hated to lie to her like this. To use his injury. 'I'm losing us time messing up like this. Can you take over? I don't want to screw up again.'

He didn't want to look at her.

'Yeah, sure.'

He checked his rear-view and pulled over and they swapped seats. Elaine took over the driving.

The A13 was rammed with traffic and Ray could feel the tension rise as they attempted to manoeuvre through the three lanes. They arrived at the derelict warehouse on River Road with just short of fifteen minutes to spare. It sat to the side of where the Sunday market was held, in clear view of the old power station. There had been no recce of the premises done. No time to get up close and personal with them.

The sky was still bright but the air felt cooler here. The Thames was behind them now and carried its salty, oily life on the breeze. You couldn't see it, but Ray knew it was there. Could feel it in the air. Like an animal stalking in the brush. Silent. Deadly.

He barked brief orders at the team. Directed them to some positions. They were to get as close as they could without being seen. Ray wanted Billy protected.

His team had to try to find spots around the perimeter of the run-down metal-cased building that would both hide them and give them a vantage point to see from.

He was frustrated as hell. To do this in such a rush was asking for trouble.

Ray checked the inside of the building. It was no longer in use but it had been abandoned without being cleared out properly. There were pallets filled with who knew what, wrapped in blue plastic that was now peeling off, and lifting equipment to move the pallets around, and at the rear of the building was a mezzanine created with slim metal girders, now rusting, underneath which were stacked several gallon drums.

Ray squatted down behind a group of the large rusting drums that were backed into a corner. He pushed his hand against one. It was cool to his touch and felt hefty. It was full. He pushed against another. Again, full. This would make do as a surveillance point. The drums were heavy, they wouldn't move – but he would have to stay completely still, as any slight movement could be spotted through the slivers of gaps between the drums. But this was the only place he would be able to get a visual for when Billy was able to give them the identification signal. It would have to do.

With no electronic visual or audio equipment, he needed eyes and ears for this to work, and he was only willing to risk himself. All he needed was for Billy to indicate that they had the right guy, and Ray could shout everyone else in.

The earpiece that connected him to everyone else involved in this operation buzzed gently in his ear, letting him know that it worked. Static filled the air as they waited it out. His thighs burned as he crouched. Bones that had knitted back together ached. He didn't move.

Several silent minutes dragged by and then a single voice, Will's, came over the earpiece.

'An old Ford Mondeo has pulled in. There are three nominals inside but from this point I can't get a good look at them.'

It had started.

Ray swore to himself that if they got through this he would string someone up by their balls afterwards.

13

Ray had a good view inside the warehouse. He was almost bent double, crouched down behind the drums, knees creaking, leg throbbing, complaining at him that it shouldn't be held in this position for any length of time. But he couldn't move, he had a perfect spot, the full length of the building was visible. He could see the door where they'd enter, and he had a view of most of the rest of the facility, other than some of the side areas. The gap between the drums provided a straight-line visual, but it wasn't great if someone stepped out to the side.

The other problem was, he was blind to the outside and had to rely on the commentary of those who were out there. And the perimeter coverage was blotchy due to the way this had gone down. He knew not all of it was covered. They hadn't had time to organise where staff could put themselves out of view but with a line of sight. As with the Beckton gas holders, it was a good place for the organising group to meet in terms of spotting any surveillance.

A message in his ear informed him that Billy was walking in with the two men from the vehicle. It had only been possible for his staff to see the men's backs, but it was likely these were the muscle and not the guy they were after.

Billy came into view. Young, black, with the same red trainers he'd worn every time Ray had seen him, and the bounce in his walk that Ray liked to think indicated joy – though he knew differently.

They walked to the centre of the warehouse and waited. No words passed between them.

Ray watched.

Tense.

'A second vehicle has now pulled in. Three nominals again. And again I can't get a look at them,' Will reported again.

There was a pause over the airwaves as Will waited to see who would exit the vehicle.

'Confirming three nominals. View obstructed. Entering the warehouse now.'

Ray watched. Only one man entered. The warehouse was vast. It was a stretch, but Ray saw two males peel away at the door.

'Two are walking the perimeter, going opposing ends around.' Will's voice crackled over the airwaves.

As this male entered, Ray saw the two who were with Billy straighten themselves. Their shoulders went back, their heads up, their feet wider apart.

This must be him.

He sauntered over to the group of three. Not a care in the world. He was tall, nearly six feet. Eastern European. Dark hair kept tidy. Dark bomber jacket.

'So this is Billy,' Ray heard him say as he approached them.

'Hey,' Billy said, and he bounced a little on his feet.

Ray was tense, both because of his position and for how this was going to play out. He had five unknown nominals and a very untidy operation in play. After a short conversation in the middle of the warehouse, which he could no longer hear, the two males that had originally entered with Billy moved to the doorway and stood guard there, leaving Billy and the male alone.

This must be the guy they were after. He had to hope the listening equipment, no matter how far away, could pick up some of their conversation. Otherwise it would be Billy's word against the male. An arrest would no doubt give them a trail to follow, but it wasn't the best way to investigate.

Ray watched as Billy bounced on the balls of his feet, nodding at the guy he was with as he talked. Then, when he had a chance he started talking himself, gesticulating with his hands, trying to get a point across. Ray hoped he was doing it well. He had no idea how dangerous these people could be if they thought they'd been set up. He wanted it to be over, to know they had done it and that everyone was safe, because it wasn't just Billy at risk, his team was also here.

It was as he was thinking this that the operation started to spiral out of control.

14

Rusnac took a step back.

The little fuck had screwed him over. Who the hell was this kid? And how had he pulled the wool over his eyes?

Rusnac didn't mess around asking these questions. He wasn't a sit-down-have-a-cup-of-tea kind of man. He drew his gun from his waistband and pointed it squarely at the kid's head – the kid who was supposed to be a computer whizz, one who lived in the depths of the dark net like a shark gliding silent and unseen, a killer predator. The type of person Rusnac needed for his organisation.

The kid spoke but Rusnac paid no attention; instead, he pushed the muzzle of the weapon into the boy's head, kept his arm outstretched and his stance wide. He couldn't get any closer. If he pulled the trigger there'd be a fucking big mess, and though he didn't mind if he made a mess of other people, he didn't like it to transfer onto him. Not if he could help it.

He'd need to turn away. He didn't want brain matter lodged in his eyes.

How the hell had this happened? Where had their original web guy gone anyway? There had been mention of an arrest. A stop and search of his vehicle. A completely random incident. So they'd needed another guy. They couldn't operate without this cog. And as the kid was running for them anyway …

Rusnac looked across as his name was called. His guys had got twitchy when he'd pulled his gun on the kid. They were spooked, eyes like saucers. He could only see two of them, the other two were out of sight, but he knew they were there, eyes on the outside.

'POLICE. PUT YOUR WEAPON DOWN, YOU ARE SURROUNDED,' a voice shouted out from somewhere inside the warehouse.

Fuck.

Rusnac's brain started to skid in different directions; he needed to pull it back to focus on the task at hand. To get out of here in one piece. He wrapped his meaty hand around the kid's arm. It wasn't difficult. There was nothing on it. He was all skin and bone. He gripped hard.

He needed to use the kid.

Jesus Christ.

What the hell had gone wrong?

15

The minute it was out of his mouth, Billy knew he had said the wrong thing. The fact that there was now a gun pointed at his head confirmed it. He found it difficult to focus on anything but the cold of the metal on his temple. Of all the things to think about, it was how cold it felt against his skin that was at the forefront of his mind. Because it wasn't just pointed at his head, it was jammed up against his skull. Pushing his head sideways with the strength behind it.

The pressure of the muzzle on his skin came directly from the tension in the arm of the man who'd introduced himself as Vova Rusnac.

He had tried to avenge his brother's death. He'd tried to be the big man, when who was he kidding, he should have stuck to what he was good at – though how could he say he was any good at acting? His acting skills obviously left a lot to be desired. He couldn't act his way through this meet. Rusnac had picked up on the scam.

No, he hadn't played his part well enough. And where did that leave him?

The cops were here. Did that mean they'd get him out of this? Billy knew it had been a struggle for them to get here. He couldn't see them. Had they even made it in time? Rusnac was clever, he knew how to avoid, how to take precautions. He didn't trust easily.

'Look, man,' Billy said.

Rusnac's head moved around, swept the area.

'POLICE. PUT YOUR WEAPON DOWN, YOU ARE SURROUNDED.'

The cops had made it. He could make it out of here. He just had to keep his cool. Keep his head.

'Look, man,' he repeated.

The gun moved from his head down to his side, where it embedded itself deep in the layers he wore, the hoody, the sweater and the T-shirt. Through it all he could feel the gun. He was sure he could even feel the coldness he had felt when it was up against his temple. The freezing cold of metal that had the power to kill.

Billy shivered.

'What did you do?' Rusnac snarled. Hard edges cutting words up short.

How could he deny it? With what he'd said, and now the police shout. What could he say? He had to keep his cool. They'd get him out of this.

'The feds, they jammed me up yesterday and then let me out. They must've followed me, put a tail on me, man.'

Rusnac was wired. Everything about him tense, his movements jagged.

Billy's insides curled, his bladder cold, weakened. But it held. He ducked his head into his neck. Tried to make himself smaller.

Rusnac's grip on his arm tightened. He started to move. Away from where they were standing. Billy held firm. Planted his weight down towards his feet.

'Move,' hissed his captor. 'Or I'll drag you limping with a bullet in your foot.'

Billy's bladder twinged and leaked. Not enough for anyone to notice. He needed to hold it together. They'd get him out of this.

He moved with Rusnac. Away from help. He hoped someone could see them from where they were hiding. Rusnac had a firm grip on his arm with one hand while the other still forced the gun into his side. They moved as one. Billy's breath came fast.

'I didn't do this to you, man. I wouldn't do that, I wanted in. I wanted to be a part of this. I still can. Once we're away.'

'You think I'll let a snitch into my organisation?' The gun pressed in further than Billy thought possible.

'It's not what you think –'

'It's not? So, tell me, young Billy, how did you say you knew our earlier customer Jamie?'

He'd blown it. He'd let his emotions lead him. He needed the cops.

16

Ray stayed crouched for the moment, out of the line of fire. Noise filled his head as panic lit up the radios. He kept his eyes trained on the male and Billy. The male was nervous. He looked around him, wanted a way out. The guys that came with him started to move; they ran towards him, then back away, orders were barked and shouting ensued. Ray didn't understand what was said as most of it was foreign.

The gun was stuck firmly in Billy's ribs. He couldn't see it, but he knew it was there. He'd kept his eyes trained on it and had watched as it transferred from Billy's head to his side. Plus, he could tell by Billy's wild-eyed demeanour that he was under threat.

Ray relayed events to the team outside the doors. Told them to stay back. There was no way he would allow one of them to become a target. SCO19 support should be on their way. Although who knew how long it would take them to get out here.

The male took his hand away from Billy's arm and grabbed his jacket collar. He tugged at it hard and suddenly they were on the move.

Like jackrabbits they went hard right and out of sight behind one of the pallets.

Ray couldn't lose Billy. This had turned to shit, but he wouldn't lose the boy. Not on his watch. He stood. His bones protested but he ran forward. 'The male is on the move with Collier; all units stay back. I repeat, he is armed, stay back. Make any arrests of the other males that have scattered, if possible.'

The noise was like a base party in his head as officers made visual contact with fleeing nominals. As he moved behind a stack of pallets he saw the other exit at the side of the building. The steel door was open.

'One IC2 male and the boy have exited the building. Anyone have eyes on them?' he shouted into the radio.

No one did.

Ray paused at the door. Rested his back on the hinges. Felt the rounded metal dig into his back. He took a deep breath and looked around the frame. The male, dark bomber jacket, was still moving, the gun still jammed into Billy.

Ray ran out after them.

'Police. Stop,' he shouted. Billy turned and looked at Ray but he couldn't decipher what passed over his face.

Billy ran for the man who held the gun to his side. He ran hard and fast and Ray could feel his bones hurt as he pushed himself to keep up. His leg, still strengthening, struggled. Pain shot up to his brain but he would not let Billy out of his sight.

They ran the length of the warehouse, out into the open air, where the smell of the Thames pricked Ray's nostrils. The male pulled Billy across the flattened, hardened dirt towards a side road. Ray wanted to stop, his body complaining. But he wouldn't. He wouldn't give up on the boy.

As the burn kicked into his brain they hit the tarmacked lane that led to a business at the edge of the Thames and the male pulled Billy to a stop. He stood and looked Ray in the face, paused, and then smiled.

A solitary bird flew overhead and squawked down at them as it passed.

Ray leaned forward, palms on his knees, gently panting, neck bent upwards, eyes forward on Billy and the male.

The male smiled.

A smile that said it all.

Ray's heart slammed heavy in his chest. He could feel it reverberate loud in his ears. Felt it bang against his ribcage. His legs shook. He straightened himself. This man had a smile on his face. He could still recognise a smile, and a smile like this didn't signify fear. This man was not scared right now.

Ray's brain scrambled for sense but he focused with all his energy on the face of the man. This was about to go wrong. He needed to focus. This was the hardest thing he would ever have to do.

In the couple of seconds that followed, a moment in which the male paused for what seemed like effect, Ray pushed his mind with all he had.

Eyes.

Nose.

Mouth – a sneer.

Short brown hair.

Six feet tall.

'It's too bad, copper. Billy would have been a good soldier in the organisation. He's shown his worth and now you've gone and killed him.'

'Don't!' Ray shouted.

He pulled the trigger.

A single loud crack smashed its way through the still air.

A look flitted across Billy's face.

He slumped to the floor.

The male moved. Towards the car that Ray now saw parked on the road behind the male. A silver BMW.

Ray dropped to his knees, sliding in the already slick asphalt, tiny fragments of the road dragging at his trousers, snagging and tearing, stinging his knees. Pressing into the deep red life fluid that seeped out of Billy and now stamped itself into Ray.

He didn't have time to glove up; he couldn't remember if he had any on him anyway. He pushed a hand into the hole that gushed and used his other hand to make the shout for assistance. All the while he watched Billy as his eyes flickered, his mouth moved without sound, like a goldfish out of water, and then the man who had shot him, climbing into the car and driving away.

The man he wouldn't recognise ever again.

17

For Rusnac it had been a split-second decision to shoot the kid. His mind had skittered about like marbles in a box. The cop had followed him and what with dragging the boy along he hadn't been able to lose him. The boy had been a dead weight tied to him, had slowed him down. It was this realisation that crystallised his mind, sharp and bright, that brought the moment into focus.

He'd have much rather exacted a slow and painful revenge on the boy for bringing the cops down on them like this. To show him his displeasure at the events that were unfolding. But there hadn't been time.

Shoot him in his side: that would give him time to escape because, unlike a bullet to the head, the boy would fall bleeding. He'd have a moment to feel the pain. A moment to realise he'd crossed the wrong person. To know he'd been punished and that payback was hell. And in all that, as long as he didn't fall down dead, like from a bullet in the head, then the cop would be forced to stop and offer first aid. To attempt to save his life. And he could make a run for it.

That split second had slowed so that every single action, thought and reaction was etched in his memory. His finger on the trigger. The tension in his muscle as he pulled back. The gun's recoil. The loud snap in the air. The shock on the face of the kid.

And the cop.

Rusnac remembered the weight in his other hand as the kid crumpled to the floor and he realised he had to let go of him.

The shock still registering.

He had but seconds to make his move.

The cop cried out.

And Rusnac felt a bizarre pleasure as he realised that his plan could work. He watched him. The cop. As the kid lay on the floor. Blood seeping from under him.

Then time started again and he ran. He ran for his life. Because he'd have no life if he was caught and locked up in a prison. He'd escaped Moldova. It wasn't an escape if he'd left one shithole for another.

He ran down the road to the car he'd parked there as a precaution, not thinking he'd need it. How wrong he'd been. He scrabbled at the handle and hauled himself inside, turned the engine over and moved away, foot on the gas, and kept moving until he was far enough away to stop.

He had never wanted to use the gun. He only had it because the Russians had given it to him. He never expected to use it, to have to use it.

When he pulled up he got out of the car and held his hands out in front of him. They shook as he looked down at them.

It wasn't the kill. He wasn't afraid of the violence. It was how close he'd come to being locked up and fed on slop, reminded of home. This country was rich beyond anything he'd ever known, and he lapped the cream from the unsuspecting idiots who didn't know how good they had it. If they were stupid enough to not realise how much they had here, then he had no problem taking from them. But there was no way in hell he would be taken to jail and treated like he'd been back home. No way.

Now he needed to regroup. Sort out any issues and get the organisation back on track. Before the Russians found out there was a problem.

18

Grey clouds had scudded over and now offered a leaden blanket as Ray tried to stem the flow of blood from Billy's side.

Billy, his breathing ragged and laboured, tried to speak. He wheezed and coughed as he tried to get words out.

'… was him… heads it. Organises …' He coughed again and blood trickled out of the side of his mouth.

'Stop,' said Ray as he tried to control the emotions that raged inside him, tried to hold it together in front of this person who was essentially just a boy. He pressed harder, keeping his palm flat as he tried to staunch the blood that kept seeping out, finding a way, no matter how much pressure Ray applied.

'Where's that ambulance!' he shouted into his radio. He'd already informed them of the BMW, though he'd only caught a partial VRM as it left the scene. His eyes were more caught on Billy than on the fleeing male.

'Two minutes out,' came the response. He pressed down again.

Heavy footfalls vibrated through the packed dirt as they ran toward them. Will, short and wide, and a female dropped down beside him.

'Aw fook, guv,' said Paula, the accent Scottish.

Ray kept the pressure on the wound, though it was obvious his hand wasn't enough.

'Ambulance is a minute out now,' said Will.

'Hang in there, kid,' said Paula. Voice low. She removed her jacket. Folded it up, gently lifted Billy's head, dropped the jacket on the ground and placed his head onto it.

'Will, jacket!' Ray snapped.

Will pulled off his jacket, balled it up and handed it to Ray, who shoved it over the bleeding wound and pushed down again.

Billy winced.

'You did good,' Ray told him.

'I'm …' Billy's chest rattled and wheezed some more. '…sorry.'

'Don't say that.'

Billy's eyes closed.

'You've got to hang in there. You have to finish what you started. Come on. Hold on. They'll be here in a minute.'

Blood pooled around them as they crouched and knelt with him. Ray could feel it as it seeped up his shirtsleeves. Through his trouser-legs. Could taste the copper tang. Smell it. Feel it bite at the back of his throat. He felt contaminated in death, because that was what this was. Billy's death.

Sirens punctured the still air.

The green uniforms of the ambulance crew pushed them away from Billy and started to work.

Ray, Will and Paula stood to the side, arms down by their sides, but curled away from their bodies. Bloodied hands and arms kept at a distance.

They watched the paramedics work.

Watched the blood.

No words.

Just blood.

Billy.

The green ambulance crew.

The announcement of a life extinct.

19

It was like a scene from a movie.

Billy lay where he fell. On his back. One leg bent under the other, arms splayed as though he'd windmilled them in an attempt to stop his fall. A darkness spread out and formed a huge right wing and a smaller left one. The dust and grit from the ground kicked up into it, spattering it, clogging patches.

Dark-coloured footprints moved around and away from him.

Men and women in white Tyvek suits worked their way to him on square silver step-boxes. Moving with focus.

One pair of footprints belonged to Ray, who had walked to a spot away from everyone. He looked over the barren, brown-dirt landscape towards where he knew the Thames ebbed and flowed, its own animal, its own life, and breathed in. Tried to clear his lungs, which felt as though they were filled with dirt from the ground, oil from the air, and blood, thick and cloying, from Billy. He was soiled, inside and out.

There were so many people here. He had no idea if there were people he already knew or who he'd been introduced to earlier. He was fried. After watching the life drain out of Billy, and the sudden influx of people, his brain felt overloaded. For instance, everyone in a white suit looked exactly the same. There was nothing to differentiate them. All identifiers were covered up.

'Ray!'

Shit. It was the voice of Detective Superintendent Prabhat Jain.

Ray turned and watched Jain stride towards him. Strong and purposeful. Blue strobes rotated behind him, criss-crossing each other from different vehicles. Signalling the drama that unfolded here. He wished they wouldn't do this. Draw attention. There wasn't any need. There was no traffic to stop.

'Guv.' He acknowledged his boss with deference to his rank.

'What the hell happened?' Jain asked as he joined him.

'You sent an unarmed, untrained child into a dangerous situation is what happened.'

'Ray,' he warned. 'We agreed.' He looked past Ray at the boy on the ground and the swarm of white-suited ants around him. 'He was already in. Had been for two years before we knew about it. We couldn't protect him then, we hadn't been able to stop him then. There were no signs that anything was amiss or that there was an armed element to this. It must have happened here, today.' He returned his look to Ray, who sighed.

'It was a complete farce. We were underprepared. They're good. Organised. Meticulous. Their prep for arranging a meet was good. We were on the back foot from the start. And then he was spooked and he pulled a gun. There was nothing we could do, we weren't prepared for it.'

'This is bad PR, Ray.'

'For fuck's sake, Prabhat.'

'Okay. I know.' He raised his hands, palms forward. 'I know. But this incident still has to be reported somehow.' He lowered his hands. 'I have to work with the media and communication unit and work out what we'll say.' He pushed his hands in his pockets and

76

nodded towards Ray's own. 'You need to get back to the nick, get your clothes into evidence bags, get cleaned up and then help me figure this out.'

Ray looked down at himself. He was unrecognisable from how he'd set out that morning, and his skin was itchy where the blood was drying, tight and cracked.

'Well, he knows it was a police operation now, so there's no point being coy about it, but we do have to be careful how much info we give the press and, by extension, him, about how much we know.' Ray laughed as he said this, it was hard, brittle. 'Or don't know. Let me get sorted and we'll get everyone together.'

Jain let out a long slow breath. 'Thanks, Ray.' He turned to leave, then stopped midway. 'Ray, you were there when Billy was shot. You saw him ...'

Ray's stomach curled in on itself.

'If we get you with an artist you could get us an image, right?'

Ray's stomach felt as though it was about to eat itself and would then throw its contents right up in front of Prabhat. He tried to take a breath before he spoke. 'I'm sorry, guv, he ran like the wind, and with him having a gun to his side Billy ran with him and they were just that distance too far. All I can say with any certainty is he looked Eastern European, but they were too far away for me to be able to see him properly.'

Rusnac had to get rid of the car. Even if that cop didn't come after him right now, it wouldn't be long before the entire Metropolitan Police force was on the lookout for it. You don't kill a kid in front of a cop and not expect them to bring the might of their will down on you.

He swung the steering wheel left onto Choats Road. The cops would come from the west, he needed to head in the other direction and then around.

He was smarter than they were. He always did play one step ahead. You didn't survive Moldova and then come to London and fail. It didn't happen. This place was soft and fluffy in comparison.

With one phone call he had a location to get to.

He had to get as far out as he could as fast as he could, and then switch up the car. If it was local it would make it too easy. The site wasn't close, but if he kept to the speed limit and away from major roads, he should be okay.

He quickly pulled over and soiled the rear number plate. Made it impossible to identify the first and last two letters. If he passed through any cameras that were tasked with the search for his plate before he got to his location, he didn't want to be stopped. If he completely destroyed the visibility of the number plate he knew he could get pulled up for that, for not having his plate on view, so he played it clever.

Adrenaline coursed through his veins. His arms vibrated as he held the steering wheel. This was simply a physical reaction to the situation, Rusnac knew that. It threw him back to the days at home when he did his first thefts, the first time he walked into a shop and walked out with a loaf of bread without paying for it. The first time he stole a phone right out the hands of a lad who was probably the same age as he was. Ready to fight him if needed, but he'd been so aggressive in the takedown that the young lad just looked at him with wide eyes and simply watched him leave.

The physical reaction didn't change the fact that he was still in control and knew what to do. He felt high. Buzzing. It was a natural high. His arms continued to fizz. His legs shook as they worked the car.

As he drove, he wondered what had happened to Borta, Popa, Lupei and the British guy, Weaver. Had they managed to get away or had they been arrested?

He'd love to have someone on the inside. To tell him where they were in the investigation so he could be sure he'd stay one step ahead. It was so easy to get that kind of information at home. Money talked. Pay enough and you got what you needed. Here, you had to be careful who you approached. Many of the cops were the real deal. You couldn't tell who would take a bung simply by looking at them, and Vova didn't have the contacts to work that system yet.

Now he realised how important it was to his business that he built up this branch of it.

Rusnac's arms shook more as he skidded to a halt in front of the row of lock-up garages. Glad to have made it.

The area was quiet. He wound the window down. Listened for voices close by. Assured he was alone, Rusnac got out of the BMW and looked around. There were some houses that overlooked the area, but he couldn't see anyone in the windows. He counted along the garages and found the one he needed. Felt along the corrugated roof, which was disgusting to the touch, filled with dirt, slime, and who knew what else, until he found the key he was searching for.

Rusnac dusted it off and tried to insert it into the lock but his hand shook so much that it wouldn't go in.

Swearing under his breath, he jumped up and down and tried to shake the adrenaline out of his body. Then he held his right hand steady with his left and tried the key and lock again. This time it slid in. The garage door groaned in complaint as he pulled it up.

With another look around, Rusnac sat back behind the wheel and drove the BMW into the darkness of the garage.

21

Elaine had a weighty feeling in the pit of her stomach, as though she'd eaten a heavy meal and it was simply sitting there. They'd been standing around for hours, unable to do anything. It wasn't a case of crime scene investigators doing their thing and the cops present doing theirs. She was a cop and she was frustrated. This time officers uninvolved with the original op had been brought in to deal with the murder scene of Billy Collier because they, the force, the Met, needed to be seen to be beyond reproach. So the team who had taken him on the op, they couldn't be involved in the crime scene. They couldn't support the CSIs. They couldn't do their jobs. Her hands were tied. But she wasn't allowed to leave either. Not until someone else higher up said she could.

The two offenders that they, the team on the ground, the team from the op – the team being frozen out – had managed to detain had been taken back to the station by a couple of uniform cars.

Elaine had then found an empty bucket, had tipped it upside down and was now sitting on it. Hands on knees, chin in hands. She could hear the hum of the crime scene. The quiet chatter of CSIs as they worked the area. Made decisions. A gentle hum in the background of Elaine's hectic mind.

Paula approached. 'He was a good kid.'

Elaine lifted her chin. Looked at Paula. 'Dammit. I just feel so bloody useless.'

'Ay, but it has to be done.'

Elaine looked at Ray, still standing off on his own. 'How's he doing? You were with him.'

'He seems … distant. We've seen murder before. Maybe it's because he was there in the final minutes. But … it feels like more than that. He feels dark.'

'Dark?'

'Yeah. Like something is brooding in him.'

Elaine looked across at him again. His hands shoved into his pockets. His face closed off.

'You think you can talk to him?' asked Paula.

'What makes you think that?'

'You were in that accident together.' Paula kicked at the ground and the dust lifted, floated, and coated her boots.

'It doesn't mean he'll talk to me.'

'No, but you've been through something tough together already. You've a head start on the rest of us.'

She had a point. Elaine shrugged. 'I can but try.'

His shoulders were tense, pulled up to his ears. 'Guv?' she said from behind him. Though Elaine understood Paula's reasoning, it didn't make this feel any easier.

'Elaine.' He didn't make a move to turn.

She could feel the darkness Paula had mentioned. Wondered what was pulling him in on himself so much. More than the rest of them, anyway. She couldn't get Billy's face out of her head. Felt sick to the heavy lump in her stomach.

'It's been a long day. I wondered how you were doing? If there's anything I can do?'

Ray turned. His face was grey. He was covered in blood. Elaine winced. Seeing the end of Billy's life all over Ray like this – it was, well, it was like being in the superintendent's path when he finally blew his top – which he rarely did, which was why it was so bad to be around when he let loose. You just didn't want to be there. To be hit by flying debris. The contrast between the calm, mellow man and the seething, top-blowing boss was something to be seen. Or not. And seeing Ray this way, it was like that.

She couldn't go to Billy, he was now evidence. Much as that term grated on her when she knew him after his many visits to the office, that was what he had been reduced to. Evidence. To be photographed, swabbed, poked, taped, collected – when she remembered him as a boyish, sweet, kind, a little angry, determined, and brave lad.

Ray's face mirrored her own feelings – but yes, as Paula had said, there was something else there.

'When we're released from the scene we need to get the incident room up and running as fast as we can,' he replied. His tone was hard-edged. His words clipped.

'You think they'll let us run the investigation?' she asked.

'I don't give a flying fuck what they want. This was on our watch. They can oversee it all and make sure we're following all protocols, policies and procedures, but we're running it. I'll talk to Jain and he can bang heads with whoever he needs to, but this was authorised somewhere else, not by me, so I'm damn well not going to let whoever organised it run it. That, in my book, would be the wrong move. Not us looking at it.'

'Can I do anything for you?'

He looked at Elaine, the words with which he'd just answered her echoing in his head as he realised she was asking a personal question.

He shook his head. Turned away and looked off, back into the distance.

22

Ray's journey back to the office had been difficult. He had been driven by a uniform officer who had not been involved in the job, so that there would be no cross-contamination. He didn't have the energy to remember the guy's name or any details about him so he sat in surly silence. The officer kept his hands on the wheel and his eyes on the road. After a couple of attempts to engage Ray in conversation, he'd received the message and stopped.

Ray stripped out of his clothes as he stood on a brown paper sheet, shiny side up, which crinkled as he moved. There to catch any tiny fragment of evidence that could fall from him as he disrobed. He placed each item of clothing into its own brown paper bag. The air cool on his skin. His mind replayed the events that had led him to be standing here, in his boxers, as a CSI swabbed his skin for trace evidence.

They needed to follow the evidence and make sure the scene matched up to the narrative he provided. He understood the procedure. But he wanted the faceless white Tyvek suit to hurry up so he could shower and get on with his job instead of standing there as evidence. He wanted to wash Billy's blood off him. Because it was evidence. Evidence of his incompetence and his poor decision-making skills. How had he managed to get this so wrong? It all looked so simple when he'd assessed it in the cold light of day from his home on sick leave; but here, up close and personal with real people's lives, it was hard. Ray gritted his teeth as the CSI worked.

Will and Paula would be going through the same rigorous procedures.

Once his various areas were swabbed and his nails clipped, Ray was done. He thanked the Tyvek suit and made a beeline for the showers.

He took a minute to gather himself under the lukewarm water that dribbled over his back as he leaned under the trickle. Closed his eyes as the blood slipped down the plughole.

Fuck! He slapped down hard on the wall in front of him, stinging his palm. Anger rearing up inside him at the mess. At the loss.

He took a deep breath in. He had a team waiting for him outside those doors. He had to push himself back into work mode. He needed to have his head on straight if he was going to get through the rest of the day. He needed to remember the visual hooks he'd attached to people so he didn't screw up, because he needed to lead as they expected him to. As they knew him to be able to. He wouldn't allow this deficiency to rule him or destroy him.

It would test him. The level of activity and movement, the sheer speed with which his officers would move about, working, would make for problematic conversations, as well as the fact that there would be several officers in and out who he'd be expected to remember. He couldn't fail, not now.

Ray placed both palms on the wall in front of him, leant into the water, tipped his face up and allowed the water to flow over him. Allowed it to soothe him.

He needed to take control. Find a way to make this right. What he could do was run his own investigation parallel to the one he would run in the incident room. He would work the job himself alongside the official investigation, put in extra hours and follow impossible leads if it meant they could get an ID for the head of this organised group. This killer.

He would rectify his mistake.

Once dressed, back in a clean shirt and tie, Ray walked into the incident room. The cacophony of noise assaulted him. Shrieked inside his head like a colony of seagulls about to be fed.

He paused, watched the room, a hive working. This was where he belonged. This was now where he had to deceive his whole team.

'Okay everyone, gather round, let's get this show on the road.'

23

His head hurt. It was like a blunt object was burrowing down into his right eye socket from his brow-bone. Ray kneaded the bone with his knuckle in the hope he could kill it dead before it dug into his eye and scoured it right out of his orbital socket.

The briefing had been frenetic. They had run an operation that had resulted in the death of a civilian – Billy. Many of his staff knew him and the loss was going to hit them hard. The office was thick with unsaid words. Stoically held back emotions. And a solid determination. But he needed them to focus until they had the full team of offenders behind bars. He was glad of the peace he had now. Tamsin, Elaine, Will and Paula were in interview with the two offenders they had locked up. One had been identified by his fingerprints as Darren Weaver of Haringey, with a history of drug and violent offences. The fingerprints of the second male had been sent through to Interpol.

Forensics had been down, seized their clothing and replaced it with plain jogging bottoms and T-shirts after they'd swabbed the men for particle evidence. They'd had no weapons of their own on them other than a knuckleduster and a pair of rather nasty attitudes.

He'd normally like to get involved and do one of the interviews, but he had his statement to type up. Jain was on his back for it. He wanted it as soon as possible. Yesterday if he could. Ray's mind continued to replay Billy's murder, which was helpful in that he wouldn't forget the details; but no matter how many times he watched the scene unfold in his mind, there was always a blank space, a faceless face. There was a vague concept of eyes, nose and mouth, but no concrete image he could grasp.

He wasn't sure how much time had passed when there was a knock at his door. Ray prodded the burrowing pain again. It was persistent. Annoying.

He waved the visitors in. One male and three females. Rare to get the ratio this way around, he knew. Curls, Tamsin and Will. One from each interview team; the other two must be Elaine and Paula.

'What do we have?' he asked, looking past them both through the office to the windows on the back wall, which were both now reflective like a mirror as the night slid down behind them. Mid-March, the days were lengthening, but they were still short.

'They tried for a no comment interview,' replied Will with a grin.

Tamsin and Will grabbed the two chairs that were already in his office.

'Tried?'

Elaine and Paula walked back out and wheeled in a couple more chairs and sat.

'Yeah,' said Tamsin, 'but much to the consternation of his solicitor, he couldn't stop himself from answering some of the questions.'

'He was a bundle of nerves, to be honest,' Paula chipped in.

'Nervous of us?' Ray asked.

'I don't think so.' Tamsin shook her head. Curls swirling around her face. 'Afraid of the guy who got away. It was when we questioned him about Billy's killer that he stuck to the no comment response, but if it wasn't related to him, then he felt he had a bit more freedom to speak.'

'We don't think the solicitor is involved?'

'No, he opted for a duty solicitor.'

'So.' Ray looked at his mug, which was empty. 'What did he give us?'

'He told us his real name, Ion Borta, where he's from, Moldova, and that he came to England about two and a half years ago.'

'So he's illegal?'

'Yeah. I think this could help us in our search for the head guy. He also talked a bit about the organ trade. Not much, but enough to know they were involved and people are willing to pay. There are huge amounts of money being exchanged, and kidneys are the easiest organs to trade because you can use live donors. That's when he got pretty passionate.' Tamsin pulled a hair elastic from around her wrist, screwed her hair in an untidy bundle at the base of her head and fastened it with the elastic.

Ray wanted to explode at her then and there, as her identifier disappeared before his eyes, until a couple of curls popped out at the front, springing around her face.

'It's as though they don't see it as much of an issue because everyone involved consents. They were very proud that they only use live donors and aren't one of these shit bastards that kill people so they can take their organs – his words,' she clarified. 'They said everyone who goes into it knows all the facts. They provide a service, and one that is crying out for help,' she continued. 'He was adamant that the people involved all consented and were all compensated well for their time, trouble and organs. And that they all walked away well. The operations were conducted by good doctors. It was simply a business that fills a need our NHS fails to fill.'

'Yeah, our guy was the same,' jumped in Will. 'Did you know there's something called transplant tourism now?' He was incredulous. 'Can you believe it, transplant fucking tourism. It's a thing. And these guys, instead of asking patients to travel abroad for their shiny new organs, they do it in their home country. It keeps costs to a minimum and keeps the risk of infection down because they don't have to travel.' His mouth nearly hung open at his jaw. 'They genuinely believed they were the good guys in this scenario.'

'Did you point out it was against UK law?'

'Oh yeah, they knew that, but this guy who's done the runner has got them believing in some God complex shite.'

'Not quite that altruistic,' Paula butted in. 'They –'

'No, but –' Will tried.

'But nothing.' She stopped him again. 'They make money from other people's misery and they damn well know it. Who gives a toss if they're not slicing up prisoners in China to do it, they're still breaking the law, and people die.'

'I'm not disagreeing with you, you twat.'

'Okay, I get the picture,' Ray intervened. 'While they were feeling so chatty about the transplants, did they give us information we can work with? Locations, dark net addresses, doctors and nurses they work with, chemists, drugs suppliers, blood banks, a goddamn taxi service?' He looked at the group gathered in front of him; each face wore a different expression, and while he struggled to place each of his long-standing friends and colleagues as easily as he had in the past, he also found the ability to read them as well as he used to was affected. Great big signals across the face he could spot, but the subtler signs he missed.

He waited them out.

It was Tamsin who spoke.

'While they don't want to give the name up of their boss, they are willing to talk to us, but they haven't given us as much information as we'd like yet. It's like falling into Alice's looking-glass. A strange and twisted land. I think we'll need that extension, to keep questioning them.'

Ray drummed his fingers on the desk as he considered this.

'We will be able to progress this investigation with their help,' she added, her tone measured. 'It's not like any job I've come across before.'

Ray leaned back in his chair. Hands clasped behind his head.

'I'll get you the extension, you've got more out of them than I expected. Let's give them the night to think about it and go again in the morning. But get me a lead we can follow up on.'

They stood to leave and acknowledged the task in front of them.

'I wasn't saying they did it out of the goodness of their hearts, you idiot,' Ray heard Will snipe at Paula as they walked out, and then a roar of laughter from her in response, which she followed up with a swift punch in the arm for good measure.

They were a good team and he had let them down in spectacular fashion today. Only they didn't know it. He would make it right.

And they'd soon know a little more about what had been behind the botched operation that had got Billy killed.

24

The apartment was warm as he walked through the door. They didn't live together but they did spend most evenings at one or the other's home. Tonight, Ray walked into Celeste's beautiful two-bed apartment in Primrose Hill. An affluent area of the city, all right. And as a highly regarded and in-demand defence barrister who had always taken care of her finances, she had managed to buy herself the light and airy place Ray found himself in.

The smell of garlic wafted through the hall from the kitchen and his stomach rumbled in response. Someone had shoved a chicken sandwich on his desk after a run to the shop at some point, but that had been it during a long shift. Gentle humming attempted to keep tune with the song that played on the radio, but tunefulness was not Celeste's strong point. A smile played across his lips as he stood and listened to her. Her carefree attitude and ability to not care if people laughed were what drew him to her in the first place, and he revelled in it for a minute. This was what he needed after the day he had had. He needed the warmth and comfort of Celeste. He needed to be brought down to a level place, instead of this strung-out feeling he was carrying around.

He remembered the heady days of their new romance. A chance meeting in the Crown Court canteen, where she had been taking a break from the defence of a client on a GBH charge, had led to long evenings of conversations that were full of life considering the two sides of the same coin they worked on, and longer nights when they explored the landscape of each other. He remembered the curve of her neck and the light, slightly floral scent of her perfume, how it would invade his senses while her long blonde hair played with the nerve endings on his skin. She was beautiful. It shone from within, her intelligence and gentleness, and all wrapped in a lithe body he couldn't get enough of. He wasn't quite sure how he'd managed to get so lucky a second time.

He knew her. Her blonde hair. The way she walked, so tall and upright. She looked after herself with yoga and other fitness classes. He wouldn't forget her. He could do this without screwing up. All he had to do was remember there would be a disconnect when he saw her. Then they could move on with their evening.

Eventually he walked through to the brightly lit kitchen with high-gloss cream units and a dark-walnut granite worktop. Two large bronze globe light-fittings hung over the dining table, tucked neatly at the far end of the kitchen, providing it with a centrepiece to admire. They were rather stunning. If they were in his place they would probably always have fingerprints on them from the kids.

Right now the kitchen was a mess, and in the middle of it all, still humming along with her back to him, her blonde shoulder-length hair swishing as she moved, was Celeste. Food was splattered up the tiles at the back of the hob; empty tins, meat packaging and used pans were abandoned along the worktop. The tense, itchy feeling that was clawing at him started to melt at the sight in front of him.

Ray coughed, smiling. Celeste jumped, turning around to face him.

'Hey honey! I didn't hear you come in.' She moved quickly to him, flung her arms around him and moved in to kiss him. The floral smell of her perfume. Ray inhaled. Took in this woman who was good to him.

But he didn't recognise her. He tried to do what he always did. He reminded himself this was Celeste. He knew this happened. But the day had pierced him and he couldn't get a grasp of his usual routine.

He pulled away. The radio still burbling away in the background. The warmth of the oven wafting dinner towards him, wafting care and attention towards him. He rubbed his face. This was Celeste. The woman he cared for.

'What? What is it?' Her voice was concerned. 'Ray? Is it work? Has it been too much for you?'

He couldn't confide about his day when he couldn't even tell her what he was hiding from her. How to leave without hurting her?

'No. I'm not hungry, that's all. Why didn't you ask if I wanted to eat instead of making all this? You've wasted your time.'

'But ... I thought –'

'You didn't think, Celeste. What if I'd have been even later: you'd have been sat alone. Alone with cold, uneaten food.' He tried to keep his voice level but he was aware his words alone were hurtful.

'But you're not later, you're here. I've made this for you and now you tell me you don't want it?'

'It's been a hell of a day and the last thing I feel like is sitting down to eat nice food when other people can't.' Shit.

'I didn't think. I just wanted to do something nice.'

Ray turned away from her.

'Ray!' She grabbed his shoulder. 'Don't push me out.'

'Stop, Celeste,' he growled. 'How are we supposed to build a relationship if you cling to me afraid I'll walk away?'

He caught the sharp intake of breath. The step back on the hardwood floor.

He lowered his voice. 'I need some space.' And walked back out of the door he'd a minute ago been glad to enter.

25

'Daddy!' The glee on the girl's face was clear to see.

'Alice.' He picked her up and swung her around on the doorstep. Her bare feet barely missed the door jamb as they swung wide before he caught her up and hitched her onto his hip, wrapped his arms around her and faced the woman with his daughter. Helen. His ex-wife.

'Ray, what are you doing here this late?'

'It's …' He looked at Alice. He didn't want to go into it all in front of his daughter.

Helen looked from Alice to Ray. 'Come in. They both should be in bed by now anyway. If you put them to bed, I'll put the kettle on.'

'Yay,' squealed Alice.

'Thank you,' Ray mouthed at Helen, and smiled at Alice. 'Okay, munchkin, let's get you upstairs to bed, shall we?'

Alice chattered about her day at school as Ray climbed the stairs with her in his arms, his bones reminding him that they were still repairing themselves and didn't need to lift weights upstairs; but he pushed on and ignored the niggle.

'Dad!'

'Matthew.' Ray smiled back at his son and the look of joy on his face.

'What're you doing here?'

'I've come to put you both to bed. So, your teeth are brushed, I take it?'

Their heads bobbed up and down furiously.

He dropped Alice down onto her feet, and his arm howled in relief.

'Great. Matthew, jump into bed. I'll tuck Alice in, then I'll come and say goodnight to you.'

Alice climbed under her pastel pink and purple duvet and snuggled down. 'Daddy?'

'Yes, sweetie.' He sat on the edge of the bed, tried to take in his daughter's neat little features.

'Are you all better after the accident?'

He felt a new stab of pain slice through his heart. Sweet Alice, the warm smell of oranges seeping from under her quilt from the bath he knew she'd had before he'd arrived. (The dampness at the ends of her hair, which had tickled his face, had given it away as he carried her upstairs.) The familiar warmth and scent unfurled his heart as he looked down at the face he didn't know and listened to the question he wouldn't give her an honest answer to.

'I'm all fine now. I carried you all the way up the stairs, didn't I?'

'Yes?' A question.

'You're right, it's still a little sore, but that's to be expected, sweet. I'll be back to fighting fit before you know it.' He rubbed her hair. 'Get some sleep now. I'm going to sit and have a chat with Mummy.'

'Like you used to?'

'Like I used to.' He kissed the top of her head and inhaled the oranges. Hovered over her that extra second to take in the scent of his daughter. To warm his aching heart.

'Matthew is growing so much.' Ray perched on the breakfast barstool with the steaming mug in his hands. 'It seems that I only miss him for a few days and he shoots up an extra inch.'

'That's old money, Ray. They shoot up in centimetres now.' Helen jumped up onto her own stool and looked at him.

He put his mug down and rubbed at his face.

'What is it, Ray? What brings you to our door at this time in the evening? Looking like shit, no less.'

Ray picked his mug back up, looked at Helen's face. He couldn't read it, but he could read the tone in her voice and it wasn't welcoming.

'You said you'd be there for me, because of the kids and, I'm sorry if it's late, but –'

'Ray, it's six months after your accident, and I want you to be sane so you can co-parent the children, but that doesn't mean you can take the piss. What, I'm going to see more of you now than when we were married, is that it?' She looked out of the kitchen window, her lips pursed. Then, without turning back to him: 'If I'd have known the way to see more of you when we were married was to get you into a car accident, I'd have driven the car into a wall myself.'

Ray stood. 'I'm sorry. I shouldn't have come. It's just … I thought …'

'That's the problem with you, Ray, you don't think. You never did.' She rubbed a shoulder, kneading it with her right hand. 'But I've made the drink now, so you can bloody well stay and drink it.' She faced him. 'And you can tell me what dragged your sorry arse over here this evening.'

Ray ran a hand through his hair. He never wanted to hurt her. Putting the job first had broken up a relationship that he now knew could probably have lasted and been good if he'd nurtured it. Now, with her being the only person to know his diagnosis, because of the children, because he never wanted to scare them again, he was at risk of putting on her, and he needed to watch that.

'I'm screwing up.' He couldn't tell her all of it though. He couldn't tell her how his diagnosis was screwing up his life. She didn't need to hear that. How it was affecting his new relationship. He could imagine how well listening to that would go down. 'I screwed up and I'm screwing up and I don't know how to deal with it all and you, of all people, are the only person, other than medical personnel, who knows about some of it.'

Helen took a drink of her own coffee before she spoke. 'I'll try not to take that as an insult.'

'Shit, I didn't –'

'You're here now. Tell me about it. I need you to be of sound mind for the kids.'

Ray dropped his head into his hands.

'I said it's okay, Ray. Don't make a habit of late-night calls, but for some reason that evades me, the kids adore you –' he grinned at

101

her '– and you need to continue to be a good dad for them. So let me have it.'

He wasn't going to say no. 'We screwed up today, Hel, and I mean really screwed up.'

'That job on the news?'

'Yeah. That civilian that was killed. I could have prevented it if I'd have fought harder for him to not be there.'

'Really? Who were you fighting against?'

'Prabhat.'

Helen laughed.

'What?'

'You never win a work fight with Prabhat. In fact, you never win a personal fight with him. He likes to get his own way and I imagine the fact that he has rank over you at work would make it incredibly difficult for you to do much of anything, so I wouldn't worry too much about it. If there's any fault here, it's on his head.'

Ray needed to hear her say this. He needed an outside opinion. One he trusted.

'Though …' She paused, looked him in the eyes, 'you know I don't understand why you don't tell Prabhat about the prosopagnosia. Why you have to keep it all a secret. He could support you. Work could support you. You're making it all so much more difficult for yourself.' She paused. 'And for me.'

'I'm sorry. But they wouldn't support me Helen, they'd retire me. I know they would.' He sighed. He hated to have to explain this to her again. To keep repeating himself. But he needed to keep her onside. Her support was the only support he had, so if she

102

needed to hear it again then he would go through it all for her. 'The organisation can be quite narrow-minded, but – I thought long and hard about this, as you know, and I thought I would never be in a position where it would cause a problem for me.' Could he tell her? Admit his mistake? His grave error of judgement. That going back had caused a young man to die, or rather, the killer of that man to walk free and him to be helpless against it. How would this have worked out differently if he'd have retired? He hated to think about it.

She took a drink, then nodded.

'What else, Ray?' He couldn't decipher the look on her face but again he recognised the tone of her voice and this one was the one that said he had to talk properly and honestly or the conversation would be over.

'I don't know if I can do this. Live like this. The pressure, the responsibility. I'm screwing it all up.' It was wrong to lean on her this way, she was his ex, but she was all he had right now, and after the accident and the diagnosis and the fear that had cut through the children, she had promised him that she would do anything she could to help so that Alice and Matthew were on a more stable footing. Her concern was for them.

'You can do this. You are a strong man, Ray Patrick. You recovered from that crash. Your kids adore you and as they get a little older we'll explain how as they change they'll need to help you in recognising them when you first see them; but at the minute they'll always be in my company so it won't be a problem. All your days at work won't be like that, and you'll adjust. You've only recently gone back. Give yourself some time. Stop being so hard on yourself.' She looked at him. He couldn't fathom the look on her face. 'You haven't told Celeste yet, have you?'

He shook his head. 'It's all too new and fragile.'

He hated to live this way. Not able to connect the faces in front of him with memories of the people. Yes, he still loved. He adored his children and they were an easier connect. No matter that he didn't remember their faces, he remembered their hair, their smell, their walk, their laugh, the way they talked to him. It was all so much easier because the love was a real natural bond.

But the relationship with Celeste was still fairly new, a bud waiting to bloom, and the strength of feeling wasn't enough to break the shock-and-fear barrier of not recognising her.

He didn't want to watch as his relationship with Celeste broke down. He didn't want it to break down. He had feelings for her that were growing, and if he told her there was something wrong with his head she might run, and he didn't want to risk that.

'It's now that you need to know if she's in it for you, Ray. If it's real. You need her more than me.'

'I know.' His shoulders slumped even more.

'But for now I'm here –' she glared at him as she finished the dregs of the coffee '– at a sensible time of day. I need you to be okay.'

'Helen ...'

'Yeah.' She put her mug on the counter.

'I was face to face with the killer today.'

'Fuck, Ray.'

26

Ray rented a two-bed apartment in Stoke Newington. He'd made the decision to live close to work rather than closer to his children. After all, it was where he spent most of his hours. Or it had been until he'd had the accident and had had to take six months off. The apartment was an attractive, high-ceilinged affair on Burma Road. He'd managed to get it at less than market price from a colleague whose mother had unexpectedly passed away a month before Ray had needed somewhere to live when he separated from Helen. His colleague had said it would do him a favour if Ray took it on, as he wouldn't have to put it on the market or worry about how other renters might treat the property. So Ray had a nice place and slept on the sofa when the kids came over.

Helen had been worried when he left her that night. She'd not only been worried about Ray and how he was coping, but also about the fact the killer had seen Ray and what implications this held for her family. It didn't take Ray long to reassure her that the man would want to avoid him at all costs and would not want to try to antagonise him and go after his family for some bizarre reason. This, after all, wasn't a movie they were in the middle of, but real life.

Once he'd calmed her fears he then had to calm her anger. Her muted annoyance at him turning up unannounced to talk through his bad day, turned to anger at him keeping the diagnosis a secret from the organisation. This wouldn't have happened if they knew. Her fears wouldn't have had to be calmed if the police knew about him and what had happened because of the crash. He had promised her he would do everything in his power to bring this killer to justice. He really didn't want to have his one begrudging ally offside.

He opened his laptop and leaned over his knees so he could see the screen as it sat on the rather low coffee table. The glow of the screen provided the only light in the room, other than a tall lamp he'd switched on in the corner as he'd walked in. The eerie glow emanated out across the room and cast shadows in familiar places.

He'd heard of the dark net and knew a little about it. He knew it was the place you went if you wanted to buy drugs online. He knew it was all encrypted and that it was incredibly difficult for anyone to get traced. Now he needed to find out more, so he opened his regular web browser, keyed in some terms into the search engine, and watched a TED talk about the dark net going mainstream. This explained the origins of the dark net, how it had started life as a US Naval intelligence project and then went open source. Further research explained that this was to protect navy operatives who wanted to send information back from dangerous operations. The TED talk also explained exactly how he could access this unknown section of the internet from his home computer. He needed to download a new browser. One that would encrypt his data so he couldn't be traced. The TED talk extolled the virtues of private browsing and of good customer care within the world of the dark net. Even for those who bought illegal drugs. All was well if customer care was up to scratch. It was unbelievable. What did surprise Ray was that mainstream websites were also in the world of the dark net: the New Yorker was there, other news outlets, and even Facebook had a dark net site.

With all the browsing and all he read, he got what he wanted: details on how to access the dark net himself. The need for the browser that would encrypt his own data. This was how Billy's brother and Billy himself had initially got in touch with the organisation. He wanted to find them online.

Himself.

To download the browser was his first step.

He was about to cross a line. The investigation was ongoing at work. All this could be done at the office. Why should he do this himself? Put his whole career at risk?

He knew why. He was at fault in so many ways. This wasn't because he felt guilty. This was real, genuine fault. He hadn't argued his case hard enough against Prabhat for Billy not to go to the meet, and the investigation was now disabled, even though no one realised it, because he was unable to recognise the killer. After he'd looked him in the eye, he was still unable to identify him. The investigation would have to rely on any forensic evidence they could gather, or evidence from other lines of inquiry that came up. And he, Ray, was going to stand in front of his team and lie to them on a daily basis. He hated himself for it.

When the TOR browser was downloaded and live on his screen he stared at it for ten minutes. He was surprised to see how much it resembled a regular internet browser, other than the giant onion image at one side, which was why the browser was often called the onion network, because in an onion network messages are sheathed in layers of encryption comparable to the layers of an onion, and TOR stands for The Onion Router.

It was certainly an education. A whole new world.

Another nail in his career's coffin, too. Because he wouldn't disclose the prosopagnosia. Because he had been face to face with a killer and was unable to identify him. Because he was the weak link in a chain of evidence. So, if there was any other way he could bring this guy in, he would do it. And he knew damn well he should have fought harder against Prabhat in the first place in relation to Billy. No matter what Helen said. She didn't know the job. His responsibilities. He would do this, no matter what the fallout.

27

It had been late by the time he'd hit the sack the previous night. Sleep had been elusive. Tantalisingly in sight, but not within his grasp. Ray had tossed and turned. Punched pillows, made tea instead of coffee, picked up a book until it blurred in front of his eyes, punched pillows some more and eventually slid into a restless, half-restful state where his mind wandered through corridors lit by strip-lights, white walls dripped with blood, and his bare feet squelched through great pools of the stuff. Too copious for anyone to have survived the loss of it. His stomach heaved as he moved further into the building. High-pitched screams pulled him forward. Screams that pierced his brain.

His legs were leaden. They refused to run, to help whoever needed him. His progress through the horror was slow. As the blood dripped down the walls the screams started to slow. The victim was losing their fight and yet Ray couldn't get his legs to move across the bloody floor any faster.

A hollowed-out laugh cut through the failing screams. Ray's legs hurt with the energy he was using to push forward. His thighs burned. His chest ached. The resistance he was up against, true.

Then cries broke through. Soft gentle sobs.

He was close. He knew where the sounds came from. The door at the end of the corridor. Not far now.

The cries continued.

Ray pushed on.

The laughter of a soulless man echoed around the whitewashed, blood-filled corridor.

And then he was there. The door was in front of him. The screaming was now only a whimper.

The laughter continued to echo around him.

Ray looked down at himself. Blood had splashed up his legs. It had rubbed onto his shoulders and arms from the walls. He looked like he had butchered someone.

His legs burned. But, he was here.

He reached out to the door handle, touched the cool metal, pushed down, felt it give beneath his bloody hand, heard it creak as it moved under pressure …

And then he woke.

Again.

The clock read five a.m. He'd had maybe an hour and a half's rest, if you could call it that.

Now he stood in the silent incident room, soaking in the quiet time. Before the team came in. Before he had to do it all again. Keep up with the difficult task of identifying his staff and keep up with the investigation that he'd already screwed up.

His head still whirred with thoughts, jumbled and incoherent, when the sound of the incident-room door swinging open broke through.

'Guv, how long have you been in?'

Ray fought to bring his mind back to the room and away from the incident.

'I didn't sleep well.' His answer for the early start. He couldn't place the shirt and tie. He was tired. Damn, it would be one hell of day.

The suit and tie slung his jacket over a chair and started to go through the motions of waking his computer. 'My youngest is teething. I know how a bad night feels.'

Ray ran a hand through his hair. Ah, new baby, one of the HOLMES team. 'I remember those days. They feel like they won't end, but they do. Hang in there.'

His phone beeped as a text message arrived. Ray looked at the screen. Celeste. This was her first contact since he'd walked out on her last night. It should really have been him making this move but he had felt too guilty and had put it off and now it was too late, she'd done it. With a deep sigh he unlocked the phone and read the message.

I'm sorry you had a bad day. It doesn't seem to be going well. This worries me. Don't push me away like that though. There was no need, Ray. Just talk to me. Xx

He ran a hand through his hair. She was worried. What did this make him? Last night had all been his fault. His doing, and she had been the bigger person and had texted him, had reached out with that olive branch and told him she cared. He didn't deserve it. She deserved better. He knew that. But for all that she cared now, Ray didn't know if she still could if she knew the truth, and it scared him. He didn't want to lose anyone because of what was wrong with him. Because he was broken. He didn't want to lose Celeste.

Dammit. He would have to try harder. He typed out his own response and sent it.

You're right, work has been hard. Sorry to push you away last night. x

It wasn't long before more people filed in.

Curly hair – Tamsin. Always in before the rest of the team. Without fail. Or she had been before his accident. He wasn't aware if this had changed or not in the time he had been away. It didn't feel like it.

A Scottish good morning – Paula.

More people. The larger team. His head started to hurt again. He was too tired to try and figure people out as they moved about the office towards their respective seats. He needed to wait until they were seated. He at least had a chance, then, to know who they were and not screw up and get kicked out of his job. He moved to his office. He needed to quieten his brain before briefing. Bring the static levels down. Quell the clamouring fear that had caused the dull roar behind his eyes.

Celeste would have had some painkillers, but he was royally screwing around with that relationship.

He just needed to relax when he saw her. Lean in to the relationship they had. Enjoy the feeling of being with her and accept the disconnect with her face as he had to with everyone.

Ray kept an eye on the incident room, watched as staff trailed in while he updated his policy documents. The IPCC had been informed and brought in to examine the incident. Prabhat had sent him at least half a dozen emails through the evening; obviously he'd worked from home, his brain refusing to switch off from such a massive investigation as much as Ray's had.

The two men in custody still had eight hours on the clock, so Ray needed to get the paperwork in order for a superintendent's authority for an extension. And the authorising officer couldn't be Prabhat. He was too close, too involved. It had to be a superintendent unconnected to the case.

Ray checked the duty register to see who was on and saw Greg Moss. He was pedantic and had been known for most of his career as the station cat, but Ray believed in the grounds for the extension, so he wasn't worried.

The morning passed in a haze of too much paperwork, requests for extra staff and ludicrous amounts of red tape.

The custody clock extension had been signed off. The two guys would stay with them for a while longer yet.

Ray was frustrated. He couldn't sit behind his desk and wait for results to come to him. He needed to be active. Involved. He needed to move forward rather than be at a standstill like this.

He walked to the doorway of his office. The incident room, busy, filled with people in suits. Filled with people needed to run a major investigation. He had the urge to step back into his office and close the door; instead, he looked for the desks of the people he wanted. Found them.

She was standing. Papers in her hand. Coffee mug in her other. Ready to go.

'Tamsin?'

She turned. 'Guv?'

'I'm going in to interview with Paula for this one.'

'Guv?' She didn't move. Ray could hear the confusion in her voice. He stepped out of his office. Closer.

'This isn't a reflection on you, Tamsin. It's me. I want to get in there.'

Deliberately she placed her mug on her desk. Paula, who hadn't yet risen, looked at them both. Waiting.

'But, guv, I've done all his earlier interviews. I've built up a rapport with him. He's more likely to talk to me.'

She didn't want to let this go.

'I want to mix it up. Throw him a little. Let's not allow him to get comfortable.'

'You think that's the right play?'

Paula looked down at her notes. Kept her eyes down.

'Tamsin.' Ray kept his voice level and calm. He understood her desire for advancement, and this job was a big one for her CV. 'Yes, I do.'

'Okay, sir.' She dropped the papers on the desk and walked out of the office, head held high, her back straight.

28

Ray peered through the cell door at the detainee they were about to interview. He was stretched out on a thin black mattress between him and the solid concrete painted slab of a bench, and looked as though he didn't have a care in the world. Arms up and tucked underneath his head, cushioning it from the hard surface it would otherwise have to rest on.

He was too comfortable. Ray pushed the key in the lock, turned it and pulled open the heavy cell door, which groaned in complaint. He was immediately assaulted by the stench of sweaty feet, body odour and microwaved breakfast. His hand tightened on the door handle.

'Up you get. Back into interview,' Ray bellowed.

In the interview, the discs were switched on and introductions and other formalities were given. Kieran Wade was the solicitor, a slender male with a hooked nose and an expensive brown leather briefcase bearing the initials KMW propped at his feet. Ray made a mental note of his nose and the briefcase. Everything else about the solicitor was pretty nondescript. He'd have trouble if he needed to pick him out of all the other solicitors who milled around the custody area, so his best bet would be to use this guy's initialled briefcase to identify him.

Ray looked at Paula and nodded. She started to talk. Reminded Ion Borta of what had been said in the previous interview. Borta looked bored. Ray needed him to pay attention. He needed him to be alert, to take this seriously. That was why he'd swapped the interview up. He looked at the man who was here, arrested for trafficking in human organs and conspiracy to commit murder, even though, with Billy's death, they had no evidence. From his attitude, you wouldn't believe he was here for such serious crimes.

'We'll find him eventually, you know,' Ray said, cutting across Paula as she finished up. He shot her an apologetic look. Borta raised his eyebrows. Thick, dark, over equally dark and brooding eyes. He had his attention now at least.

'We'll find him eventually. So what surprises me is why you're protecting him. The only reason I can think of is that you're afraid of him.'

Borta stiffened.

'Is that it? You're afraid of him?'

'I'm not afraid.'

Ray stayed quiet a moment. The guy had bristled, and he hadn't qualified what he wasn't afraid of. That was interesting.

Silence stifled the room and Ray had to fill it. It was one tactic to try to get the offender to speak with an uncomfortable silence to fill, but this guy was good. He'd kept his mouth shut. If Ray continued the silence much longer it would be seen as oppressive.

'What aren't you afraid of, Ion?'

The man opposite him laughed. 'You, for one. You think your small prison here make me afraid. You know nothing.'

Ray leaned back in his chair, stretched his legs out. Made himself comfortable. Appraised the male in front of him. 'You've nothing to fear from us other than a long prison sentence. The more helpful you are, the more the judge will take that into account at any sentencing if this goes to trial. I'm here to ask you questions, nothing else, and to be honest, Ion, it's not you that we're interested in, so why don't you do yourself a favour and tell us about your boss?'

Borta sat back and appraised Ray and Paula, who made notes as Ray spoke. Ray took it, gave him the time, waited to see what would come.

'You consider yourself the boss man?'

'I am of a higher rank than some of my colleagues.'

'But above you there is a whole machine turning, yes?'

'The police service is an organisation that is structured so that it runs well, yes.' Where was he taking this?

The solicitor looked confused and was furiously making notes as his client and the officer spoke.

'All organisations need structure. Need a boss to front sections. You think you want me to tell you who my boss is. You have no idea what you ask. You want me to be disloyal to an organisation and give up one of our –' he put his fingers in the air and used air quotes '– "rank". Because that's all he is, one of the rank.'

117

29

Ray took Will's hanging mouth to be shock at what he and Paula had disclosed in the interview's debriefing. Elaine on the other hand said, with a deep stare Ray couldn't hold, 'What the fuck?'

'So it would seem,' Paula confirmed, at the existence of a whole other shadowy organisation behind the one they were investigating. One that was a whole lot darker and supposedly scarier, and one that was run by Russian mobsters.

Will's jaw still hung from the hinges of his skull, threatening to drop off if he didn't pick it up soon.

'So what we're really investigating is a Russian mob?' Elaine again.

'No,' said Ray.

They all turned to look at him. Even if he could read every expression on each face, which he couldn't, he understood what they would be feeling now. Confusion.

'We're not set up to run over to Russia to dismantle a Russian mob who send guys over here to do nefarious deals with our citizens. Jesus, even our governments can't deal with Russian mobs, what the hell makes you think we can deal with a criminal ring of this scale?' The shock and outrage lessened. Understanding slid into place. 'No, our job is to deal with what we have here and now. What we've already been dealing with, and that's to identify and locate the male who killed Billy. It's the best we can do.' There were nods around him. He looked at Tamsin. She was unreadable.

As she hadn't been a part of the interview she couldn't claim any success for this development. She couldn't put this on her CV. Cracking an interviewee of a major organ trading ring. He wasn't sure she would have got the same result had she been the one to go in a second or third time. Their thought processes were all different, and maybe her train of thought would have led the interview somewhere else. Maybe not. They'd never know.

'I'll write it all up in my policy log,' he continued. 'I'll also make Detective Superintendent Jain aware of what we have, so that he can move it up the chain of command and anywhere else he feels this needs to go. Probably the National Crime Agency so they can follow up the Russian lead. They're more equipped for it.'

'So what now?' asked Will, who had picked his jaw up from the floor.

'Now we carry on debriefing both these interviews. See what matches, what doesn't. We're waiting on forensics to see if usable evidence comes back from the cartridge, and once we have the bullet from the morgue we can check to see if the weapon has been used in any other offences – but that will take some time. If we can get them charged with the offences for which they've been arrested by the end of their time limit, then we get them remanded and we continue the investigation. If a lead comes back from forensics, then it's another lead we follow.'

Nods all round again. Notes were made on hard-backed blue pads.

'We follow every lead we have to get this guy in the UK. We can't have this organisation removing organs from UK citizens and giving them to the highest bidder because they can't be arsed to wait on the transplant list.'

'I'm not sure it's as simple as that, guv.' Tamsin had decided that now was the time she would break her silence against him. She was tough, dedicated and principled.

'I know that, Tamsin.'

'It's not like they're out to buy a new car, though, is it?'

'That's not what I said. I was maybe a bit flippant. But you can't jump the queue because you have money.'

'I doubt they take the decision lightly. This is a last resort. The transplant list isn't a lifeline for everyone. It's a chance, but it's not a given that you'll get what you need. People die waiting on that list. I'd imagine people need to be pretty desperate to make the decision to buy themselves a new organ.'

Ray was starting to lose his patience with Tamsin but he wouldn't rip her one in front of her colleagues. 'They might be desperate, Tamsin, but that still doesn't give them the right to put someone else's life at risk and potentially kill someone else to save their own life. We know life is fragile.' He looked at Elaine. The slightly pink scar that ran down the side of her eye and along her cheekbone. He felt the throb in his leg. He looked at the faces he could clearly see but wouldn't recognise if he walked out of the room and walked back in again. Fragility. 'Look at Billy's brother. No one has the right to do that to another human being. To another family. We have to take what life throws at us and we have to deal with it.' He looked hard at her now. His voice laced with steel, but quiet and smooth. 'Like it or not.'

120

30

The handle clattered into the wall as it always did as Elaine opened the door into the ladies' toilets. It was a shabby room, painted, yes, but not in the longest time. It was scuffed and dirty, though not unclean: there was a fresh scent in the air, as the cleaners made sure the air-fresheners on the windowsills were always refilled. The current one was pumping out vanilla and cherry-blossom. The sweet fragrance was a little overpowering and sickly, but Elaine preferred the syrupy scent to how it could potentially smell in here with multiple visitors throughout the day.

'You in here?' she asked of the apparently empty room.

'No,' came the reply from one of the stalls.

Elaine sighed. 'Tamsin, it's been a tough couple of days for all of us. Come out, let's talk about it.'

The door opened. Tamsin's eyes were dry where Elaine had expected them to be damp. It must have shown on her face because Tamsin smiled and pulled her up on it. 'He's not going to make me cry. I'm tougher than that.'

'I didn't think –'

Tamsin gave a hoarse laugh. 'Oh yes you did.' Then her face dropped. 'But what the hell, Elaine? Does he not realise we're hurting over Billy? That we've known the lad for weeks and for him to then be killed on our op … ? And then for him to do that to me … and it's not that he did that, no, it's his … he can do that,' she stuttered, 'he's the boss … but in front of everyone. You just don't.'

Elaine was leaning back on the wall. She watched the emotions play out across Tamsin's face. Her own stomach twisted as Tamsin spoke of Billy, her affection for the lad cutting deep. 'I don't know. I really don't know. For some reason he seems a little –' she paused, looked for the word '– different, with this job. I spoke to him at the scene yesterday and he looked dreadful, Tamsin.'

Tamsin looked up. 'You know he opposed the op?'

'No?'

'Yeah. Jain told him he had to do it and he had me back him up. I went into Ray's office and I told him everything would be okay.' Her eyes filled with tears now.

'Oh, Tamsin.' Elaine reached out and put her arms around the other woman. Pulled her into a hug. Felt her curls tickle her face. Her own emotions were so tangled that she couldn't decipher them, but she could clearly feel the hurt radiating off Tamsin. 'You couldn't have known.'

Tamsin pulled away. Scrubbed at her eyes with the backs of her fingers, then wiped her face with her palms. 'Look okay?' she asked.

'You look fine,' answered Elaine, 'But – are you?'

Tamsin pushed her shoulders back. Rubbed at her face again. 'Yes, I'm fine. We need to get on with this job. For Billy.'

'I'm here if you need to talk.'

'How are you always so in control?' asked Tamsin.

'The perks of having two tearaways,' laughed Elaine.

Tamsin smiled.

'This is going to be a tough job, there's no doubt about that, but we will get through it. And I'll keep my eye on the boss. He does seem to be acting a little out of character.'

31

After tearing a quiet strip off Tamsin, Ray wanted to understand the transplant system better. He wanted to know the process for being placed on the list: the criteria for being added and particularly for being refused. And he wanted to know what the waiting time was for people on the transplant list, especially for organs that could technically be harvested from living donors. It had emerged from the interviews earlier that this seemed to be the business plan of the organisation they were dealing with. Living donors only. People who were willing to come forward and sell parts of themselves for money. To fund whatever it was they needed the money for, or to get themselves out of debt. He'd heard of a case of a person who had attempted to sell an organ on eBay of all places. As though it wouldn't be noticed or stopped. People so desperate to break out of the debt cycle that they'd offered themselves up with little or no knowledge of what it entailed.

Ray wanted this information.

He spent a couple of hours researching transplants, then made an appointment with a consultant at the Royal Free Hospital on Pond Street to discuss the whole process with her so that he understood it. If he could get his head around it and find out what the organisation they were up against needed, then they would know what other lines of inquiry they needed to follow.

There was a knock at his door. Ray looked up. Tamsin stood there. Arms locked across her chest, a barrier. She'd had a bad day.

'Come in, Tamsin. Sit down.' Ray gestured to the seat in front of his desk.

Tamsin did as he directed. Again she held her upper body in that stiff purposeful way.

She was silent.

He waited.

She locked her ankles around each other and pushed them back under the chair.

Still he waited for her to speak. Allowed a peacefulness to settle in the room. Gave her space to breathe and find her voice. He made a quick note of the time he was to meet the consultant in his diary as he waited.

'Sir.'

'Mmm?' He kept his head down. He didn't want to force her hand, to push her over the edge. He valued her on the team but he was aware how her drive to succeed could push her into the middle of problems. He'd avoid it for her.

He opened his email inbox.

'About today.'

'Yes?' Ray selected his recipient and entered the subject line.

'If I overstepped the line ...'

He stopped typing and looked at his subordinate. Struggling to find her place when her determination had pushed her over lines she hadn't realised were there.

'Tamsin, I admire a desire to succeed and how much you bring to the table. How many hours you put in. How passionate you are about the jobs we do. I don't ever want you to lose that thirst for the job. I don't want you to turn into a jobsworth, clocking in and clocking out, not caring about the people we deal with day in and day out. You're a part of this team because of the person you are.'

His young DS had chewed the side of her mouth while he talked, but now she'd stopped, her mouth a little ajar.

'But, I thought –'

'I know what you thought. Yes, I disagreed with you, and yes, I need you to learn when you can and can't push a topic, that's all. Learn to read people a little more. Figure out when you can push and when, for instance, I'm not in the mood.'

'Yes, sir.'

'And, Tamsin.'

'Yes, sir.'

'Taking you off the interview this morning was not a reflection on you. I wanted to get my feet wet with this job. It meant a lot to me.'

'Okay.'

'Have a glass of wine tonight. Sleep and come at it tomorrow afresh. We've a lot of work to do yet. Plenty of work –' the phone on his desk started to ring. He looked at Tamsin '– to get your teeth into.'

Tamsin nodded, her curls now moving around her face. Ray picked up the handset on the third ring. Listened to the caller, uh-huh-ing down the phone as he did.

Tamsin stood to leave. Ray looked up, still listening, and held up a finger for her to wait. He told the caller a couple of them would be right there, asked for the address again, grabbed a pen and scribbled it down on his open notepad.

'We have a burnt-out silver BMW in Plaistow.'

'You think it's ours?' Tamsin asked.

'I've no idea. It was lit up inside a garage. Could be kids. But we'll have to check it out. Want to come?'

The bright clear day was now punctured by the ugly blackened steaming shell of the garage in front of them. Fingers of smoke damage leisurely grasped hold of each side wall to the adjoining garages. Its door, which was completely off the frame, lay on the floor, bent and crumpled, blackened. The brickwork was scorched, licked from the inside, like a dragon had breathed outwards. The corrugated roof sagged as though there were a weight at its centre.

Inside, the car was a charred shell.

The fire had been ferocious.

The air was clogged with the stench of burnt oil and rubber.

Ray and Tamsin stood back and let the firemen work, hands in pockets to keep the cold at bay. It always seemed that the brighter the day the colder it felt. Even with the residual heat that came from the now extinct garage and car fire, steaming from being recently put out. It hissed and groaned in complaint.

'He really wanted to destroy the evidence.' Ray looked at the firemen who walked around the outer scene. He couldn't stop them trampling all over his scene: they had priority if there was a fire.

'We might be able to check the vehicle through the VIN number and then make enquiries as to who owns the lock-up?' Tamsin ventured.

'Yeah, once fire have said it's safe, we'll take it in and get it examined. See if there's any area left untouched by fire that may hold a print or partial print that we can run and get a match for.' He looked at Tamsin. 'Because this is our guy, no doubt about it.'

'What do you think the odds of that are?' she asked.

Ray took a step back and looked at the ground. The guy was good. He'd shot Billy, not in the head, not a death shot, but one that would make Ray stop and help so that he could get away, and now he'd fired his vehicle in situ so as to not trigger any cameras. He had brains, and Ray didn't like criminals who used their brains. It always took so much longer to catch up with them, which often meant more people ended up hurt.

'Slim,' he answered, as he faced down.

'I feel bad.' Tamsin kept her eyes on the ground.

'For what?'

'When I walked into your office the other day, when you were in conversation with the guv about it …'

Ray knew what she was about to say. 'It's okay.'

'No. I was so focused on the outcome I didn't think through the risks properly. I said it should go ahead.'

Hands still in his pockets, Ray looked right and left the length of the garage lock-ups and then back down to his feet. It was reasonably clean.

'We all feel it, Tamsin. The truth is, I don't think any of us could have stopped Billy. So now we have to finish it for him.'

He took another step back. Then another. Then another.

'Tamsin?'

She finally looked at him.

'Step back here with me, will you.' She moved back as he'd asked.

'What do you see on the floor?'

She looked down. 'Not a lot.' She looked back at him, confused. 'Why, what should I see?'

'I'm not sure, but let's get the CSIs to do the area around the length of the garages and see if he's dropped anything. I'm certain this is our guy.'

32

With the sat nav on it took him half an hour to navigate to the hospital.

In that time, Ray ran through the questions in his head that he needed answers to. It was a complete unknown, so the old phrase 'you don't know what you don't know' sprang to mind as he manoeuvred through the late-afternoon London traffic. Out of Stoke Newington, through Islington, and into Camden to Hampstead. He had an appointment at the Royal Free. One he hoped would shed some light on the matter.

He was flustered by the time he arrived. Getting accustomed to driving places he used to know by heart, with the help of an electronic device, wasn't easy. It irritated him. Made the journey twitchy as he continued to follow the hollow-voiced instructions. He'd been informed by the doctor who had talked to him about his condition that losing his sense of direction might be one of the side-effects of the disorder but wasn't one that all prosopagnosics struggled with. Ray was annoyed that he was one of those affected this way.

Finding a parking space had proved close to impossible, and then navigating the large hospital had nearly sent him into his own private meltdown as time and again he found himself back in a room or corridor he'd already visited. He felt like a child lost in a maze. The corridors looked identical, a linoleum floor and scuffed painted walls; the signs were no help at all, as the arrows seemed to point in random directions or nowhere in particular. It took a kindly cleaner who he had passed at least three times to take him by the hand – very nearly literally, and he could have done with it – and show him where he needed to be. Ray couldn't thank him enough and pleaded a late night at work for his incompetence with directions today. He dreaded the thought that he'd have to find his own way out, and cursed, yet again, the injury to his head.

Ray took a minute to compose himself.

Mrs Moira Sandford sat behind her desk, glasses down at the end of her nose as she bent toward the computer monitor reading whatever it was that held her interest on the screen. Ray rapped on the open door. Sandford pushed the spectacles up her nose and looked up at her visitor. Ray struggled to place the look on her face. Eventually she asked, 'Can I help you?' a slight tone of exasperation in her voice.

'Oh, yes.' He straightened himself, aware that he may have been slouching on the door frame a little. 'I'm DI Ray Patrick, we spoke on the phone.'

Sandford now pushed the square-framed glasses to the top of her head, which pushed her loose brown hair up with it, the spectacles acting like a child's Alice band. 'Yes, yes, of course. Come in. Have a seat.' She waved to the two chairs in front of her desk. 'Can I get you a drink? Tea, coffee? It's from the doctor's lounge, but I can't promise it'll be much better than what comes out of the vending machines. I'm informed I'm not the best at making it.'

'A coffee would be great, thank you. Black, no sugar.' He was in need of it after the trials of the drive over.

'Give me a minute. I'll be right with you.'

Sandford rose; she carried a little extra weight but she was attractive and well presented, wearing a dark, slim-cut pencil skirt and a floral pale-cream blouse. Her hands, he noticed, were well manicured, though not polished, the nails short. Her eyes when she looked at him were the palest blue. All details he could take in on the spot.

Once she'd left he looked around her work space. It was equally tidy and clean as she presented. There was little on her desk. The computer she had been working on, a framed photograph that faced away from him, and a file of papers.

There were a couple of metal drawers against the walls which looked like they'd hold patient files, and some posters on the walls which explained what specific organs did for the body. She didn't, he noticed, have her credentials tacked up on her walls as some doctors he knew did. She was obviously comfortable with who she was and what she had achieved. She didn't need to convince others of her skill.

Ray heard her heels tap on the floor before he saw her, and turned as she entered; he recognised the blouse and skirt as she handed him a mug with a pharmaceutical company name on the side.

'Thanks. I need this.'

She went back to her seat. 'Don't thank me yet, you haven't tasted it.' She smiled. Relaxed. 'So, what is it I can do for the Metropolitan Police today?'

Ray leaned back in his chair. This was difficult. It was likely to shock. He didn't want to give too much away. He didn't know if they would end up identifying medical professionals involved from their NHS. That would be a complete disaster. But that was some of what he needed to know: who and what this organisation needed to carry operations like this off. He took a deep breath.

'It's a bit of a delicate matter.'

'Detective Inspector, everything that comes into my office is delicate,' Sandford replied with a smile that made her face light up. The weak afternoon sun lit her from behind and made random strands of hair stand out as though electrified.

'Ray,' he replied.

'Ray,' she said. 'There's no need for subtleties in here. Not with me anyway. Little can shock me in my line of work. You have to be quite hardened. Or good at compartmentalising, anyway. Otherwise you'd go home at the end of some days a quivering wreck and wonder how or why you even put one foot in front of another.'

This time it was Ray's turn to nod in appreciation. His job did the same to him. Human nature made him wonder if the kindness of strangers existed or if it was just a phrase someone had created to keep hope alive so that they would all continue to put that foot in front of the other one.

'Okay, good. I have an investigation that you may be able to help me with. Not directly, but I do need a lot of help to understand the peripherals of the job and who the people involved might be, both on a professional level and a personal.'

Sandford put her mug on the desk and leaned forward, elbows resting on the wood. 'I'm all ears.'

Ray took a drink from his mug and wondered why he'd bothered. She hadn't been kidding when she'd said she didn't know how to make coffee. He did his best to keep his face straight and not let on how awful it was.

'We have a case of illegal organ trading and I know very little of the transplant world, I'm afraid,' he said.

Sandford didn't appear shocked. It surprised him. Did he need to bear her in mind for this, as one of the doctors used?

'Yes, I've heard of transplant tourism. The World Health Organisation keeps us up to date with these issues.' So that was where she was coming from. 'You've had victims travel out to foreign countries to buy new organs?'

'No, I'm afraid it's closer to home than that.' He didn't want to give too many details away, but this needed to be a two-way street. He needed information from the consultant, and she asked direct questions, ones that were difficult to ignore or answer around. Ray supposed that came with her job, the ability to ask the right questions; and that was why he was here, to get the information she knew.

'It's here in the UK?' Now she did look incredulous; it was so plain on her face that Ray could recognise it.

'I'm afraid so.'

'How can you be sure?'

'Mrs Sandford, let me assure you, our investigation is thorough and our information solid. This is happening and it's happening now on UK soil. And people are dying.'

134

'Oh my God.' She leaned back in her chair. The colour had drained from her already pale face. 'What can I do?'

'I need a crash course in transplants. Specifically living transplants.'

'That's a lot of information, can you be a little more specific?'

Ray put his mug down. He wouldn't drink it anyway. 'To be honest, the best way for us to get ahead of this is for us to understand it, so I need to know as much as I can.' He bent down to the soft leather briefcase at his feet and pulled out his hardback notebook. 'I've jotted down some of the first questions that came to me, to get us started, if you have the time for us to go through them?'

Sandford waved her arm across the room a couple of times as though wafting away a fly. Ray took this as a sign that he was to carry on and he had the floor. She'd give him the time he needed. A light scent of vanilla with a floral undercurrent floated up to him as she moved the air in front of him. It wasn't unpleasant.

Ray opened his notebook and clicked on his pen.

'How many people, bare minimum – not what you think you need in case of emergency, or in case you are sued, or any other random factor, but bare, bare minimum –' Ray looked at her to get his point across and she nodded '– are needed to do the transplants on living donors, both for the donor op and recipient op, and what equipment is needed? Again,' he eyed her for impact, 'bare minimum, for these ops?'

'You've asked me two questions, I need to answer them individually, okay?'

'It'd probably be more helpful to me. To help me follow.'

'Okay, we'll go with the first question, people, and I'll try my best to pare it down for you and not give you all the people we would have in the theatre, which, to be honest, some days is like a merry-go-round with people coming in and going out.'

Ray was grateful that she understood his meaning. 'Thank you.'

'You obviously need an anaesthesiologist and a surgeon. If you're looking at bare minimum, I'll take it that you'll use the same team for transplant as you do for the retrieval. Which is perfectly reasonable, particularly with a kidney as it can be held on ice the longest of all retrieved bodily organs, at thirty-six hours.'

Ray whistled. 'I did not know that.'

'Not many people do. They think the turnaround time is short, which it is for other organs. The liver is eight to twelve hours. This is incredibly short if you want to get it from one end of the country to the other.'

'Hence the allowance for blue lights on transport vehicles.'

'Yes, and the use of helicopters. But back to our transplanters.'

Ray got the impression that she didn't quite have as much time as he'd imagined. That, or she didn't go in for small talk, even if it did relate to their subject.

'You'll need a scrub practitioner and I'd say a recovery ODP, but your scrub could probably do that job if they were short on staff. I've dropped several staff out of this equation. Staff that I'd say were quite vital, like an assisting surgeon and a surgical ODP.'

'I do appreciate that. So. These are very specialist medical staff they have on their books.'

'They are, and it worries me that this is happening, that these staff are available to people like this.' Sandford moved the file of papers from one side of her desk to the other. 'I do hope you manage to track them down.'

'With this help from you, it'll make it easier. Before I spoke to you I had no idea what was involved.'

Sandford picked up the file again, tapped the edge of it on the desk, straightened the papers. 'The equipment is a more difficult topic to cover, particularly in the way you want me to answer it.'

'In what way?'

'In that there is so much medical equipment needed for retrieval and transplant. Stuff you really can't do without. The people who pay for the transplant stage of the process will pay huge sums of money for a new organ. They'll risk it all, but they think it's worth it because they feel let down by the system, the waiting list, they feel their life won't hold out long enough for the NHS to save them. So, on that premise they give huge sums of money for a third party to provide the service. And when they pay this amount of money they expect to see certain things – I imagine, because I certainly would.'

'They'd expect to see a proper surgical theatre is what you're saying?'

'Exactly. And all that goes with it. The operating table, the lights, the apparatus that supplies the anaesthetic, the surgical equipment that goes on the trays, pulse oximeters, capnographs, resuscitator, defibrillator, ECG machine –'

'I get the picture.'

'Really? Because I wasn't even halfway through. Then there's also your ancillary equipment and medications to manage emergencies, which no surgeon in his right mind would operate without.'

Ray rubbed his head at the sheer volume of medical kit Sandford talked about. 'And what about premises?' He knew Sandford had got his point about it not having to be to her standard.

She looked at him. 'Bear in mind the equipment we've discussed, they could set it up anywhere discreet. So long as they have power and they can make the surfaces sterile – because I presume if they run it as a business, they don't want patients to die – then they can set up in any room they wish. There is absolutely no way to narrow down a location for you. But, as I've mentioned, it will probably look semi-professional, or I'd hope so, otherwise these customers –' she put her fingers up and made air quotes round the word customers '– who buy the organs take their lives into their hands coming off the NHS waiting list to do it this way, more than I already think they are. They'll also need a ward of sorts, and twenty-four-hour nursing staff to take care of the recipient – you can't kick the recipient out straight after surgery. You can do that relatively quickly with the donor, especially nowadays when you can do the retrieval laparoscopically, but the recipient will need to walk away with a whole host of anti-rejection meds. This needs to be a well-run business if it's to be a lucrative one.'

It suddenly felt so very grim. Ray picked up his mug and drank, then remembered why he'd put it down.

'I told you I make dreadful coffee.' She smiled.

He thought he'd managed to keep a straight face.

'Do you want to finish this in the canteen, grab a decent drink?'

With a steaming mug of fresh coffee in front of him and a slice of lemon drizzle, Ray opened his notebook again. Left it on the table and started to eat the cake. Sandford had tea. No cake.

'I get why people might think it's easy money to sell an organ they don't need.' He paused, reconsidered what he'd said, and started again. 'Okay, I don't quite get it, but people are desperate and take desperate actions all the time.' He shoved the rest of the cake in his mouth, swirled his finger in the air like a washing machine as though Sandford couldn't see he was eating, and waited until he'd finished before he continued. He hadn't realised how hungry he'd been. 'What I don't get is why the recipients act so desperate. Why they put themselves at such risk. If they're already on a transplant list, waiting for an organ, why then go to a shady organisation, to a shady place, to have an op that needs continual medication afterwards, with such high-risk factors when the NHS has you sorted?'

She stared at him with the look he recognised from earlier: that one of incredulity. He didn't know if it was due to the fact that he'd paused the conversation long enough to eat cake, or because of the question he'd asked.

'You think everyone who's on the transplant list will get well?' she asked.

'Won't they?' Ray swallowed some coffee, draining away the remains of his cake.

She nearly laughed and he felt a little stupid, but she managed to stop at a wide smile. Not a comfortable feeling though. 'Do you realise how many people are placed on the transplant list every year? In fact, let's talk about kidneys, shall we, because that's the main living-donor organ we transplant.'

'Okay, give it to me. That's what I'm here for.' Ray knew they were headed into serious territory now. Not that any subject they'd covered so far hadn't been, but they were talking about real people on National Health waiting lists who were waiting for other people to die. He put his mug down and picked his pen back up.

'This year we have a little over five thousand people on the kidney transplant waiting list alone. Five thousand people. Imagine that.'

He did. Five thousand people needed to offer up kidneys or five thousand people needed to die and their relatives needed to agree that their organs could be harvested. That was a lot of people, by anyone's standards.

'And for each of those people so many criteria must be met for the transplant to go ahead, and then if the patient finally gets to the top of the list –' Sandford stopped and looked at Ray '– and when I say gets to the top of the list, I don't mean the list works in order of who goes on it first rises up fastest, it doesn't work that way, there are so many criteria involved in matching available donor organs to those waiting – so when I say they get to the top of the list, I mean when their time comes, okay?'

Ray agreed. Made more notes in his pad.

Sandford continued where she had stopped. 'So if a patient gets to the top of the list –' she looked at Ray and he waved his pen to show that he understood her meaning '– and a donor becomes available, we have to cross-match the donor and recipient, and that doesn't always work out the way you want it to. Do you know the patients who hold the majority on the long-wait list?' She fiddled with a napkin on the table, folding corners over into neat right-angles.

Ray shook his head. It was swimming.

'Black and ethnic minority patients. They're more difficult to match, as well as patients with blood group O, which may surprise you. And patients get matched by their life expectancy after the surgery.' Sandford's face was serious, eager now, she wanted him to understand. 'They need to have a good chance of life after the transplant. But the problem is, if they've been on the transplant list a long time, their health has deteriorated and therefore their life expectancy chances have decreased. It's a vicious decreasing circle and these people are desperate.' She made another fold; this time she halved the napkin and seared the fold close with her nail.

'Jesus.' Ray had no other words. Policing was tough but these people were in a limbo like no other. Sick and in need of someone else's death, and the quicker the better.

'And that's not all,' Sandford continued. 'Since 2012, the number of people who have donated organs, be it either as a deceased donor or as a living donor, has halved as of this year. Halved.'

141

33

Ray lifted the lid of the laptop, a can of beer open beside him. It was already dark outside. The day had been a long one, though the daylight hours themselves were short. Night stole in, silent and heavy. Ray tended to like this time of year as the season changed. Signs of life started to creep in again. Light was the main clue that spring was creeping towards them, but Ray could also feel the wet and freezing winter slip away, the days become less harsh. Easier on the soul.

He opened the TOR network browser again, and, in another window, the hidden Wiki page with listed websites. He needed to go in and keep up his search. It wasn't an easy place to navigate. The people who found their way here, he decided, were both desperate enough to do it and also intelligent enough to figure it out. That, or, when it came to those who wanted to sell, knew someone who would point the way.

He took a deep slug and stared at his screen. Joe had outsourced this work to the eCrime Unit before Billy had given them a direct URL address, and since Billy's death the website had moved. The group were really twitchy. He didn't know how much work eCrime would be able to do, how deep they'd be able to go or if indeed they'd be able to get any information if they found the website. That was the whole point of the dark web. People wanted to be untraceable. That was why he had to do this off the books. He would hold back, though, and see how the investigation went. He wouldn't be stupid enough to screw up the investigation by trampling his size tens all over it. No, he'd wait and see if they could get somewhere the proper way, and if not, then he'd have to see what he could do from this point of view.

The front door opened. Keys dropped onto the side table with a clatter. Heels clicked, then stopped. Ray knew stockinged feet now walked towards him. He took another swig of his beer. Remember, there's going to be a disconnect, he told himself.

Then another swig of beer.

He could feel her waiting behind him. Waiting for him to put the can down. Ray leaned forward and placed it on the table, next to the laptop, which was still open. He pushed down on the screen, clicked the laptop closed.

Celeste wrapped her arms around his neck. Her face came to meet his. A routine they'd got into. A closeness they enjoyed.

Ray could feel the warmth of her, heard the soft hum from her throat as she pulled in close, the back of the chair still between them, smelled the sweetness of her perfume mixed with the chill from the night; her body heat was pushing through but the cool from the street had clung to her as she'd swept into the warm house. The familiarity of all this made his chest contract. He'd missed the intimacy. Missed her. Craved normality back in his life. He lifted his hand and touched Celeste's cheek where the chill and warmth battled.

A physical sigh went through his shoulder as she leaned over him.

Ray didn't want to break this moment. This was the relationship he remembered. This was him and Celeste from before. He needed this. If he turned around now he'd be shocked by the lack of connection between the person in front of him and the memory of her. Of them. He was still adjusting and it was still a jolt when the face of those closest to him didn't connect to the memory. The wiring had disconnected and it wasn't easy for him to hide how he felt.

'Good day?' he asked

'Mmm. You?' she murmured. Her voice so familiar and warm.

'Busy – you know how it is.'

'You smell good.' Her nose nestled into his neck. Ray closed his eyes. Her hand pushed its way down the front of his jumper. This was the woman he was falling in love with. He knew her voice, recognised her touch, her scent. Ray relaxed as her hand caressed his chest and then slid down. A moan escaped. He could be in the here and now.

Suddenly Celeste was laughing.

'Ray, I can't reach your jeans from back here. I'm not Mr Tickle.'

She moved. She was at the side of him and then she was in his lap, moving in to kiss him. They stopped to face each other.

Ray looked into her eyes.

'I'm sorry, Celeste.' He stood. Celeste stumbled from him, all arms and legs. 'I've got a shit-load of work to do tonight. I was in the middle of it when you came in.' He looked to the floor, hated how he felt, how he was behaving, but he couldn't stop himself. Then he looked back to her face where she was now curled up in the chair Ray had a second ago leapt from. Her mouth ajar, no words, a shocked expression on her face. Ray's stomach twisted. A knife sliced through his insides. He felt like a heel. He had felt the old connection he'd had with her, but the minute he looked at her the disconnect threw him, even though he had tried to prepare for it.

He hated this. He had been managing while he had been off work, but since the Billy op, since his problem helped a killer walk away, the self-loathing was creating a barrier that he just couldn't break through, and Celeste was taking the brunt of it. They always say those closest.

'What am I missing, Ray?' Her eyes were damp.

'You're not –'

'You've been a little off since the hospital.' She stood in front of him. 'Since the accident.' Her eyes bore into him. 'Did they say something you're not telling me?'

'No, Celeste.'

'I don't know if I can believe you. The timing of it fits. I can work that much out for myself. And it got so much worse when you went back to work, as though work is aggravating it. So if it's not that, what is it?'

'It's work.' He stared at her. 'In the normal sense. That's all. I told you about the kid that was killed in the middle of an op. It's a big deal.'

'Don't give me that.' Her voice was hard. 'This started way before that. I need to know. We're a couple. If there's a problem with you, then I need to know to be able to help. That's what couples do, Ray. So. What aren't you telling me?'

'There's nothing.' He desperately wanted to tell her now but the fear of her leaving was worse than the immediate anger they were dealing with.

'You know what I can't deal with?' Her back was rigid, her arms crossed.

He knew what she was going to say but was helpless to stop it. 'What?'

'Lies, Ray. Lies.'

He looked at the floor.

'I can deal with the problem you aren't telling me about. We can work it out together. I'm with you. I won't walk away. But what I can't deal with is lies. No matter how bad you think it is. I'm in it with you.' She narrowed her eyes. 'Even if that means we have to switch to client confidentiality.' Her voice was low.

'Jesus, Celeste. What do you think I've done?'

Her voice lifted now. 'I don't know, Ray, that's the point, you won't tell me!'

Ray turned his back on her. His shoulders slumped. 'Because there's nothing to tell you.'

'I don't understand why you won't talk to me.' She walked back towards the door. Leaned to put her shoes back on. 'You know where I am.'

Heels clicked against the floor and the door opened and closed as she left.

The laptop screen light shone bright as Ray leaned over it, determined to find answers. This time it wasn't the dark net he searched, but the everyday internet. There had to be something he could actively do to help himself. Like physiotherapy for the mind. He wasn't one to sit back and accept a problem. He would assess it and search for the best answer, and that was what he would do now.

With the slammed door still ringing in his ears he planned to find a way to make his brain rewire itself. He'd heard of neuroplasticity, that the brain could repair itself, that it could relearn, that it was an amazing part of the human body that was more uncharted than the depths of the world's oceans, the last human frontier. If scientists still knew so little, then he wouldn't sit back and simply believe that there was no treatment for his condition. He would find an answer and retrain himself.

Sitting and waiting wasn't a part of his DNA.

In the bar of his search engine he typed: Memory exercises for prosopagnosia.

The first result was the NHS website. It cited no treatment.

Psychology Today cited no treatment.

Further listed sites offered no hint of treatment options. No random or quirky try-at-home ways to retrain your brain.

Ray picked up the laptop, anger ran through his veins. Frustration. Hopelessness. Then all the feelings that coursed through him exploded and the laptop flew up in the air towards the wall. It missed the television by a few inches. Metal and glass crashed through the silence in the living room as it dropped to the floor. The lidded screen-hinges parted from the keyboard and Ray could see a huge crack appear on the dark and empty screen. A crack that resembled his life.

He returned to his seat and picked up his beer.

34

They were running out of time on the custody clock and needed to pull all the strands of work together. The conversation with Sandford had been eye-opening, but Ray still wasn't sure how well it could be used within the investigation. Though there were plenty of leads they could follow.

The morning briefing was due to start. Through his door Ray could see the incident room. Staff were milling about, checking computers, making notes, carrying mugs of drinks to desks. He looked at the seating plan he'd drawn, frustrated.

It was easy to figure out who was who when they were seated where they were supposed to be as per the written plan, but when they were out of their seats it screwed with his brain as he had to rely much more on quick thinking. He had to check hairstyles, listen to language, search for rings, gender, all manner of characteristics that identified all the individuals in the office and in his life. It was hard work, and work he could do without today.

What he could do with was a coffee.

Ray headed to the staff kitchen, filled the kettle with water and his mug with coffee granules, and stared out of the window as he waited for the kettle to boil.

'It's that bad this morning, is it?'

Ray recognised the voice behind him as that of his friend and guvnor, Prabhat Jain.

He replied without turning, 'It is, this morning. Days like today I can understand why people turn into functioning alcoholics.'

'Want to tell me about it?'

The kettle clicked off as it reached boiling point. Ray turned. The face before him failed to register, as he knew it would. 'This case. Billy. Responsibility.'

'Ah, want to add world peace to that list?'

'I'm serious.'

'I know you are. So are the Independent Police Complaints Commission. You don't get to have the monopoly on responsibility, Ray. When the investigation is over into Billy's death someone will lose their job, I can guarantee you that. Heads are rolling upstairs. I'm shielding you from most of that because you're fresh back after six months' sick leave. I've figured you're finding it hard. I think you're still in some pain. So I've kept all the flak that's flying around away from you. And in turn I don't want the responsibility word thrown back in my face, no matter what you may think you mean by it.' Jain paused for breath, and then said, 'Do you understand me?'

'Yeah, I should have realised an incident like this has major repercussions. I must have been so wrapped up in my own guilt that I didn't pick up on it. Will you let me get you a whisky one night?'

'A whisky? You'll be buying a bloody barrelful, the amount of trouble I'm keeping away from your shoulders.' And with that he walked out of the kitchen.

Ray looked back out of the window at the awful, dull, flat, eight-storey grey building behind them, then poured the hot water over his coffee and walked to the incident room, full of faces he didn't recognise, to do a briefing that frustrated the hell out of him.

The plan was to put a file in to the CPS for a charging decision on the two held offenders. They should have enough for conspiracy to commit murder, but not the trading in human organs offences yet. They would have to continue to investigate while they were on remand.

Ray told the team about the meeting with Sandford, and set actions for inquiries into medical professionals who had been struck off in the last five years; he also wanted to consider the finances of all transplant surgeons, although he wasn't sure if he could get the authority to do that. It was a fishing expedition. They also needed to pay attention to the transplant lists and see who no longer needed a transplant, who no longer turned up for dialysis. The list of actions on the case was endless and Ray's head swam as he kept up with it all. Everyone had notebooks out, pens scribbling away.

Ray scrubbed at his face with his palms.

'Okay, guys, we've got a lot of work to get through so I hope you've had a decent night's sleep or have a strong cup of coffee with you, because you'll need it.' A couple of days into the inquiry, they still looked alert. Give it a couple more days and they'd start to turn a shade of grey as fatigue and the lack of a decent meal took its toll on their bodies, and stress at home from lack of interaction with loved ones created ripples of conflict. Ripples that everyone knew would level out again once the first wave of the investigation was over, but that had to be ridden out in the meantime.

Ray continued to run through all they had and all they needed to do.

'We also have the BMW in the CSI garage and they'll go over it with a fine-toothed comb,' he went on, 'as well as a full examination of the garage it was housed in. I don't hold out much hope that we'll get anything actionable back because whoever torched it did a pretty good job of it and we all know how destructive fire is.' A sea of faces watched him. All disconnected from any previous interactions. Yet all people he trusted and knew.

'We do have one light that shines in the darkness of this case though: I picked up an email from yesterday's CSI this morning – a cigarette butt was found in front of the garage. It was a Doina, which is not a common brand, in fact you can't buy it in the UK, not over the counter anyway, and it's possible it could be from our arsonist. It'll be tested for DNA and I've put an urgent rush on it so we should know soon if we get a match …' He paused then, rubbed his face with both hands. 'A match within the UK. If not –' he rubbed some more '– then we wait again while we send it to Interpol to search their systems, which I expect to have to do if we bear in mind the ethnicity of our killer and the home location of one of his goons.'

'Elaine.' He looked to Elaine's desk. 'Keep up with the inquiries for the VRM I gave you so we can confirm it's the same vehicle that left the scene.'

There was no response.

He waited.

'Elaine?'

'Guv? Sorry, I was in late so I dropped into the nearest desk there was.' The voice came from nearer the back of the room. The woman in Elaine's chair wasn't Elaine, which was why she hadn't known how to respond to him.

Damn.

How to recover?

'Shit. Will you look at that? Only a couple of days in and already my brain is fried so much that I didn't notice it wasn't you in your own chair. I think I need another coffee!'

Laughter echoed around the room.

He'd done it. But really? These were intelligent people. They would never guess what was actually wrong, but some of them would be suspicious of the fact that he'd spoke to a colleague and thought it was Elaine when it wasn't. They'd be concerned. Maybe think it was drink. Drugs. He might get away with stress and lack of sleep if it didn't happen again.

He had to be more careful. He hadn't checked for the scar before he directed the question at her because her seat was occupied. But now he had to push himself more. He had to double check. He had to check the seating plan and he had to check the person's physical descriptors and characteristics. He couldn't slip up again.

'So,' he said as he looked at the correct version of Elaine, 'the BMW inquiries?' He smiled, making light of it.

She laughed. 'Yes, guv.'

35

It had been a long day but the team had managed to put a file together for the CPS to get a charging decision for the two men in custody. It was thin, but charges had been agreed on: conspiracy to commit murder. It was decided that they knew the guy carried a gun and that he was willing to use it should it turn out that the person they were meeting was not all he said he was.

As expected, there were no charges on the trading in human organs, even though they had talked about it a little. There was no evidence of any description, other than the brief comments made by both men that what they did was for the good of all people concerned. This was not considered enough.

'I understand this,' Ray told the team in front of him, 'but it doesn't mean I'm happy about it, because this was the entire reason Billy came to us in the first place. We now have to keep doing what we're doing and we'll get there. These two idiots are not the end of the line.'

There was grumbling around the room.

'Hey, we can do it. We'll have less of that,' he chided them. 'That's two locked up, it's a good job. Pat yourselves on the back and then get your head down and keep at it. You all have a lot to get on with.'

'So, beers tonight then, guv, as we've locked two up?' piped up Will.

Shit. He did usually take them all out for a beer if they closed a job or CPS authorised a charge on a good job, but it wasn't something he'd done since he'd come out of the hospital. Going into a scenario like that, a busy pub, people all over the place, moving about, changing places, going out of view and then coming back into view. Damn.

'I can't tonight. But I promise we'll make it a good one when we close this job properly, what do you say?'

'I say we'll keep you to it, guv.' Paula, Scottish accent.

'You'd better. I think we'll have earned it,' he replied.

With that, he walked into his office. They were a good team. He hated to deceive them. They'd be so much further ahead if he'd been able to identify the killer from the get go. And now he'd made an excuse to not take them out for a drink. He was going to go to hell.

There was a quick knock at the office door and a female walked in. Ray scanned her for markers and eventually went to her face and found the scar. It was Elaine.

'Hey, everything okay?' he asked.

'You got a minute?'

'Of course, what is it?'

She sat on the chair in front of his desk, looked him in the eye. A move that now made him uncomfortable.

'Are you okay, guv?'

'Am I okay? Why do you ask?' He shut the lid on his laptop. Sensing where this was headed.

154

'Well, this morning you were so tired and distracted you failed to notice I wasn't in my seat, and now you don't want to go out for a drink. It's ...' she shifted in her seat, 'not like you.'

Ray forced a smile onto his face. 'Don't worry. I'm fine. Honestly, it's fatigue. I think I tire easier since the accident. I think it aged me ten years. I don't know about you but I feel like an old man with these broken bones that ache when it's cold and remind me I'm not invincible.'

Elaine pushed a few strands of hair behind an ear. 'I know what you mean. But I thought I'd check.' She stood and went to walk out of the office, but stopped and turned before she left. 'I hope you don't think I've overstepped, but ... well, we've kind of been through a lot and ...'

'It's fine. But I'm good. Thanks, Elaine.'

Then she was gone and he felt like a complete heel, playing on their injuries from the accident. It was from the accident all right, but it wasn't the physical side.

He needed to up his game.

36

Elaine grabbed the lime and soda from the bar and walked to where the rest of the team were sitting. Voices loud and raucous, happy with the result they'd had that day.

'Don't forget we've got more work to do when we get back in tomorrow,' she said as she sat beside Tamsin.

Will groaned at her. 'Can't we just take this small win?' he asked. 'We're one step closer. Two charged. It's not a bad result.'

'It's not bad, but we haven't got justice for …' She shook her head. 'Never mind. Just make sure you're fit for the job tomorrow.'

Will lifted his pint glass in the air. 'Yes, ma'am.' Then slugged it back.

Elaine shook her head again.

Tamsin smiled. 'You seem tense, you okay?'

'Did the guv give you any clearer a reason for his not coming this evening?' She watched as a group of three women entered the pub. They were laughing at something that had been said before they had entered.

Will turned and watched as they approached the bar.

'Will, put your eyes back,' Tamsin advised, then turned back to Elaine. 'No, I only heard what he said to the team, that he couldn't make it. Why, did you want to talk to him?'

Elaine took a sip of her drink, thought about how much she could say to Tamsin. They were friends. She trusted her. She placed her drink back on the table. 'It's not that.'

'What then?'

'I'm worried about him.'

'The guv?'

'Yes.' Elaine looked at the team; they were making fun of Will, who had an eye for the ladies and was giving them plenty of ammunition now that he had his eye on the women at the bar. Will was taking it all in his stride. Elaine suspected that at some point in the evening he would probably go and talk to them. She was glad she wasn't in the dating scene anymore. Not that Will was supposed to be. He had a girlfriend, but chose to forget that fact when opportunity arose.

'Why?' asked Tamsin, leaning towards her, voice lowered. 'What's wrong?'

Elaine pushed herself back in the seat, away from the table, putting as much distance as she could between herself and the rest of the team, even if it was only a matter of inches. She dipped her head. 'Haven't you noticed anything odd since he came back to work?'

'I can't say I have. What are you seeing?'

'When he called Annette by my name in briefing?'

'He said he was tired. He's been putting in a lot of hours and he's not long returned to work after six months off sick. It's not surprising the hours he's putting in are getting to him.' Tamsin looked confused.

There was a scrape of a chair. Elaine looked past Tamsin and saw Will getting up. To talk to the women already? But he moved past them and went to the men's room.

'I'd believe that if he hadn't also taken a wrong turn when we were heading to Billy's op that day. He made the same excuse then, that he was tired and in pain.'

'I wondered what had happened.'

'Yes, the guv was driving and it was as if he didn't know where he was going. We had to swap seats and I drove.'

Tamsin laughed. 'The guv not knowing where he's going? You are kidding, right?' She'd dropped her voice and twisted at the waist more so her back was to Gareth. He wasn't paying attention anyway. Paula had the group in stitches, as she was taking the piss out of Will in his absence. Not worried about his return, as it was something she was more than willing to do to his face as well.

Elaine shook her head. 'That's what it felt like to me. In the car with him.' She was beginning to wish she hadn't brought this up now.

'So what are you thinking?' asked Tamsin.

'I don't know. I really don't. But I do know I'm worried about it. It doesn't feel right. Something is wrong. There's something he's not telling us.' She spun her drink on the table. 'Maybe it is tiredness. Maybe he shouldn't be back at work, it might be that he's not fully recovered. But in that vein, maybe the accident messed with his head and he's still concussed or something.'

'You know what I think?' Worry lined Tamsin's face.

Did she really want to know? 'What?'

'I think you could do with a little more sleep as much as he could.' Her eyes were soft, kind. There was no malice. She wanted nothing more than to help her friend, Elaine could see that.

'You're probably right.' She gave Tamsin a tight smile.

'Hey, you two, are you with us or are you talking shop?' Paula shouted across the table.

Tamsin straightened herself. 'We're here. Don't worry about that.'

Elaine knew something was amiss. She could feel it. She would keep an eye on him. Even if she'd be doing it alone.

37

A few days of pulling together the paperwork for the court file and attempting to progress enquiries that would lead them to the guy at the head of the organisation, had caused some in the team to feel a little stir crazy. Ray watched from his office as Will and – he presumed it was – Paula, because it was always Paula, bickered about hell knew what. He would berate her and she'd laugh, causing him to get more annoyed. In the end, he turned his back and walked away. Ray rubbed his hand through his hair and looked at his own monitor, reading through the post-mortem report for Billy again. He understood the frustrations the unit were feeling, as he was itching with the very same irritation.

The phone rang and he picked it up. Tony from the control room. Said there was a message in the night from Basildon hospital, Essex, that he might be interested in.

Peartree Close at Ockendon, Essex, was as nondescript as any place Ray had encountered. Low three- and four-storey blocks of flats, maisonettes and garages crammed together. Cars parked all along the edges of the road and in front of garages, blocking them off. Space at a premium.

He looked at Elaine. 'Glad to be out the office?'

'Definitely. Though I wish it didn't have to be for this.' She put the handbrake on and switched off the engine. Looked at him. 'So your leg is really playing you up, is it?'

Ray cleared his throat. 'You wouldn't believe. Driving makes it worse. I'm probably going to have to sort out some more physio.'

Elaine dragged her coat from the back seat and exited the car, pulling the coat on.

'I'll sort it. I'll get in touch with a private physio and get it seen to as soon as I can.' Ray slammed his door shut.

'It's not a problem.'

'It may be safer with you driving.' The laugh was forced, sounded brittle in the quiet of the street, and Elaine narrowed her eyes at him. He turned away. His stomach telling him to move away from the situation. He was making it worse.

The door was opened by an older man. Creases lined his face like a well-worn road map. His hair was a bright white mop on his head. Strands sticking out in different directions. Smells of cooking seeped out of kitchen behind him.

'Mr Kayani?'

A single silent nod of the head.

'I'm Detective Inspector Ray Patrick from the Metropolitan Police and this is Detective Sergeant Elaine Hart, we're here to see Mrs Kayani if she's available. I believe she's expecting us?' He held out his identification for the older man to see. He leaned forward, squinting at the ID card. Laughter lines radiating out. Though laughter was not an emotion he was going to be feeling any time soon. He looked at the photo and up at Ray. It was several years old and Ray had greyed a little more since it was taken.

The older man stepped back. 'Come in please. She's in the living room. Can I get you a drink?'

161

'I'll have a coffee please,' said Ray.

'And just a water for me,' answered Elaine.

They walked through the busy kitchen, pans on every ring of the hob, each one bubbling away, with aromatic smells rising from its interior. Bowls and plates lined the work surface beside it and Tupperware boxes filled with foodstuffs lined the opposite counter.

In the living room the woman was surrounded by people. Beside her sat an older woman, her face grooved like the male who had let them in. Her eyes dark pools but red rimmed. Other men and women all squeezed into the small room, as well as a couple of teenagers and a younger boy, filling the sofa, chairs and space on the floor.

'Mrs Kayani?' asked Ray.

People parted, gave access to the woman. She stood. Arms crossed around herself, rubbing at her upper arms as if cold. 'Yes?' Her voice gentle.

Ray made the introductions again. 'I'm so sorry for your loss. Can we talk?'

Halima Kayani inclined her head and sank back on the sofa. A young male who had been sitting on a chair in the room vacated it and indicated that Ray could take it. He thanked him and took the seat. Elaine stayed on her feet. No one offered her a seat. The children stayed in the room on the floor.

'We need to know what happened with your husband. It's really important that we get to the bottom of this.' He paused, looked Halima Kayani in the eyes. 'So that no one else has to go through it.'

Her eyes were wide. Her clothes looked loose on her, as though she'd lost weight suddenly.

'Your coffee, Detective Inspector.' Mr Kayani came in from the kitchen and handed Ray a steaming mug. He took it and thanked him. The coffee smelled good and he was grateful for something to hold. This was always a difficult call to make.

'What is it you need to know? Maybe I can help. My daughter-in-law is struggling to get her head around the loss. As you can imagine, we all are. But I can tell you what I know.'

Ray accepted the older man's help. 'We need to know the circumstances surrounding your son's admittance to the hospital and his subsequent death,' said Ray. 'From what we've been told it doesn't appear to be entirely natural.'

The old man looked down at his hands. Twisted them together.

'It's okay, you won't be in any trouble. We just want to stop this happening again.'

'You have to understand, my son was responsible for supporting his family. For keeping a roof over the head of his wife, his three children, his mother and me; and occasionally he'd need to support an uncle and aunt too. Times were tight. The factory he worked at cut his hours, and because he was on a zero hours contract he couldn't do anything about it.'

38

Dr Mei Zhang was the Home Office forensic pathologist who had done the post-mortem on Balbir Kayani, and she had been kind enough to make time for Ray and Elaine that morning between cases and paperwork.

'It's a disturbing one, I thought we should deal with it so that you can get on with what you need to do to prevent further deaths of this type,' Dr Zhang said, her voice soft and lilting. She was a petite woman. Dark, glossy hair pinned up in a chignon at the back of her head. Small-framed glasses perched on her nose.

'Thank you. We appreciate you making time for us,' said Ray, before taking a sip of his second coffee of the morning.

The office they were in was small, compact, but tidy. The sharp tang of hospital antiseptic, strong down here in the mortuary area. Ray watched Elaine wrinkle her nose. It creased the scar under her eye. He looked away.

'I mean what I say, this needs to be stopped before it takes more lives.' Dr Zhang's face was set.

'Of course. We're working hard on this. We already have a couple of people charged.'

She lifted an eyebrow. 'With this?'

'Well, no.' He coughed. 'It wasn't possible, but they were involved. They indicated as such, but we didn't have the evidence.'

Elaine looked at the floor.

'Let me show you something, officers.' The petite doctor stood, pushed her chair back and walked out of the room without another word.

'She's serious about this,' said Elaine.

'She's not alone,' answered Ray, rising and following her out.

Dr Zhang walked with purpose, her rubber soles making soft thwacking sounds on the hard floor as she strode to her destination. Arms swinging at her sides. Ray's shoes and Elaine's boots clacked in comparison as they kept pace with the doctor.

They turned into a well-lit room that was cooler than the rest of the hospital and was steel-lined floor to ceiling and had small doors within the wall. Ray knew immediately where they were.

Dr Zhang walked straight up to a door that was at floor level, bent over and opened it. Yanked on a bar that was inside the door, and a tray slid out, wheels giving a small obstinate squeak on her first pull. Laid on the tray, wrapped in a clean white sheet, was a body.

'This is Mr Kayani. I think you need to see him. To understand what is happening to these people.' Her voice was clipped now.

'We understand, Dr Zhang. We know exactly what this group are doing and what they're capable of. You don't need to show us another body to prove a point. We're here for your help. For your knowledge.'

With gentle, soft movements, she unwrapped the cloth that surrounded Kayani, exposing first his face, then his chest, and eventually his abdomen. He looked peaceful. Or he would have, had it not been for the Y-shaped incision, neatly stitched, starting at his shoulders and going down to his pubis.

'Come this side please.' Her voice was gentler. More conciliatory. 'This is what you need to see.'

Ray and Elaine walked to the Kayani's left, and Dr Zhang indicated the curved incision which was also now stitched back up around his left side. Going from the front to back. It was about fifteen centimetres in length and must have been an angry red colour, though it had faded in death.

'Isn't that what kidney removals usually look like?' Ray asked.

Dr Zhang started to wrap Kayani back up. 'Not anymore. They can remove the kidney laparoscopically nowadays.' She looked at them. 'Keyhole surgery.'

'So what does this mean?' asked Elaine as she helped tuck the final areas of Kayani's cloth around him.

'That they went for the quickest option rather than one that would be easier for their patient. Doing an open surgery like this is faster than doing it laparoscopically. They save time. But not care. And this wound was more infected than it looks. It was filled with pus, although that was cleaned away during the post-mortem process. He was in a real mess and would have endured quite a lot of pain.'

Ray winced.

'They removed his left kidney. Then they failed to provide proper aftercare or advise him what to do if he had any problems, or what those problems could be. This man didn't need to die, Detective Inspector Patrick.'

Ray nodded. 'We understand the effects of this horrendous trade, Doctor Zhang.' He felt his skin crawl, standing here with the male stripped down in front of him. Stripped of his clothes, his dignity and his life. During interview the offenders had sold the business as that of saving lives. As doing good. All parties involved were consenting and treated well, they said. But this man that Dr Zhang was now sliding back into the darkness had not been treated well. The only people gaining from this operation were those who were running it.

The loss brought home the utter devastation he felt about Billy and how useless he was in the hunt for his killer: the head of this group that was responsible for taking the lives of people desperate enough to sell anything, themselves included.

They returned to the small office space that they'd not long ago vacated. Dr Zhang perched on the edge of her chair. 'There are senseless deaths and then there are deaths like this where they walk right into it through sheer desperation.' Her voice was subdued.

Elaine leaned forward. 'We do understand. We're desperate to identify and locate those responsible for this.'

That word. Identify. If only she knew.

'You have leads?'

'We have people connected but they're not talking. Anything you can tell us would really help.'

39

People were milling about. Talking, updating each other on different aspects of the job, and socially as well, from what Ray could hear

'Okay, let's get seated and get this briefing underway, shall we.' He wanted to bring the room to order. Not because he was desperate to get the briefing going but because his head was swimming from the ebb and flow of his team. He needed to stem it. Seat people. Halt the tide of confusion.

A rumble progressed through the incident room as individuals settled. Once silence had draped itself over the room, Ray thanked everyone. 'As you know, Elaine and I drove to Essex today after a report of a death that could be related to our investigation. I'm afraid to report that the body in the mortuary is in fact linked. Mr Balbir Kayani died after donating a kidney to a back-street organisation and getting an infection. His wife said he was too afraid to seek help from the NHS after he did this, because he feared they would report him to the police and then he would not be able to care for his family, and caring for his family was why he went ahead with the procedure in the first place. He felt it was his duty to look after the household, and he struggled. He was unable to get the help he needed from the group that had taken the organ from him, so he suffered in silence, not realising it was slowly killing him.'

'What do we know, guv?' Will asked.

'Speaking to the pathologist, we know that the medical personnel involved in this racket are in fact trained professionals. It was a good clean incision, removal and stitch-up. As opposed to the organisations abroad, where we know the work is shoddy, where we know that little thought or consideration is given to the donors; all they're after is what they can provide. Here, it would appear, they have genuine doctors on their books.'

'So what happens, why are people dying then?' Curls. Tamsin.

'It's the lack of aftercare. It's a big surgery. The people who are selling their organs aren't in a position to take it easy for as long as they need to and they aren't looking after themselves. Something starts to go wrong, something that would be easily solved if they saw a doctor, but they don't. It progresses. Infection sets in and they die. It's not the surgery itself that kills them. It's what happens after, as in the case with Billy's brother.'

'But what kind of doctors would do this?' Her accent was Scottish. Paula.

Ray leaned back on the table behind him. 'Doctors who are fully trained in organ transplants, Paula, I'm afraid to say. So we need to focus on this line of enquiry even more, please. Interview everyone who has been struck off in the last five years, and if no one stands out, go back ten years. Of course, there's no saying they're struck off, but I think it's the best place for us to start.'

A murmur moved through the room like a ripple on a still pond. Everyone had something to say about the fact that a trained transplant doctor, someone who worked to save lives, could or would be involved in an underground practice.

'I know. I know.' Ray tried to bring them back to focus. 'That's why we need to up our game on this. It just got a whole lot more serious. Not only are we investigating a murder, an organisation trading in human organs, but we know more people are at risk of dying at the hands of this team. We have a medically trained doctor, potentially still on the register and seeing patients, working with a group of people stripping UK citizens of their organs. We're up against it. We need to find out who these people are before we have to go and visit another family, another mortuary, and tell them we still don't know who these people are.'

40

The next week was filled with the day-to-day running of the investigation. A myriad inquiries, meticulously run through. Contact with the General Medical Council, and lots of long days spent going through background checks of each doctor struck off, before planning for home visits to see what they would throw up. Without anything specific, anything suspicious, it was impossible to home in on any one of the doctors who had been struck off, so a lot of work had to be done.

The incident room was busy with people constantly walking in and out. Other than briefings, Ray tried to keep himself to his office.

When he had decided to return to work and not disclose the prosopagnosia, he hadn't quite realised how overwhelmed he'd feel during a homicide investigation. Time was gradually allowing him to memorise people at a quicker pace, but it was still a slow process looking for the individual identifiers, and it was a process that frustrated him.

This morning it would be just him and Elaine, so Ray felt more settled. It would be a much easier day.

She was dressed in a black trouser suit. The jacket nipped in at the waist, with a plain cream round-neck T-shirt underneath.

Today they were to attend Billy's memorial. Yes, the church would be filled with people, but not people he would be expected to recognise. It was a memorial because a funeral couldn't be held yet: the coroner wouldn't be releasing his body for some time. This was to give police the opportunity to find his killer and avail any defence team of the discretion to request a second post-mortem.

It was often a difficult concept for families to get their heads around, to not have a loved one returned; but it was a part of the legal process.

The memorial, meanwhile, would provide Lilian Collier with a time and place to say goodbye to her second child.

A tightness gripped at Ray's chest at the thought, and the love he felt for his own two children seeped into his bones. To have them torn away from him would be like having his very body pulled apart.

'Ready?' asked Elaine as she shoved an umbrella into her bag. The sky was loaded with grey clouds and the forecast threatened showers all day.

'Yeah, it has to be done.'

'You'll note everyone who attends?' asked Prabhat from the doorway.

'Bloody hell, guv. Creep up on a guy why don't you,' Ray grumbled.

'But you've got a pen and notebook on you? You're not there to simply pay your respects.'

'Yes,' Ray huffed. 'I'm not new to the game.'

'I know how you feel –'

'I've got them,' Ray cut in, his tone sharper than he intended. He couldn't bear it when someone told him they understood how he felt. Especially now.

Prabhat threw him a look. He couldn't read it but he didn't need to. If he was in his shoes, he knew exactly what that look would say. He kept his mouth shut and patted his pocket, made sure he had his wallet.

Elaine jangled the car keys in front of him; he looked at them and a horror emptied him of all other feelings as he realised he wouldn't be able to use the sat nav with Elaine in the car, especially as it was only in Stoke Newington, and yet there was no way he'd find the church without it. They'd go around in circles all day before he got there.

'This weather ...' he indicated out of the window at the overcast sky, 'it seems to be playing havoc with the break points in my leg. It was a painful drive into work this morning.' He looked at Elaine, keys still dangling in her hand. 'Would you mind?'

She threw the bunch in the air, caught them as they came down and shoved them in her trouser pocket. 'Nope. I'm all over it.' She turned to walk out of the door and bit her bottom lip as she walked.

A stab of guilt cut through the horror he'd felt as he followed her through the incident room, past his team, where all heads were unnaturally down, and out of the door.

Ray knew that Billy's brother had died, but he hadn't been aware of how small his circle of loved ones was. Only a handful of people were at the service. And looked even fewer in the vast ornate interior of the church. His mother was there. A petite woman – she couldn't have been an inch taller than five foot four – dressed in a skirt and blouse that hung from her small frame. Her face was hollowed out; dark smudges underlined her eyes as though someone had dipped their thumb in an inkpot, then smeared it below each eye. Creases and folds of skin, soft and dry, hung where it once must have clung to sharp cheekbones. Eye sockets jutted out like landmarks on a map. Her collarbone created a deep crevasse below her neck. Whoever the woman had been, losing two sons had sucked the life from her while she had been inside. She was handcuffed to a hulk of a female guard who could easily have given Billy's mum her much needed weight and still had enough to live off. Though she was as tall as she was wide, she had a gentle smile for Mrs Collier when she looked her way. It was hard to believe that this small woman was the angry drunk they had heard about at the briefing not so long ago.

'We can cross her off our suspect list,' Ray whispered to Elaine, who shot him a warning look. He knew it wasn't the time or place for gallows humour, but nerves had got the better of him. He'd agreed to come to the memorial in case the offender turned up, but what the hell use was he. Lilian Collier was the only person he could guarantee it wasn't.

St Mary's Church on Church Street had few parking spaces outside. Elaine had managed to slide the car into one. This was the second church of St Mary's; there was an older building known as the old church, across the road, that was now used as an arts and community space. It was one of the oldest known churches in the country and had quite a history, rebuilt in 1563 and again after the

London Blitz of 1940. It was a survivor. Ray liked that about the old church.

Ray and Elaine seated themselves behind the mourners and attempted to be unobtrusive, but a white couple at a black-attended service made them stand out for what they were.

The other mourners looked to be friends. They were all of similar age to Billy. Their dress sense reminded Ray of him, too: jeans, trainers and a sweater. Ray's stomach clenched at the memory of him alive and well in the briefing, before the op that had gone wrong.

There were five of them. They were what Ray supposed were called 'tight'. They appeared to move as one entity. In sync. Like a shoal of fish. Without the need for communication, they stayed in their pack.

Ray nudged Elaine and looked towards the group. 'Know who they are?'

'No. Billy said he hadn't told anyone what he was doing. How d'you want to play it?'

The organ music started, deep and mournful, and Ray had to wait to finish the conversation. The pack moved into a line of chairs to the right, not too near the front, although there was no one else in front of them.

A few pews in front of Ray and Elaine were an elderly couple, both shaking their heads at regular intervals, as though to remind themselves that this couldn't be happening.

Ray couldn't see that anything positive would come from today but it was a task that needed to be done, and it gave him the opportunity to pay his respects to the lad who'd tried to do some good, no matter the way he'd gone about it.

As the vicar started to talk, his face so bland that Ray didn't even attempt to pick out any identifying features, and with a voice to match, the door of the church opened with a gentle creak and a male slipped in. Elaine was to the right of Ray, in the way of the door, so he couldn't make out the latecomer.

Ray leaned forward and looked past Elaine at the man who now sat adjacent to them. He was smart, tidy, suited-up, white – but he didn't recognise him. He'd wait and see what Elaine said.

The voice of the vicar droned on as he talked about Billy's early life, where he'd grown up, how he'd stuck at school even though it wasn't his thing, and then, strangely, the vicar's voice lit up as Billy's must have when he talked about Billy's love of drama and how he wanted to pursue it; but then he lost the joy in his voice as the loss of the youngster hit again.

Lilian Collier could be heard sobbing, her heart breaking. Smashing, hard and crystalline, against the jagged edges of the life her boys had lived. And died in. Shattering and skittering across the hard floor for all to hear and see.

Ray's own heart contracted in his chest. He fought to grab his breath as he tried to capture an image of his own children and failed. Anger knotted in him and compounded his grief.

He balled his fists. Ground his teeth.

Lilian Collier's shoulders juddered hard. The guard placed a large padded hand on her shoulder. The sole mark of care and respect the woman was likely to get.

The monotone vicar paled in front of his small party of mourners.

Then it was over and 'Wretch 32' was played incongruously over the speakers as the vicar indicated that the mourners could leave.

Silently, the vicar helped the prison guard and Lilian Collier leave the church, leading them out first so they would be able to receive the rest of the mourners.

Ray waited. Watched, as the group moved out first, and then the old couple, holding each other, still shaking their heads, and then again he looked across at the white male who had walked in late.

He turned to follow Elaine out of the row of chairs as the man stood and waited for them in the aisle.

'Elaine, nice to see you again.' He smiled at her. A friend of Elaine's?

'Joe, I didn't expect to see you here.' Her voice was friendly.

'I had to pay my respects. I started this, I agreed he could do it in the first place ...'

Elaine let out a deep sigh.

Bald head, sharp suit: Joe. It was the DI, Joe Lang. Ray moved past Elaine into view and held out his hand. 'Nice to see you, Joe, I'm sorry it's under these circumstances.'

Up close, Ray could see that Joe looked drawn. His eyes dark and sunken. He wasn't the only one to have taken this hard.

Joe took his hand. 'He was a good kid.'

They stood in silence a moment, a time to remember Billy and what he had sacrificed.

There wasn't a lot of room to move. The church wasn't endowed with spacious grounds. Statuesque as the church itself was, it was the building you were here for, there was no burial site on this side of the road.

The guard looked at her watch. The movement had been a sidelong glance but Ray caught it. Time to get back, he saw. A day job to do. Sympathy only went so far. But she stood still as the group of young men offered up their condolences to the woman handcuffed to her wrist.

It was difficult to both be security and to appear to offer privacy at a difficult time, Ray could see, as the guard pushed her free hand into her pocket and turned her head a fraction to the left, away from the conversations of the grief-stricken.

Ray hadn't yet decided how he wanted to go, whether he wanted a burial or cremation. He didn't know if he believed in a God. A watchful one. So he didn't know what he would do, or rather, how to advise his nearest and dearest – whoever they might be. He grunted to himself. It should be something he sorted out, considering his most recent brush with mortality.

'It doesn't seem so, no.' Elaine was talking to Joe. Ray focused again, looked at them for clarification.

'Your offender – not turned up?' Joe answered.

'Not if you consider who was at the service,' Ray replied. 'I'll have a wander, see if I can spot anyone familiar lurking around the outside the building, on the street.'

41

Rusnac didn't want to attend the memorial. Knowing the boy was dead was enough. But to cover his bases Rusnac had to make sure the kid hadn't talked to anyone else. That he hadn't told his mum about the organisation. Or his mates. It was bad enough that the musor, or – what did they call them over here? – Old Bill were investigating, so he had to conduct damage limitation and make sure there was nowhere for the musor to turn to get any further information. All the information Billy knew needed to have died with him.

Rusnac trusted Borta and Weaver not to disclose locations or give him up, but after what happened at the warehouse he couldn't trust that the kid had only told the musor of the meet and had given them no other intelligence. Not that he knew much, but the smallest thing was a risk that Rusnac was not prepared to take.

The few parking spaces outside the church were taken up, so he parked where he shouldn't, a little further down the street, and stayed with the car. If a traffic-watcher person came with tickets, he would be able to move and then slip back in when they had walked on.

He looked in the rear-view mirror, pushed his fingers through his hair, lifting it slightly at the front. Rubbed a non-existent mark from under his eye, and was ready to sort out his business.

It was cool and he wore a thick coat that covered the Glock pushed down the back of his trousers. He had no intention of using it. The gun was precautionary. And today it was to be used only as a threat, if needed.

Rusnac had witnessed first-hand the look of fear that imminent death brought to a face. It wasn't particularly flattering. And it wasn't the first time he had seen the look when he'd shoved the Glock in the kid, Billy's face. No, back in Moldova he had seen his share of violence. Those who helped his mother. Who helped him into this country. Who set him up in the lifestyle he now lived. Who had organised the operation he now ran. Those people knew how to instil fear. They knew how to get their way. People did as directed or faced the consequences. And you knew the consequences were fatal.

The Russians were hard-faced, stony men and Rusnac had watched them dole out punishment time and again. He knew the cool metal in the small of his back was worth a thousand words. He was never any good with his words. Always better with his fists. The Russians gave him the Glock as a gift. Told him that in his position he needed to carry it. If he was to be the boss of the organisation in England, then he needed to act like it. People need to fear him.

Rusnac had thought people feared him anyway. He had that presence. The way he carried himself. His threats. They were never idle. He never shied away from turning a face into a pulpy mess. He preferred to feel the release as bones gave way under his fist. Melted, practically. No feeling like it. But the Russians, they preferred him to carry a gun, and who was he to say no. Not after they'd saved his Mama and set him up over here.

The thing was, when he used his fists and he felt bones break and muscle slide away from its moorings, the poor shmuck who was on the receiving end lived to remember the event. They lived to fear Rusnac another day. To remember to stay in line. And more importantly, they lived to spread the word of his dominance.

With a gun – there was no living to say anything.

But, like a good subordinate, he carried his weapon. And once away from them, he never considered himself a subordinate.

The air was crisp in the grounds of the church.

He looked at his watched. 12.10 p.m. The service was underway. He wouldn't have long to wait. They seemed to be on a conveyor belt here.

Rusnac snorted.

Dignity.

This didn't feel dignified, watching from the outside. Watching people mourn this way. Back at home there was a sense of movement, of voyage. People gathered. Yes, there were tears, but there was food, lots of food, eaten with hands and shared. This was so formal and stiff. It felt unnatural.

Rusnac stamped his feet and lit a cigarette. He breathed in the familiar taste that reminded him of home, taking in a deep lungful of smoke. He held it a moment, savoured the feeling. And released. The air around him swirled as the smoke rose in front of him.

He felt calm. Relaxed even. If there was a problem here he would deal with it. There would be no need for the weapon. He alone would drive fear into the heart of the problem, and then, if needed, away from prying eyes, he could deal the issue on a more permanent basis. He wouldn't risk his position here. He was too comfortable now. This mess would be cleared up and the operation would continue as before.

Rusnac tipped his head back. Looked into the grey sky, acknowledged to himself that all was good, blew out another lungful of smoke. His watch read 12.20 p.m. The exit doors were opened by the dreary funeral staff and he wondered how they let their hair down at the end of the day. How did you get your kicks when all you looked at was death and grieving fucking relatives hour after hour? It must take some hard-core shit to get your rocks off after you've been driven to the depths of such tedium on a daily basis.

The first person out was small and thin. A woman, her shoulders shaking. His mother, Rusnac assumed. Standing to the side of her, a hulk of a white woman. As they moved he saw that they were handcuffed to each other.

Well, he'd be damned if she wasn't a convict. Billy really wasn't all he said he was at all. Mam, dearest, was a jailbird. Rusnac wondered what she had done to get her time. He finished his smoke, threw the tab-end on the floor and smashed it into the tarmac with his heel.

A group of youths emerged from the church. These were who he wanted to talk to. He wasn't sure he could get close to the mother, but then he doubted Billy would have talked to her about what he'd been up to. He would pay his respects and get a feel for her, but it was the group he was interested in. Instead of walking straight up to them he decided to give them five minutes. He didn't want to deal with the shit of their emotions.

Christ, his Mama would kill him.

He wandered across the road to an older church where there were some gravestones, and stood over a small headstone. Natasha Barry. He worked the dates out. Natasha Barry had only been thirty-six years of age. Older than he was now, but not by much. There were fresh flowers at the headstone, so her family or friends still grieved or still cared. The only person who would grieve him would be his Mama.

He gave himself a moment to think of her. He missed her. Missed her cooking. Her whiplash tongue and her gentle smile.

She'd brought him up alone after his dad got so pissed one night he fell into the river and was unable to get out. She'd cursed him for his stupidity, for weeks and months. Wailing at him for his idiocy. For wandering about in the dark. What had he been looking for? she'd wanted to know. He was a stupid, stupid man, she'd said. She'd been furious with him.

She'd ranted and she'd raved.

Until she burnt herself out.

Then she pulled herself back up and took care of herself and Vova. She told him that she was now the main breadwinner. She had to care for the house, for the child, for both of them. She didn't stop. He loved her for it. Hated his father for it.

Rusnac knew at a young age that he needed to go out and bring some money into the house. He was a smart lad, but lazy. He wanted to make money fast, and in town the easiest way to make money was crime.

He started small. With some thefts. Found he was good, and the money easy. He branched out into drugs. This was a much bigger part of the pot and Rusnac clawed his way up, fought with anyone who tried to stop him.

The natural progression from drugs was the girls. If you moved drugs you may as well move girls.

He thought his life was as he wanted it. He was at the top of his little empire, but then the news came from his Mama that her heart was failing. They could offer no treatment. She needed a new one but they couldn't do it for her there. They just couldn't. She didn't have the funds.

Rusnac had contacts. They were Russians. They had crossed paths but generally kept out of each other's way. Now he wanted their help. At whatever cost.

They had done it all. His Mama had her transplant. Vova hadn't questioned where the heart had come from. And now he was here.

Indebted to the Russians.

He shook himself free and turned back to the task at hand. He looked at the mother, but there was already someone with her.

The group. He needed to talk to the group.

The sky was grey overhead, like a slab of slate had been laid above him. Heavy, loud and obvious in its presence, the damp in the air a precursor to what would likely be a substantial downpour. He needed to move: the group would disperse once the rain came.

Rusnac raised himself to his full height, pushed his shoulders back and stopped the group. They weren't pleased with the intrusion but it was of little consequence to him. Though he did want to get this done with as little public fuss as possible. He wasn't a stupid man. Stupidity got men dead. Or locked up. And he didn't plan on either of those.

He introduced himself as a new friend of Billy's. The group looked sceptical, and then bemused by the interruption, confused that Billy would have a new friend that looked and sounded like Rusnac.

Rusnac took offence and wanted to smash each of their sneering little faces in until they bled from their judging eyes. He would listen with pleasure as they popped from their sockets. And it was as he imagined this sound that he heard the man speak behind him. He wanted to introduce himself. Rusnac stiffened. He liked to be prepared and he had no idea who had managed to sneak up on him. He was annoyed. Now here he was in a vulnerable position.

'I'm DI Ray Patrick from Stoke Newington police station.'

Fuck. Police.

He had the option of the Glock.

The kids he had talked to disrespected the cop and moved away. That was an option. He did the same. No need to cause a scene. He'd done what he came here to do. Now to leave and be done. His back was still to the cop.

The cop wouldn't be done though. He wouldn't stop. He shouted and hollered. He followed. He was drawing attention to him. People would stare and they would remember him. Drawing in a breath, he put his hand on the butt of the gun in his waistband and turned to face the cop.

Fuck. It was the cop he had killed the kid in front of. His fingers tightened around the handle. His forearm tensed and the material strained over them.

He couldn't. Not here. He'd be the most wanted man in the city. He turned away, hoped he could make it away before the cop grabbed him. But instead of hearing the cop run, he shouted him, told Rusnac he wanted to talk to him.

Talk? Seriously? That's what they did in this country after they saw a kid killed in cold blood?

Rusnac looked at the cop. Stared at his face. It was definitely the same guy. He'd never forget that face. The dark hair streaked through with grey over dark probing eyes. Strong chin.

Whatever was going on, Rusnac didn't want to hang around to find out.

42

Ray was standing motionless.

'So who was it?' asked Joe. The rain had started to come down heavier now. Umbrellas were put up.

'No one.'

'No one? It looked like it was someone, Ray, the way you ran after him and the way he didn't want to talk to you.'

Elaine watched her two supervisors with interest.

'It's not important.' Ray started to move towards his car.

Joe put a hand on his arm. A light touch. Ray spun as though burnt. Eyes flaring. 'I said it's not important, Joe.'

'But here, Ray. At Billy's funeral. Today of all days. In this location. Does it have anything to do with the investigation? You have to see I have no choice but to ask?'

There was a heavy silence. Mourners moved about. A hearse pulled up with the family car behind it. Daddy in flowers, in pinks, whites and lilacs on the side of the coffin. The sky felt low, dark, oppressive. A blanket smothering the day.

Elaine pushed her hair behind her ears. Waited. The men stared at each other. Neither backing down.

'I can understand you asking. Of course, I can,' Ray replied at last. 'But I assure you, it's bad timing, is all. I saw someone I wanted to talk to in relation to another case. You know what this job's like. People pop up anywhere. You know he didn't attend the memorial, so he wasn't part of Billy's crowd, which is what we were interested in. He's local, was probably passing, saw someone he knew, one of that group, and came to say hello. It's a small world when all is said and done.'

Joe waited a moment. Digested the information. 'Okay. Sounds reasonable. You know I had to ask though?'

'Yeah. I'd have done the same,' Ray answered.

'Shall we go and grab those kids before they disappear? See what they can tell us about Billy that we maybe didn't know?' asked Elaine, breaking in. She could see from her guv's face he was far from happy, that something was wrong. The guy he'd chased, somewhat weakly, had been important to him in some way, but she didn't know how.

'Sounds like a plan,' he replied.

They caught up with the group as they walked away from the church towards town. People were going about their daily business.

'Hey, can we talk to you?' shouted Joe as they approached. A lad with his face down to his phone, which he held close to his body, protecting it from the rain, jerked his head around to look at Joe, panic on his face. Joe shook his head, then indicated further ahead. The lad sighed, crossed the road and went back to his phone.

Ray was still distracted, Elaine noticed. It wasn't as simple as he'd made out to Joe. Whatever the male meant to Ray it was important, and he was brooding. His mind wasn't in the game now.

The group stopped. Seemed to turn as one. Looked at the white cops approaching them. Looked them up and down.

'Cops, yeah?' one of them asked.

'Yeah, we're cops,' replied Joe. 'But you're not in any trouble. We're here for Billy.'

'Much good you did him, yeah,' said another. A sneer on his lip.

They were closer now and Joe lowered his voice so as not to shout and sound overbearing.

'I know you're upset. He's dead. You have every right to be. You've lost a friend. We need your help to make sure someone pays for that and Billy's death doesn't go unanswered.'

The rain was hammering down now. Elaine struggled to hear over the noise on her umbrella. A dull, inconsistent beat. The group were hostile. Kids who hadn't had much good come out of interaction with cops.

'Fuck, man, you think we're upset? We're angry. What've you ever done for us? Now you want us to help you?' The speaker turned his back on them. The rest of the group followed suit.

'Did you know Billy came to us?' Ray asked. Hands in his pockets. Rain streaming down his face. Joe looked at him. Surprised by the disclosure. They hadn't agreed on what they would tell them.

The group paused. No one turned.

Ray spoke again. 'He was into something big and he wanted us to help him sort it out.'

The smallest of the group turned now. 'And you got him killed, yeah?' Anger in his voice.

Ray took a step back as though he'd been physically hit.

'What Billy got himself involved in was too big and too dangerous for him. He didn't allow us to know too much. We weren't in a position to help him as we'd have expected to,' Joe

189

answered. 'That's why we're here. To see if he talked to any of you guys about it.'

The group were engaged now.

'So. Can we talk?'

43

It was a downpour but Ray barely noticed. He wanted the information from the group in front of him but he wasn't blind to the scowls that were directed at him. To faces wiped off only to be drenched again a moment later.

'I don't want to keep you long,' he said. 'It'd be useful to know what he spoke about before he was killed. The smallest nugget might be useful to us.'

'How we's supposed to know what's useful to you, man?' one of the group asked – red trainers, the same kind as Billy wore, Ray noticed.

'Okay, how about we move to the pub? I'll get the drinks in and you can tell me what you know there?'

This time the group looked at one another, a silent conversation, and then they nodded in unison.

The Rose and Crown was on the corner of Church Street and Albion Road. Ray wasn't too far away from home. It was an old-style pub with a wood-coffered ceiling, tiled floor, wood panelling and a real fire, which was lit but low. It offered a gentle warmth and felt welcoming, friendly.

The bar was already half full. It was a weekday and these were likely to be regulars. Ray wondered if they stood out as cops. He was always picked out as a cop. Elaine less so. With her slim, petite figure, she wasn't what people expected a cop to look like. Though he never knew what female cops were supposed to look like. Ray imagined Joe would be easily picked out as well.

He ordered drinks, five pints of lager and three Cokes. They were on duty, and now it was clear they were cops. With the drinks on a tray Ray turned around and realised he wouldn't be able to find his group. He'd said he would buy the drinks and fetch them over. It was natural instinct: instead of asking Joe to help him carry them and then being able to follow behind Joe as he walked to their table, he had done what he would have done before the accident, coped on his own.

Ice ran through his veins. He took a step back and felt the curved edge of the bar dig into his back.

There were so many people in here. Didn't they have jobs or homes to go to? Why were so many people in the pub? Why were they here! The tray started to shake in his hands.

People were scattered all over, going all the way to the back of the pub. A couple of glasses on the tray clinked together.

Calm down Ray. You can do this. Remember who you're looking for. It's a specific group. Five black males, a white male and a white female.

He took a deep breath. Yes, they were identifiable, he could do this. With another deep breath he steadied himself, looked around as anyone would who needed to search for friends or colleagues who had wandered off to sit down, and identified his group.

Ray handed the pints out, then realised he wouldn't be able to identify the lad with the red trainers now that they were seated at a table. It didn't matter. He didn't need to know who was who; all he needed was to know the information they had about Billy.

If they had any.

It wasn't clear if he had passed any on to his friends. He said he hadn't involved anyone, but you never knew what could have slipped out. And they needed all the help they could get.

Ray looked across at the table opposite them. He wanted to know who might be within hearing distance. A couple, thirties, too much into each other to be interested in any conversations going on around them. They looked to have been in the bar a while, as there was no sign of them having been caught in the rain. He had his chair pulled right up to hers and she'd hooked her leg around his, and in response his arm was snaked around her neck, where he twirled a piece of hair in his finger. She talked low so as to not be overheard, and the male couldn't take his eyes from her.

'… isn't that right, Ray?' Joe looked at him.

Ray returned his look. Admitted with it that he hadn't heard.

'I'm confirming again that we only want to talk about Billy, we think he was a great kid and he's never been in any trouble with us.'

Ray took a large swig of his Coke. The drink was cold and fizzy and he wished it was a beer. 'I didn't know Billy long because I'd been absent from work, but the little I did know of him, I recognised him as a strong and vibrant person who was ethical and brave, who wanted to do the right thing, and that has resulted in a tragic loss that I personally want to right. I know I can't bring Billy back but I can damn well bring his killer to justice. And that's exactly what he'd have wanted. I know that from the short conversations I had with him. You know him better than me, was justice his thing?'

There was silence around the table. The group didn't do their usual – look at each other and manage to converse in silence; instead, they dropped their heads, considered their drinks.

Had he got it wrong? Pushed too hard, maybe? He looked at Elaine. She shrugged.

They waited.

'He was our mate, you know.'

'Yeah, we know. We're genuinely sorry for your loss,' said Joe.

The speaker looked toward Ray. 'We knew he was up to something. He kept disappearing. Answered his phone but refused to take the call in front of us. Said it was better for us that way.' His voice dropped. Ray leaned in. Arms on the sticky table. 'We thought he might be getting himself into trouble. We followed him one night.'

Ray could feel his pulse start to race. He didn't dare turn away from the lad who was speaking, now. Didn't dare break the spell. Not even to acknowledge to Elaine that they might be about to find that they had witnesses to one of the organisation. 'And?'

'He met some guy. In Abney Park cemetery. He had this really thick neck. That's what stood out about him. They talked. Billy was animated. Passionate about summat. His arms were all over. He wanted to get his point across. The dude stood there and took it. Then it was over and Billy walked away.'

'Sounds like Borta,' said Elaine.

'Who's that?' One of the lads popped his head up now.

'One of the guys we already have in custody,' replied Ray. They were no further forward.

'So we decided to have it out with him.' One of the others had decided to pick up the story. 'He wasn't too happy about it. Disgusted with us, he were. That we'd followed him and that.'

Ray listened, let them talk.

Elaine drank her Coke. Eyed the group over her drink. Her pocket notebook and pen in front of her, where she'd made some notes.

'But in the end he said to us, if anything happened to him, to tell the feds: dedit.'

'Dead it?' asked Elaine. Pen poised.

'No. One word. He spelled it out for us. D.e.d.i.t.'

'What's that?' asked Ray.

'Don't know, man. We've given you what we know. Now you have to find who killed him.'

44

Ray, Elaine and Joe nursed their Cokes. Not in a rush to fill up with another. Not in a rush to get back to the office. Billy's friends had left. They had no idea what they'd discovered. A word, that was it, one word had come from meeting Billy's mates at the memorial, and no explanation.

'So, what the hell is dedit?' Joe looked at Elaine and Ray with confusion on his face.

'Beats me. Maybe it's an abbreviation, you know, how they miss out some vowels in words nowadays, so short for "dead and it", and we're supposed to figure out what is dead?' Elaine tried.

'Billy's dead.' Ray felt flat. Defeated.

'But Billy said this when he was alive. It doesn't mean Billy,' countered Elaine.

Ray pulled his phone from his pocket. Woke it up, pulled up a browser window and tapped in 'dedit'. Joe and Elaine looked over his shoulder as he worked. He read through the results and looked at his colleagues.

'Found anything?' asked Joe.

'According to our friend Google, dedit is the Latin word for giving; a Canadian law for a sum forfeited by one who has failed in an engagement; and according to an urban dictionary, it's an insult, emphasising an embarrassing moment.'

'Seriously?'

'Yep.'

'What the hell do we do with that?'

'I don't know. We take what we've been told and what we know back to the office and we cross-check it all against everything we already have and see what comes back.'

There was a hum in the office when Ray and Elaine walked back in. He could feel it the minute he was through the door. It wasn't the busy hum of wading through enquiries, paperwork, red tape, the drudgery of the job, the plodding necessity, this was the hum of excitement at a lead having broken through. The expectation of not having to sit at those desks, those computers, for another minute more because now they had a concrete lead. Ray looked at his phone; there was a missed call from Prabhat. It must have been while they were in the pub with Billy's friends.

Elaine looked to him as though he'd know through osmosis just being in the room, simply because of his rank. He shook his head. She walked to her desk and fired up her computer. Turned to a colleague beside her. 'What's happened?'

'The DNA from the cig found at the burnt-out garage came back from Interpol. We have an ID.'

'Name?' Ray demanded, his chest contracting, squeezing until he realised he'd been holding his breath and took in a deep breath.

'Guy called Vova Rus …' The speaker looked down at a sheet of paper. 'Rusnac. Vova Rusnac. He's from Romania, which is next door to Moldova, where Ion Borta is from.'

'We have any idea where he is?' asked Ray, now pulling off his coat, ready to get to work. All thought of dedit forgotten.

'Not yet, guv. That's what everyone is trying to do now. Trying to locate him. It's not likely he's registered legitimately for anything anywhere, but we are checking all our systems and cross-checking them for associates and intelligence.'

'Okay, good. Let me know as soon as we have him. I'll get in touch with firearms, put them on standby and talk to Jain.'

With the call in to SCO19 Ray went in search of Prabhat and found him in his office, deep in conversation with a woman slightly older than he was, her short hair also greying, not dyed as many women he knew would do, and sensible shoes on her feet. He obtained all this information through the glass window in the office wall. Prabhat looked up and saw Ray standing outside, looking in. He held his hand up, held him back while he finished his conversation. The woman turned to see who was waiting. The flicker of recognition he felt, that tip-of-the-tongue feeling that he knew her from the side without seeing her face, was gone in an instant – because he'd now seen her face and it had thrown him.

He attempted to go through the files in his head for the identity of the woman in the chair. She didn't have a coat with her so she was internal staff, he should know her. But he was tired, and without context it didn't drop into place. He couldn't make another mistake when she walked out, as he'd done in the incident room last week.

He'd talk to her as if he knew her. After all, he had figured out she was staff. All he had to do was be polite.

'Afternoon, sir.' A young male in a suit walked past.

'Afternoon.' No idea.

Hurry up, Prabhat.

The door opened and the woman walked out; Prabhat stood behind her. 'Thanks for that, Julie. I'll get you the updated figures by the end of the week.'

'I appreciate it. Thank you for your time.' She turned and smiled at Ray. 'DI Patrick. It's good to see you back at work.'

'Thanks, Julie.' And thanks to Prabhat for using her name. 'It's good to be back. They certainly make sure they get their money's worth.' He returned her smile and she walked towards the secure outer office doors.

'What is it, Ray?' Prabhat walked back into his office, folded himself back into his chair. Ray followed and seated himself in the chair opposite.

'We've had a hit on the DNA on the cigarette found outside the garage where the silver BMW was burned. It's a Romanian guy. Close to where one of the guys we arrested is from. It looks like we're on the right track. We're trying to locate him now, but it may be more difficult than we want. It's not like he'll register himself anywhere, but all resources are on it. SCO19 are aware and ready to go. We'll hit him as soon as we can.' He hadn't paused for breath. He wanted this guy.

Prabhat looked at him. Didn't speak.

Ray waited for him to say something.

He didn't.

'What is it?'

Prabhat steepled his fingers under his chin. 'I know. That's why I phoned you. The main reason I wanted to talk to you though, is that you know you can't go with the team to bring him in even when we know where he is, don't you?'

'What? No.' Ray stood. Pushed back the chair with his legs. 'Why?'

'We need you to do the ID procedure, Ray. You might not have thought you saw him enough to do a photo-fit on the day, but you were the one who chased him, so you're the one who will have to do the identification. To make that secure, you can't go and arrest him. It can't be said that you picked him out because you were a part of the arrest team.'

45

The look on her face when she opened the door reminded Ray how late it was. It had been like wading through treacle trying to locate Vova Rusnac, but eventually Ray had told the team to go home and that they'd pick this up again first thing in the morning. It wasn't as though they had the identity and location of a voting-registered nominal from the UK. This was a killer who had entered the country and purposefully kept his head down. It would be a more difficult task to establish his whereabouts.

'I'm sorry,' was all he had to say as she stood aside and let him in. 'The kids in bed?'

She gave him a look. 'Of course they're in bed,' he answered himself.

She didn't respond, just walked on through to the kitchen. He followed. Helen was already pulling a bottle of wine out of the fridge when he walked through the door behind her.

'You driving?'

'No. I walked.'

'Sarcasm?'

Ray shrugged.

'You might have been desperate for a drink and got a taxi over.'

'And made presumptions?'

She pulled two glasses down from the cupboard and began to fill them. It was a good half-hour drive over to Church Langley and Ray had thought the drive would blow out the tension that ran through his head.

It hadn't worked.

He gladly took the glass from Helen.

'What brings you here at this hour … again?' Her voice held no malice. No anger. It was a straight question. She was calmer this time, calmer than the last time he'd turned up on her doorstep.

After the bottle was back in the refrigerator, she took the seat that faced him. The fall of her hair just touching her shoulders was the only familiar and recognisable detail. That and her voice.

He could close his eyes.

'Work. It's work.' He did close his eyes.

'What is it?'

'I'm sorry I came again, Helen.' He meant it.

She shook her head. Her hair gently swishing along her shoulders.

'It's a mess, a real mess. I'm screwed, Helen, and I don't know what to do. I'm about to screw up the whole investigation and Billy's death will have been for nothing, and that fact will all be down to me.' He shook his head also, unable to take in how much he'd screwed up.

He sucked in a breath.

'Ray?' A hand touched his. Light. Gentle. Warm. And rested where it dropped.

He opened his eyes. The pounding lessened. The clamminess remained.

'What did I do, Helen?' He searched her face for a connection to the past. It was lost.

'You didn't do anything. But maybe failing to disclose this condition to work wasn't the smartest move. What's happened?'

'They've identified someone.'

'That's good. No?'

'Prabhat wants me to ID him after arrest.'

'Oh, Ray.' She squeezed his hand.

He looked her in the eyes and she let go as though burnt.

'I won't pick him out.' In all his career, he had never felt such helplessness.

'I know.'

'We need more concrete evidence, not the flimsy shit we have now. It's so thin that they've pinned all their hope on me picking him out. Even after I said I didn't see him. The case needs to be stronger. We need to worker harder. Smarter. Not this.' His voice had a hard edge to it. His eyes flashed. He was no longer clammy. He felt cool, yet fired up.

'Then do something about it, Ray. Don't lie down and give in because of this. Do what you do best and work the case. Find the evidence and get him with a strong case. If anyone can do it, I believe you can.' She smiled. 'This is what you do, Ray. This is what you spent all those hours doing when you weren't spending time with me. Do it now.'

'Helen ...'

'Don't, Ray.'

'You know –'

'We're past it, Ray. Leave it in the past. Focus on the now. Focus on this, here and now.'

He wanted to reach out, touch her face, thank her. But the time for all that was behind him. He'd lost the right to do that when he left her home alone while he spent hours at work. And he had Celeste now. So why was he feeling churned up about Helen? Was it simply because she was the one who knew his secret? There was something about that safety net she provided, no matter how reluctantly, that drew him to her.

'Ray?' She was watching him. Her voice quiet.

'What is it? One of the kids?' His stomach twisted.

'No. No. Not the kids.' A weak smile. 'But I do have something to tell you.'

The twisting in his stomach wasn't doing much in the way of letting up. He hated conversations that started with any phrase similar to "We need to talk".

'Okay.' He stretched the word out. Maybe it could fill the gap enough that she wouldn't have to speak next.

'I've started seeing someone.'

It was like a gut punch. He didn't know why. They were divorced. He had Celeste. Helen was fine with Celeste. He had to be okay with this. For her. 'You're not letting him meet the kids yet though, are you?'

She looked at him. A reprimanding look. Damn. He didn't mean to say that.

'I mean, we don't want to upset them, if it's new, and they get attached ... Wait until you know he's going to be a permanent fixture for them.'

Helen nodded.

'Where did you meet him?' Did he really want to know?

'You know I go to a book group once a month; well, he just started going and, well, we hit it off. He asked to take me out and I, well, I said yes.'

Ray nodded.

They sat in silence for a couple of minutes, Helen allowing him to digest the information she'd given him.

'Just don't let him hurt you, okay?'

She smiled at him. 'Okay. But – back to you: you're going to work this case, right.'

It wasn't a question.

He watched her as she drank from her glass after she'd encouraged him to push harder on the case, her dark eyes dancing in the light of the kitchen, and he knew she was right. He had to do something. He had to push this case harder because he was about to throw it off a cliff.

Walking through the door, Ray threw his keys onto the kitchen worktop, listened as they clattered across the laminate, grabbed a cold can out of the fridge and took a deep long draw. Savoured the cool velvet nectar as it slid down his throat. He pulled at his tie, loosened it and left it to hang unevenly as he dropped into the chair in the living room.

He was exhausted. Not just physically but mentally. Keeping up this charade took it out of him. But he knew he could train himself to manage better. Better than he was doing now at least. What had happened with Billy was an extreme circumstance. No copper in his lifetime usually ever had to experience that. And Ray would never have to experience it again – so there was no reason that once this was over he should have to disclose the condition. Now he'd decided to hide it, he had to stick to that. He just had to do something about the situation he found himself in.

But it was more than a situation, it was a life, and he felt so damn helpless. No matter how much he told himself that this could never happen again or that the murder would have happened with or without the diagnosis, the fact that he was unable to bring the killer to justice was eating him up inside and he didn't know how he would be able to keep up the façade if they couldn't bring a prosecution soon.

Ray didn't expect Celeste to come by. They'd exchanged a few text messages throughout the week and she'd said she was going to spend a few days at her own place. She didn't give any reason. She didn't blame him, or give their relationship as a reason, and nor did she say she had other plans; she simply said she wanted to spend a few days on her own at her own place.

Ray knew he could take that whatever way he wanted. He could choose to believe she was pissed at him, or that she was giving him some space because she loved him; she might even need a couple of days' space herself, for other reasons. There was no point trying to figure it out. She was a woman; men were never meant to understand women.

The can he'd pulled from the fridge was cool. Damp to the touch in the warmth of the room. He drank a third of it, then put it at the side of his laptop. He'd had to buy a new laptop. There was no using his last one after he'd thrown it in temper the other evening. So, rather than spend a fortune on repairs, he'd splashed out on a cheap new model.

Finally the screen was awake. This would lead him somewhere or it wouldn't. He downloaded the TOR browser again.

Alice through the looking-glass.

He pulled up the list of dark net sites he had found, his eyes tracking down the names and descriptions. A world even darker than the name gave it credit for.

He was about to give up hope – it had been a long shot anyway … But then there it was, looming out of the gloom like an iceberg in front of the Titanic.

Dedit.

Dedit was the name of a dark net site that organised living transplants.

They traded in the sale of human organs.

Ray picked up his can, the cool condensation slipping between his fingers. He finished the can. His mind swirled at the implications of what he had found. They'd not had anything back from eCrime yet; he didn't know if they were even looking in the right place.

Knowing that it was wrong to go in and potter around on his own, and not doing so, were two different things. Ray needed to find the answers for Billy. He needed to right the wrong he was doing to the investigation. This, more than anything, was what drove him forward. He placed the empty can back down and directed the dark net browser to the Dedit site using the long, obscure mix of numbers and letters that was the site address.

The unusual thing about the dark net sites was how normal they looked in comparison to many of the internet sites people use on a day-to-day basis.

Dedit had a clear and welcoming home page that invited you to search the site, read, ask questions. If you were in need of a life-saving transplant, then there was a redirect to another page, and if you were there to offer to save someone's life there was a redirect to a different page.

Ray clicked through to the About page for needing a transplant. Again it was warm and welcoming. Looked to all intents and purposes like any above-board web page. But this one, this page, informed you that if you were tired of waiting for the government-run NHS to find you a liver or kidney, or you were running out of time, then you had come to the right place, because, for a fee and with some simple tests, a match could be found and a new organ transplanted.

Ray leaned back in the chair. Wrapped his hands behind his head and let out a deep sigh.

He'd found it. He'd actually found it.

But what now?

Could he go into work tomorrow and hand over what he'd found? Tell Prabhat that he'd unlawfully nosed around the dark net without proper authorities in place? On his own time. He wasn't even sure if they could identify anyone through the site. Finding this was only the beginning. These places were notoriously difficult to infiltrate, to identify the owner of the website, to bring it all to a close. Yes, it had been done with a few, but they had been long-running cases and a lot of hard work and man hours had gone into them to crack the hard shell around heavily protected, heavily encrypted sites. All Ray had done was find a location. Nothing more. Nothing to get excited about, in policing terms.

But still he was excited.

He felt a sliver of that excitement burst into life in the pit of his stomach as he laid his head back on the chair and contemplated. Felt it fizz as it grew from a seed into a new entity. It welled up in his chest.

He'd found the door.

Now all he had to do was find the key.

46

The corridor was narrow. A single light bulb swung from the ceiling and cast little in the way of light. Shadows crept up the walls, which were lined with closed doors.

Ray stood alone staring down the length of the corridor. He had a familiar feeling but couldn't place it. He had no memory of how he'd got here. With no one with him there was no context. How would he recognise anyone he might come across?

A piercing scream split the air. It came from behind one of the doors but he couldn't figure out which one. He'd have to try each in turn.

With his right hand he reached out and pulled on the handle of the door he was standing beside. It opened easily. A male stood there. There was nothing remarkable about him. He didn't speak, just shook his head. Ray mirrored the action, confused.

The scream came again, this time more desperate.

Quickly Ray stepped over to the door opposite and opened it. Another male. Again, the inability to identify him. He may or may not have known him. Work with him, be a friend of his, have arrested him. Any of these could be true and he wouldn't know it.

Tension started to crawl under his skin.

The male shook his head.

Ray moved to the next door, opened it; this time, a female. Same result. She shook her head. The penetrating scream went up again. It wasn't her. He moved again to the opposite door. Frustration started to fill his head like an echo of the screaming.

A moth must have flown to the bulb in the ceiling, as a flickering shadow boomeranged back and forth above his head while he moved back and forth between the doors.

Suddenly the screaming became frantic. Ray started to run down the corridor. He pulled open the next door and the next and the next, with the same results at every one.

The moth continued to zip around. The screaming pierced his skull. Ray was beside himself. Then he saw the blood pooling under the next door.

The screaming was louder now. Insistent.

He placed his hand on the handle. A small charge ran up his arm. He kept hold and turned.

The door was locked.

Ray pushed and pushed but it wouldn't give.

He took a step back, lifted his leg and pushed his foot hard into where the locking mechanism would be. It held fast. He booted it again and again, barely keeping his balance. The door stayed closed.

The screaming stopped.

The corridor was silent.

Then a single shriek pierced the air, cleaving straight through his head.

It was then Ray realised that it was his alarm. He threw his arm out from under the duvet and smashed his hand down on the phone, prodding at the screen to try to make it stop. His head was spinning. He felt disorientated.

With the alarm off Ray lay for a moment, in the quiet. Still. Gathering himself.

It was not yet light and he felt cocooned by the darkness. Enveloped and safe where he was. He knew that today he faced the possibility that they'd locate Rusnac and he'd fail the ID procedure.

The conversation from the night before with Helen entered his head, as well as the dark net search he'd done at home. If they focused on the evidence, they could still bring this guy in. No matter what happened.

He must keep telling himself that.

Ray arrived at the office early as usual. There was an email in his inbox that had arrived late the previous day. He made a quick call, pulled his jacket back on and left the office.

He was met at the reception by a small, very slim man with large jowls and wisps of hair going across his head in an attempt to fend off the obvious thinning process. His handshake, when he took Ray's hand, however, was strong, firm.

'Hi, I'm Russell Wade. I picked up your job when it came in.'

His voice was low, gravelly, at complete odds with his image.

'Great to meet you, and thanks for seeing me this morning.'

Wade took Ray through to an open office space. The London hub of NABIS, the National Ballistics Intelligence Service, was a hive of activity. The room looked like any other office space Ray had seen. Desks with computer terminals and piles of folders. There was a large map of the UK on the wall and information on current statistics for the movement of weapons around the country alongside it.

Ray knew that past this average-looking office space were the high-tech rooms where they did all the ballistic work. Fired any weapons that had been seized, examined striations under high-resolution microscopes and matched ballistic materials to weapons and crime scenes. He'd been through there a couple of times, but today Wade walked him round to a desk in the far corner of the room, past a set of filing cabinets up against the wall where a half-eaten birthday cake sat with a knife and a few plates on top. Wade sat in front of his computer and indicated for Ray to pull up a chair himself. A small plate filled with cake crumbs sat on the corner of the desk. Ray picked up the sweet sugary scent and felt his stomach rumble.

'So,' Wade started. 'We got the casing and the bullet after the forensic lab had finished testing them for fingerprints and whatever else they did to them.'

Ray nodded that he understood the process.

'We've not had them long, but there was a rush notice on them.'

'Yeah, an op went sideways and it's important we get a lead on this job.'

'Well, it's an interesting one.' Wade tapped at his keyboard and a new screen appeared on the monitor in front of them. 'This is the job,' he said to himself. 'Okay, then. Let's have a look.' He studied the monitor for a minute. Ray gave him the space and waited him out.

'That's it.' He leaned back in his chair, hair wafting gently above his head. 'For basic information, the weapon you're looking for is a Glock 19, but I can give you a print-out, or email you all the details of that, because that's not the interesting part. There were no links to any other firearms jobs in the UK.'

Ray leaned forward. 'So the type of weapon isn't interesting and there are no links to other UK firearms incidents – so what is it that has piqued your interest?'

Wade pulled another page up on the monitor. 'I read all the case information and noted that one of the offenders you arrested was Moldovan, so I put a search in iARMS.'

Ray gave him a quizzical look.

'The INTERPOL Illicit Arms Records and tracing Management System.'

'Ah.' Ray was starting to understand where this might be headed.

'Yes.' Wade highlighted a section on the form on the screen. 'Your bullets have been used in Moldova and have intelligence links to a Russian gang.'

Ray's phone rang. He apologised to Wade, who shook his head that it was fine. Ray checked the screen. It was Jain. He cancelled the call – he'd get back to him in a few minutes, when he finished up here.

'Sorry about that. It was the Super.'

'No worries.'

'So our job definitely has Moldovan links and has Russian links as well?'

'Seems that way. Though it's intelligence not evidence that links it to a Russian group.'

'This is great. Thank you. Can you email me everything you have?'

'Absolutely. If you have any questions on reading it, call me, or pop over again. And if you find the weapon in question, we'll have no trouble matching it up for you.'

The phone was like a dead weight in his hand. And more than that. It was as though it held all the matter of the universe, as though it was the fault of the phone itself that this was happening. Ray's arm hung limp at his side with the weapon of destruction pulling down to the ground.

He couldn't think straight. He knew it had been coming. He'd been given notice. And he was more than tense about the impending ID procedure. He was about to throw the whole murder investigation, and tense didn't even begin to cover how he felt. He was sick to his stomach.

He needed some time alone. Space to pull himself together.

The Haberdashery was a small café restaurant on Stoke Newington High Street, filled with neat wooden tables and mismatched chairs. It had a vintage feel to it and was a place that invited you in; it was a place Ray loved to sit and think. He'd found himself a small round two-seat table at the side of the room, and sat there with a small black coffee, nursing it as his brain spun in circles about what awaited him back at the station.

Two young women entered. They were laughing at something they'd said before they'd come in. Clutching the hand of one of the women was a small child. He looked to Ray to be about four years of age. His small round face lit up when he saw the cakes on display. Ray watched the women order coffees and cakes and arrange themselves at another table. Their chatter was constant, unworried, carefree. Jackets were thrown over the backs of chairs, a large bag pushed under a free chair, a napkin tucked into the neck of the child's T-shirt.

Only six months ago his life had resembled this image. Maybe not quite the same, they weren't a family unit, but though his days were busy, his out-of-hours time hadn't been spent in a state of constant fear that he'd upset someone by not recognising them if he saw them in an unexpected setting, or of screwing up relationships because of the lack of connection, or this waiting to screw over a murder investigation.

He picked up his drink, smiled at the child, who was now staring at him, and knew he would never recognise him again.

47

Rusnac had been in smaller rooms, his living room at home was probably smaller, and he'd even been in rooms that smelled worse than this one – his own would give it a run for its money. It was a square grey box. Bare grey walls, a grey concrete floor and, to finish it off, a painted grey ceiling. The metal toilet in the corner was emanating a pretty disturbing smell. It was the first time he'd found himself in a British cell. As the solid metal door had clanged heavily closed on him, he'd been surprised to find he was nervous. Being arrested for murder tended to be a wake-up call for one's confidence in one's invincibility.

All the measures he'd taken to protect himself, and yet he still found himself in this position. Pulled over as he was driving. He thought he'd been stopped for minor speeding or for going through a red light, but as soon as they'd got him out of the car they'd arrested him.

He sat on the bench that was built against the wall opposite the door, a thin black plasticky cushion providing what he supposed they thought passed for some level of comfort, and wondered how much information and evidence they had against him.

The interview room was of similar size but held a table, four moulded plastic chairs, and recording equipment. A red alarm bar ran the length of each wall.

Rusnac didn't trust lawyers, but neither did he trust the cops. It had been a toss-up between which he trusted the least, but he'd opted to have a lawyer present. The man, when he'd spoken to him in a side room, proved to be inept and had advised him to reply no comment to every question the police asked. He was an inadequate man, balding, a thin patch of hair running around the side of his head, and small round metal-framed glasses. He informed Rusnac that it was up to the police to prove their case against him, and that they'd provided him little in the way of disclosure. Not enough to feel happy with anyway.

This was enough information for Rusnac to decide on his own plan for the interview.

The two cops could have walked straight out of some TV drama. The guy was short and round, though he wasn't bad looking, with his own head of hair and – what did the Brits call it? – a fresh face? The woman, she looked smart in her suit, her hair tied back from her face, which he thought was rather plain. It was when she opened her mouth that Rusnac heard the accent. He couldn't understand what she said half of the time, but he understood what it was like to be in a country and to not sound like the rest of them.

They were polite enough introducing themselves. Like polite would make him answer their questions. The drip of a lawyer sat and scribbled in a notepad on his knee. Scrawny nicotine-stained fingers bent tight like an owl's claw around the pen. Rusnac had to turn away.

The interview dragged on for hours. The detectives may have looked as though they'd walked off a television set but the interview itself wasn't what you see on screen. On screen, he'd have been in and out within the hour. It was what he had expected, but no, they tortured him with the mundanity of their questions for hours. They stopped so he could eat a cardboard meal out of a microwave box, and then dragged him from the first boxy room into the other boxy room to go again. He was getting bored and the drip of a lawyer didn't say a word. Because the questions had been so boring and tedious, Rusnac had happily answered no comment to most of them and this had kept the head of his lawyer down. He'd have been surprised if he'd stayed awake.

They covered his business. The transplants. He knew from his lawyer that they had nothing on that so he replied 'no comment'. The male detective led the interview. His tone and manner at ease in the room. Not perturbed by the lack of meaningful responses. The questions kept coming. Not at speed. Relaxed, as though they had all the time in the world.

He was bored.

It was then that the woman, the one with the voice that split his brain open, told him they were bedding him down for the night and would talk to him again in the morning.

How dare they!

What did this mean? How confident were they?

Rusnac looked at the black plastic mattress in his cell and wanted to roar in anger.

There were no apologies for holding him all night. No apologies for the shouts and bangs that had kept him awake through the night and no apologies for the shoddy plastic food that passed for breakfast, or the piss that passed for tea. The same two faces in the interview room and the same useless lawyer. This all served to sour Rusnac's mood more and more. But he still had his plan of action for when the interview got to where it was heading.

One question passed through his head, and that was the whereabouts of the detective who saw him kill the kid. Why did he not question him? He would have no way out of this, then. He was still confused as to why he hadn't chased him at the memorial service. He'd expected to have to run for his life. To have to evade dogs and helicopters as well as an army of boots on the ground. But nothing happened. Not even one set of footsteps behind him, never mind the full force of this very English police force.

They were so polite. They introduced themselves all over again. He had no interest in their names. Was he supposed to remember them? Care who they were? Why the politeness, this Britishness at the start of each interview, at the start of each recording? And that voice of hers, so – grating.

His mood was not good. His tolerance level for this process was low. He had to hope Mihai Popa, his second in command, had all the transactions in order, and also that they were secure, that these idiots hadn't infiltrated them and pulled others in. It was too lucrative a business to lose it. All he needed was for this to be dealt with and any other moles rooted out and terminated.

He brought his mind back into the room, away from his organisation and what was happening out there in his absence. The two TV detectives had a look of expectation on their faces.

He raised his eyebrows.

'Please state your name for the recording,' said the woman with the dreadful voice. Had they really got no further than this?

It was going to be a long day and he was tired.

They covered the old ground from yesterday, making sure they understood his responses. How could the idiots not? His response had been no comment. They wanted to know if he wanted to add anything.

'No comment.'

Eventually they made it to where he had something to say. The guy was still leading the interview. They'd stopped for another break. Rusnac had no idea what time it was, but he'd been given some lunch and informed that an extension had been granted on his custody clock while they finalised the interview, after which there was something else they needed to do.

He wasn't informed what.

But the questions came.

About the garage lock-up. If he knew of it and had been there. When he'd been there. His lawyer had told him they had some evidence that placed him at a scene that tied him to the murder. This was it. He knew it had to be. He had no idea what he'd missed but he wasn't a stupid man. Far from it, so he'd speak and he'd place himself there.

'Yeah, I think I know the place you talk of. An associate of mine, he stopped off one day in a car. I was with him.'

A look passed between the television cops.

He was right.

'Mr Rusnac,' the lawyer spoke up. 'I advise you to stick to my advice.' His pen tapped on his pad.

'Is this my arrest? Is it only advice?'

The cops exchanged a look again. The lawyer's face changed from a pasty white to a rosy pink. 'Well, yes, of course, but it's advice that I urge you to listen to, for the reasons I provided.'

'It's advice I decline.'

The lawyer turned to the cops. 'I'd like a break to confer with my client, please.'

'Of course, I'm stopping –'

'No.' Rusnac was firm. 'I understand the advice. I took the advice all this time. Now I talk about this.'

Again, in a hushed voice, the lawyer strongly advised Rusnac to no-comment his answers. Rusnac didn't need to use words to silence him this time. A look closed him down and sent him back to his notebook.

The cops once more looked to each other and continued.

They tried to pin him down to specifics. He played it vague. Only placing himself there, while stating that he wasn't sure of dates or times. Unwilling to provide details of his associate. After all, it was him they were questioning. They pushed and wheedled for this information. He wouldn't budge. Threw in the odd 'no comment'. With a smirk at his lawyer.

The questions continued, they moved on. He stopped answering.

Then it came.

The evidence.

They had a cigarette end with his DNA on. How would he account for it being at the scene of the fire?

Rusnac thought back. He knew he'd had a smoke outside as he'd watched. It certainly wasn't in the car. They still couldn't prove anything.

'As I already told you. My associate was running an errand around there. I was smoking in his car and threw it out when I was done. I have no idea where it landed or where you found it. Unfortunately it was clearly near your scene.'

'One more thing, Vova,' said the male detective. 'We now need you to do a video for an identification procedure.'

48

Ray's office had never felt so small and claustrophobic. Jain had told him to wait in there until the ID suite was ready to receive him. It had to go smoothly. They had to do everything by the book. Rusnac's solicitor would be present and had insisted that they bring another ID officer over from another station. One that didn't know Ray. So that there could be no sneaky signals about which male should be picked out.

Ray rubbed at his face. He wasn't likely to pick up on sneaky signals, the way he felt at the minute, even if he wanted to. Even if they were corrupt enough to try it. And they weren't. He felt nauseous, and had the sense that the walls were closing in on him.

But he waited. Pretended he was working. In reality he scrolled through the intranet without reading a single word that rolled past his eyes.

Time ticked by in a surreal kind of vortex. Incredibly slowly and yet at the same time far too quickly, because there was a knock at the door now and Jain was there with a quick nod of his head, indicating they were ready.

Damn, how could he even do this? How could he have managed to get himself into this position? It was one thing to lie and say he hadn't seen the face of the killer, but to put himself in the position where he had to do the VIPER (video identification parade electronic recording) viewing, this was on another level entirely.

He acknowledged Jain with a nod of his own and closed down his computer. Stood and made his way towards his worst nightmare.

'You never know,' said Jain, falling into step beside him. His voice sounding far too happy. 'Seeing him might jolt something in that brain of yours. This might be the break we need. Even the side view of him could be the trigger and you've not realised you saw enough.'

Ray remained mute.

'Relax, give yourself time and look at each face.'

Again Ray didn't respond.

Jain laughed. 'Listen to me. Talking to you this way. Giving you the speech either one of us would give a witness. I don't need to tell you how to do this!' He clapped Ray on the shoulder and wheeled away from him towards the safety of his own office. 'Let me know how you get on.' And with that he was gone.

Ray tried to steady his breath and still his mind as he took the stairs to the identification suite, but all he felt was a heaviness take over his body and his mind. It wasn't as though he didn't have enough problems with his head, and now there was a dull weight taking over.

It was easy enough to figure out which of the two people in the room was the solicitor. He was suited, thin and reedy, with skin that gave away what must have been a difficult time for him as a teenager. The other male, on the other hand, wore the uniform black trousers and T-shirt with the force logo on the left-hand side. Ray introduced himself. The identification officer gave his name as

Ash Reid. He had a permanent smile on his face. Even when he had stopped talking and was prepping the computer.

Ray stood quietly in the corner as Ash pulled out the paperwork, asked Ray the questions he needed to ask, marked his answers, again smiling, and shuffled his papers to the side.

'Come and have a seat, DI Patrick.'

Ray sat. The tension had brought on a headache. A deep throb over his eyes that squeezed like a vice around his head.

It was nearly here. He knew what to expect. He'd sent more people than he cared to consider to these viewings, and now here he was, about to sit through one himself, knowing full well he would fail it, regardless of whether Billy's killer was here or not. And if he was, he was going to tank the entire investigation.

Ash explained what was to happen; even though Ray knew the procedure, Ash said he still had to go through it all. He looked at the solicitor. It was protocol, he said. Ray waited him out.

And then it started. The video, which Ray knew would last roughly three minutes. Nine video clips of nine males against a grey background, all facing forward, who would then turn left and right so you could see a profile view of them, before the video moved to the next person.

It started.

Grey background.

An Eastern European male.

Turned left.

Turned right.

Ray had no idea.

Another Eastern European male against a grey background.

Turned left.

Turned right.

This time he had a different T-shirt on.

It happened a further seven times.

Ray stared at the screen. He didn't flinch. Not a muscle moved.

'Okay. I'll play it again before you make comment,' said Ash.

Ray could feel the solicitor standing immobile in the corner of the room, watching behind him.

A trickle of sweat trailed its way down his spine. The video started up again. His shirt clung to his back.

Grey background.

Male.

Left.

Right.

Next.

And again. And again, and …

'Okay. All done!' Ash switched off the monitor. Pulled the paperwork back in front of him. 'Did you see the man who shot Billy Collier?'

'No.'

49

Rusnac walked away from the lawyer without a backward glance. The weasly little man was trying to talk to him about what would happen next. What he should or shouldn't do. His neat leather briefcase banging against his legs as he tried to keep up with his client. His voice lost amongst the noise of life on Stoke Newington High Street.

Rusnac had no intention of listening. He had no need of his advice. He wasn't a good honest citizen of the country who needed to obey the rules or fear the consequences. Scared of the slightest little infraction. He was bigger than that.

The street was noisy. Traffic moving, people walking, talking, shouting, pushing. Shops spilled their goods out onto the pavement, fruit and veg, the usual and unusual, small hardware shops displayed handy utensils. Handwritten signs, quirky coffee shops and takeaways. Hustle. Bustle. Food.

The sky overhead was leaden, oppressive. Like his mood. And mixed in with the darkness was confusion.

What he needed to do now was buy a phone, as the police had seized his on arrest and had informed him that they would keep it for as long as he was on bail so that they could examine it.

Once he had a new pay-as-you-go phone he could organise to be picked up from the godforsaken place and assess if there was any damage to the organisation, to his business.

The High Street was rammed with phone shops, and within two minutes he held a new one in his hand. He knew the number he needed. It was always a risk back home that the cops would take your phone simply because they could, so he'd taken to memorising numbers as well as storing them. Not like the idiots here who took it for granted that every number lived forever in the phone's memory.

It was then that Rusnac realised he'd managed to lose the inadequate little man who had been clinging to his coat-tails as they left the police station. He hadn't even noticed when it happened.

The call made, Rusnac found a bar to sit in. Ordered himself a drink and waited in the darkest corner he could find.

Why was he here, out in the world, waiting to be picked up? He checked the door of the pub; no one had followed him in. It didn't seem to be a ploy to tail him in order to round others up. Why would it be, when they had the killer and the head of the organisation in their hands?

That left a problem with the cop who had seen him fire the gun into the kid's side. That cop must have been the one who did the identity procedure, and yet they'd released him. The cop hadn't identified him, because if he had, along with the DNA evidence – which Rusnac decided he'd done a pretty good job of explaining away – he'd still be rotting in that damn stinking cell right now and not drinking a bottle of beer in the pub.

The beer was cool and felt good as he took a drink, enjoying the taste after the swill he'd been given over the past couple of days.

The corner of the label peeled back easily as his fingers searched for something to do while his mind searched for answers.

What did the cop get out of not chasing after him at the memorial and not identifying him today? What did he want? Did it mean he was bent?

All Rusnac had was an endless stream of questions and an inability to answer them.

Popa rolled up in a well-worn Audi. It wasn't easy to continue to get his hands on vehicles, he'd had to burn one and the police had seized one. Popa looked relaxed, one elbow on the edge of the window where it had been rolled down, even though the air was cool.

'Wind it up, you dick,' Rusnac moaned. It hadn't been particularly warm in the cell and all the bastards had provided him with was a scratchy grey blanket that wouldn't have kept a skinny girl warm on a hot day.

Popa pressed the window control without comment, moved his arm out of the way.

'What happened while I've been gone?' asked Rusnac once Popa had manoeuvred the car into the traffic.

'Nothing.'

'What do you mean, nothing?'

Popa looked across at Rusnac as if he'd asked a trick question.

'You going to answer or –'

'Just that, nothing of significance has happened while you been gone.' He looked nervous now. Not understanding what his boss expected to have happened.

'The cops haven't been to any of our places? Done anything online? Spoken to anyone or taken anyone else in? No jumpy clients?' He glared at the young male beside him, ready to grab the steering wheel and make him pay for his lies.

Popa's hands shook as he gripped hard as he drove. 'I promise, Vova. All is safe. They've been nowhere near us. They don't know anything.'

Rusnac told him to take a hike while he showered and changed. He felt as though he had a layer of grime covering both his clothes and his body, as though the filth had seeped underneath the material of his jeans and T-shirt and made themselves at home. He had an urge to scrub himself. It felt as though that would be the only way he would rid himself of the smell and the feeling that clung to him like a second skin. He wanted to scour himself. He wanted to burn his clothes.

The smell, he thought as he stripped out of his jeans, was hard to describe; it was like the toilet basin in the cell, mixed with someone else's bad foot odour, along with microwave meals. He wanted to retch. To clean his insides as well as wash his skin. The inside of his mouth felt as though it belonged to someone else, someone who lived in a bog.

His bathroom was tiny. The bath and shower was pushed so close to the sink and toilet that he could piss in the toilet and wash his hands in the sink while he showered if he so wished.

As the water drove down over him, the temperature as high as he could push it, Rusnac thought back to the cop and the memorial service. The way he looked when he turned to face him – what was the look he wore? Did he have a bent cop on his hands? The possibility to turn one? But how would he do it? If he was wrong, then he was in serious trouble. One option was to wait for the cop to come to him. He now knew where he was. But in the meantime he had to be careful with the business. He had to protect it. He also had to protect himself from the Russians. They couldn't know how close he had come to having it all come crashing down around him. They'd finish him in a way that would be a lot worse than the idiots who had spent hours questioning him.

He didn't like this uncertainty. He needed answers.

When he'd finished his shower, he called Popa and told him to return.

'Boss?' His voice held a quiver.

Rusnac held a bottle of Becks. He wasn't interested in being sociable and didn't offer the boy one. He was here to work. 'We've a busy time ahead of us.'

'Yes, boss.' The quiver less prominent now. He squared his shoulders back.

'I want all clients, both sides, buyers and sellers, contacting and reassuring. I want the medical staff checked on. I want visits to them all at their home addresses to make sure we don't have another leak, and I want the name and home address of the cop who saw me kill the kid, the one at the memorial service, the one who

232

did the ID procedure.' Rusnac looked at the boy in front of him, young but eager to please. 'I'll get you his photo.'

'Yes, boss.'

A silence pervaded the room.

'Well, don't just stand there.'

50

'What the hell, Ray?' Jain slammed the door to Ray's office, not bothering to keep his voice down before it had fully closed. He was furious, and Ray couldn't say he blamed him. He looked at the photo of Alice and Matthew on his desk. The two small faces no longer connected in his brain, no longer provided him with the comfort he could do with right now, and only served to remind him of the abject failure he'd been.

'I told you I didn't see him, that he was too far away as we were running. And he had his back to me.' Ray threw Jain a glare, going on the offensive. 'And then he shot Billy, remember Billy? And –'

'Don't give me that "remember Billy" crap. That's why he was dragged in. That's what all this is about. That's why I'm so pissed off. If we're talking about remembering things, try remembering the IPCC investigation I'm shielding you from,' Jain spat back.

Ray stood. The feeling of being at a lower level to Prabhat, who had not seated himself, was not comfortable. He was tense, his whole body cried out to move, his muscles aching for action. He was on full alert. He tried to lower his tone to compensate. 'As I was saying, my eyes were focused on Billy, his injury, trying to stem the bleeding, not on the man running in the opposite direction.'

Jain paced around the office. Arms waving as he spoke. 'He's admitted to being near the garages, he was in an associate's car who was running an errand – a bloody errand – and though he doesn't remember, he said it's likely he could have been smoking and thrown a tab-end down. He's placed himself quite legally at the scene of the fire. But not inside, and we can't place him inside because it was torched so goddamn well, even though we can ID the car as the one from that day from the VIN. No evidence has survived to place anyone in it. And now you can't ID him for the murder.'

'I can't and I'm sorry I can't, but what do you want me to do about that?'

'I want you to catch Billy's killer, Ray. Is that too much to ask?' And with that he stormed back out, slinging the door behind him with as much force as when he'd entered.

51

The email glared back. As though daring Elaine to suggest it wasn't real, or that it was untrue. She ran her hands through her hair. Looked around the office.

Will and Paula were fighting over whose turn it was to make the coffees. Will was adamant he'd made the last two, and that, though Paula made the shittest coffee in the building, it didn't exempt her from having to make it. In fact, Elaine heard him complain, he wouldn't put it past her to make it like pigswill on purpose so that no one would want her to make it again.

Paula then jumped into a diatribe about Will calling her lazy.

She looked back to the screen.

The email was still there. The pixelated black letters on the solid white background.

Her mind had already run through the meaning, added up the sums and come up with the answer, but she didn't like what she'd found. She didn't understand it.

In his office, the guv was at his desk, head bent over his keyboard, tapping away, occasionally looking up at the screen to check his typing before he continued. He was hell-bent on finding Billy's killer. He'd been devastated when the op had gone wrong. She knew he'd had it out with the Super. It had gone around the station like wildfire. Internal arguments like that tended get be hooked up to the gossip grapevine pretty quickly.

The investigation had also been pushed hard. They'd done long hours. Hours when she hadn't been able to put the children to bed, to read them a bedtime story or ask them about their day. She only saw them in the morning, when they were fractious, as was she. Overtired due to the hours worked, which ruined the only time she had with them. Paul was still awake when she got home, usually in bed, either reading or marking, jotters thrown across the bedcovers. His reading glasses perched at the end of his nose. They tried to talk about their day, but they were both exhausted and a quiet settled over them before sleep.

She'd told herself that they all knew it was just for a short period of time, as it always was when a murder inquiry first got off the ground. It was always the same. Family routine would soon return, and she held on to that.

But reading the email again, Elaine faltered. Where had her strongly held belief in what they had been doing gone?

Had she neglected her family for nothing? Put her marriage at risk? The emotional health of her children?

She looked into Ray's office again, ran her hands through her hair, scrubbed at her scalp. If this email was to be believed, then her guv, Ray Patrick, was not to be trusted.

52

Rusnac pushed himself back into the dim shop doorway and pulled the scarf tighter around his neck. The evening cold nipped at his face. He blew into his hands. Breath visibly shifting through his fingers into the night.

It was already dark, although the shortest day had long been and gone, back in December, when the wind had relentlessly whipped the rain through the days one after the other. But the days still fled too soon and left darkness to wrap its fingers around the buildings, streets and people far too early. Now spring was supposed to be upon them; there were occasional weather breakthroughs but the lighter evenings were only gradually creeping in.

Two men walked by. Arms wrapped around each other. One leaning in, smiling up into the face of the other, who was laughing at a shared joke.

Rusnac didn't understand the need to be so close to someone that way. To be so reliant on someone that you leaned on them, rested on them, changed the way you walked. Altered your mood around them. His life was about taking care of himself and his mother. It was about survival. The rest was there to get in the way and put you at risk.

Twenty-five minutes had passed. He had no idea how long he'd have to wait out here, and standing still in one place made his bones ache. The cold seeped in and gnawed at him. This annoyed him. The winters were so much harsher back home, he was turning into a wimp here.

It had to be done. He had to watch the large glass and green steel-fronted building. Lit up and glowing with perceived warmth in the now dark night. But he had to be discreet.

Fifty minutes and he was getting frustrated.

An hour and a half and he wanted to walk away because of the boredom and the inane idiots that continued to pass him, especially the ones that insisted on saying 'good evening' to him as they did so. His response was invariably a grunt. He had patience, though, and he was the only one who could do this. And it had to be done.

He stamped his feet.

Two hours.

Rubbed his hands together.

Two hours twenty minutes.

The glass door opened and Rusnac lifted his chin out his jacket. This was it.

But it wasn't.

He swore quietly into his collar as he pushed his chin back down.

Three hours five minutes.

A lone figure walked from the rear of the building. Walking out of near darkness. Rusnac watched. He was the right height. He pulled his phone out of his pocket. The figure had his hands pushed deep into pockets. Shoulders hunched up to ears. Rusnac continued to watch. Then the figure hit the light from the street lamps and Rusnac raised his phone. Tapped through to camera, zoomed in and clicked a couple of times to make sure he had a decent photograph.

53

Elaine wished spring would hurry up and show its face properly. These patches of blue sky did nothing but tease her about the season she preferred.

Ray had given them a day off. Part of the team, anyway. To attempt to revive them, as they'd been working through without a break. It was a Saturday but with a big case they often worked through a weekend, so it was helpful to the parents in the team.

It was cold and grey but dry. They'd bundled the kids up in coats, hats and gloves and were now crossing Silver Street towards Pymmes Park after managing to grab a parking space on the main road. The sky was clear again but a wind was blowing. The children both moaned about how cold they were and how they'd rather watch television: Teletubbies and CBeebies, specifically. Elaine knew she dumped them in front of the TV more than she would like to, and tried to get out of the house as often as the job and her energy levels allowed.

Now she gripped Hayden's hand tighter as he attempted to pull away. The road was busy. 'We need some fresh air. You're wrapped up. The TV will still be there when we get back,' she said with a sharpness to her tone that she wished she could take back.

Paul looked at her, a question on his face.

'When we get there,' she answered, and they headed towards the park area. Bare trees lined and filled the park. Brittle and cold. Small thoughts of life showing as shoots poked their way out of the branches.

The television was forgotten as soon as they walked through the gate and the vast space opened up for them. Elaine let Hayden slip from her grasp and Paul did the same with Halle. They ran and screamed, allowing the cold air to grasp their howls of joy from their mouths as they ran around each other. No matter how much they complained about being dragged out, once they were given the freedom of space they opened up and let go. Running, screeching, grabbing and twirling.

Elaine could see a few women walking about, chatting and laughing. They were wore running gear, Lycra leggings and T-shirts or Lycra tops, and Elaine remembered they held the park run at Pymmes Park every Saturday at nine a.m., so they'd have missed it by about half an hour. It was something she'd considered taking part in, but with the inconsistency of work she'd never taken the hobby up.

Clutching the flask mug she'd made up at home and taking refuge in its warmth, Elaine steered them over the bridge that leaned over the dull slow lake, towards the colourful park and the benches, where she sat. The wooden slats of the bench cold through her jeans.

Paul waited for her to speak, looking out at the children, who now clambered up the steps to the slide. Woollen gloves making their hands slip on the metal handrails. Progress slow. Then they were down at the bottom of the slide and running around to climb the steps again.

'It's work,' said Elaine.

'I figured as much.'

She watched the steam wind its way up into the air in front of her face. The deep smell of coffee reminding her of home, of the kitchen, of Paul marking homework at the kitchen table. 'You know I've always trusted Ray, his decisions?'

'Yeah.'

Halle pushed Hayden, even though she was the smallest, using her weight on his shoulder, wanting to get up the steps first. He took two steps back and she scrambled up the steps. Gloved hands slipping in her eagerness. A picture of innocence.

'Something's happened.'

Paul turned away from the two playing children and faced his wife. It wasn't often she brought work home with her. 'What is it?'

'It's complicated. But he's hiding something big and it affects the investigation.'

'So give me the short version. You brought me here to tell me.' He flicked his eyes back to the children. Elaine's had never left them.

'We went to a memorial service for the murder victim we're dealing with, where my suspicion was piqued by a man Ray had talked to. I took his car number plate. Later we brought a suspect in. Ray failed to ID him.'

She paused. The rest of it stuck in her throat like barbed wire. Sharp. Pointed.

How to dislodge something so painful?

'What did the results of the number-plate check show, Elaine?'

Her focus never left the children. Her hands tightened on the cup in her lap. Trying to draw the warmth into her bones. 'It had been pinged by an ANPR camera close to a garage that was torched, at around the time it was torched. It wasn't the burnt car, but it's too much of a coincidence.'

Halle and Hayden moved to the swings, kicking their legs, trying to make themselves move higher.

Paul waited.

'The thing is, the guy Ray failed to ID was picked up as a suspect for the murder on evidence around the garage that was torched, and after he spoke to him at the memorial service.'

'There could be a perfectly logical explanation, Elaine.'

'Like what?' She rounded on him. Her tone sharper than she'd wanted. The barbed wire that had been stuck in her throat, exploding out in frustration. Spitting out at her husband.

He didn't change, didn't pull her up on it. 'Bad coincidence. You often tell me that bad guys use each other's vehicles. Maybe that happened this time. But whatever it is, I doubt that Ray is tied up in the crime you're talking about.'

Elaine put the cup on the bench between them, then placed her head in her hands and closed her eyes. Blocking out the stress she felt. 'I know you're right,' she murmured through her fingers.

'You need to talk to him.'

54

The place was loud. Kids ran in socked feet, screaming.

Ray had just walked through the door and he had the sudden urge to run back out again, screaming himself. But there was a part of him where a warmth surged. Being here, in the family pub with Helen and the kids, held a certain familiarity that he needed right now.

As they walked to a table, Helen told the children they needed to remove their shoes before they went into the climbing area. And that they were not to run while in the seating area. It was dangerous. People were carrying glasses around. She said this as a child of about six whizzed past in a blur of orange and black, like a bumblebee.

She bent down and collected Alice and Matthew's shoes from where they'd abandoned them and they continued to a table, choosing one where they could see into the climbing area but where the decibel level created by the playing children was also louder. No wonder the seats were free and most parents took tables further away and left their kids to play, hoping they were safe. Ray never took that chance. He understood the dangers too well. Helen had often chided him for his over-cautiousness, but it was inbuilt now and he couldn't stop it.

He'd memorised Alice and Matthew's clothes when he saw them at the house, knowing they would be running about, leaving his sight, coming back and going again, to and fro, backwards and forwards. Alice had pigtails in but he couldn't guarantee that other girls wouldn't have those, so he memorised her outfit. A layered, ruffled blue skirt and white T-shirt with ruffled sleeves. All ruffled today. He also recognised the way she ran, with her right leg kicking out to the side slightly.

Matthew was a bit more difficult. Much the same as many boys his age. Jeans and a football shirt. He'd tried to get him to change his shirt and Helen had helped him in that task, understanding why he was doing it, but Matthew was adamant that he wanted to wear this one, so he'd had to bite his tongue as his own frustration grew. Helen had touched his arm to calm his frayed nerves. At least she would be with him. He wouldn't lose his children or try to walk off with someone else's child.

On this, their only day off, he'd asked to have the children and said he'd bring them here but then got wound up when he realised that he could get lost as he drove there or back. So not only could he lose his children while he had them in person, but he could lose them while he had them physically in his sight because he'd get lost as well. The frustration levels he felt were extreme.

During a long phone conversation the night before, where he updated Helen on the failed ID procedure, he mentioned the problem with his sense of direction and she'd offered to come with them and drive. He couldn't thank her enough and she'd told him to stop it, to pull himself together. She was doing it for the children. This was actually one of the scenarios she had imagined helping him with when, at the hospital, she had told him she would support him with the children and this diagnosis.

Today, he was so glad she was here. He felt comfortable. Settled. For the first time in days a calmness descended on him.

He ordered a bottled beer for himself, a lime and soda for Helen and two fruit-flavoured drinks in plastic bottles for the kids.

'So Prabhat?' asked Helen as she looked down the menu. The food in places like this wasn't much to write home about but that wasn't why they'd come, it was about being together and spending time together.

'Yeah?'

'Rough?'

'Let's just say he wasn't happy.'

Helen kept her eyes down. 'You didn't tell me much last night – what did you say to him, about your failure to pick him out?'

'Millie!' a woman screeched over them, 'Let go of that boy's ears!' The boy in question was getting redder in the face by the second.

'I told him the same as I told him the day Billy was ...' Ray looked around and lowered his voice, 'killed. That I didn't get close enough to see the guy, that he was running away from me so I never saw his whole face. There was nothing I could do to change the outcome.' Millie had let go of the boy, who was now rubbing his ear, eyes bright with unshed tears.

Helen dropped the menu. Looked at Ray. 'How do you feel?'

'How do you think?'

'I don't know, that's why I asked.'

'I feel like hell. I saw him. He looked right at me. And now I can't pick him out so he walks out the station. How am I supposed to reconcile that?'

Helen reached out and placed her hand on top of Ray's. 'You'll get him with solid police work like you always do. Keep working, don't give up. Keep beating yourself up and your work will suffer. You have to move forward to catch this bastard. Work hard. Focus. You can do this.'

The noise in the pub didn't seem as loud then; people were all around them but the volume had dipped and Ray felt as though they were enclosed in their own bubble. Out of the corner of his eye he saw a girl coming out of the play area. Noticed the blue and white ruffles. Felt the warmth rush him.

His phone vibrated in his pocket. He pulled his hand from under Helen's. It was Celeste. Something in the pit of his stomach twisted.

'Hi.' He tried for bright. It sounded tight, even to his own ears.

'Where are you? I thought we might do something this afternoon into this evening as you're not at work.'

How did she know he wasn't at work today? He didn't remember telling her, but he must have.

'I'm sorry, I'm already out, I have Alice and Matthew.'

There was a note of disappointment in her voice as she acknowledged that of course he must make time for his children, especially with all the hours he'd been working. Maybe she could see him later. Afterwards.

'I'll call –'

'Mummy, can we eat yet? I'm hungry!' Alice shouted as she ran over to the table.

'Mummy?' Celeste's tone was sharp. Pointed. 'Mummy is there with you?'

'Well –'

'I don't understand this, Ray. Something is going on with you and I'm trying to give you time and I'm trying to understand because I believe it's because of the accident. I think you're mentally affected by it and you're pushing people away as you deal with it. But what I don't get is why Helen doesn't get pushed away as well?'

'It's not the accident, Celeste, and –'

The line went dead.

55

Helen and the children dropped him back home after what few would call a relaxing afternoon, although compared to how most recent days had been, Ray thought it had been perfect.

After spending most the time running up and around, climbing frames and slides, jumping in ball pits and stuffing their faces, Alice and Matthew were now subdued in the rear seats.

Helen pulled up at the curb. 'You'll be okay?' she asked as the engine ticked over. Clear that she was about to head straight off.

'Yeah. You were right earlier. I need to get my act together and make this case, no matter the issues I've already come up against.'

'And Celeste?' Straightforward. The woman who had been married to him. Who didn't need to pull her punches or need to worry about what he would think or say.

But Ray didn't have an answer. He shrugged.

'You need to at least talk to her, Ray. Let her know what's going on and ask her for the time to work it out, rather than giving her the runaround.'

'I can't.'

'Why?'

'How do you tell someone that you don't recognise them every single time you see them? I've researched this online and people lose friends because they get upset when they think they've been ignored.'

'You know what they say about looking up issues online, don't you?'

'I know, but still. I run no more risk this way than I would if I told her. I'd rather try and sort it out in my head and at least then maybe time is on my side. If I can sort myself out, then there will be no need to tell her.'

'You hope.'

'Give me some credit.'

Helen looked in the back of the car. Startled, Ray checked the seat behind him.

'Don't worry,' she said. 'They're half asleep and not listening to us.'

'They were so quiet I forgot they were there.'

'My point exactly. This will get out. Better you control it than it controls you.'

Ray leaned over and kissed her cheek. 'Thank you.' Helen inclined her head. 'I forgot to ask,' he smiled. 'What's his name?'

'Whose name?'

'This bloke you're seeing.' He kept his voice low this time.

'Liam.'

'And you're still seeing him?'

Helen gave a slow gentle smile. 'I'm still seeing him.'

'What's with the smile? Is something wrong?'

'Nothing. No, nothing is wrong. Quite the opposite. It's going really well. I like him. We've seen a lot of each other. As much as we can without introducing the kids yet, anyway.'

Ray turned his face away, looked out of the side window a moment. Watched a couple of boys kick a football down the street, probably heading to a park.

'What would he think about today?'

'He'd be fine because he knows we have a good relationship because we have great kids. I told him all about us before we got started so he knew what he was getting into.'

'He sounds very new-age.'

'Not a caveman like you, then.' She nudged him with her elbow. He grunted and she laughed at him again, resulting in another grunt for her trouble.

He turned to the back seat again, raised his voice. 'See you, kids. Thanks for a great afternoon.' He needed to get out. Get home.

Their faces lit up. 'Can we do it again, Daddy?'

He looked at Helen, who regarded him calmly. 'I don't see why not,' he said. Though things were changing.

The apartment had a chill to it. Ray switched the heating on, grabbed a bottled beer from the fridge, dropped onto the sofa and opened the laptop, waited for it to wake.

Yes, he'd told Helen he would work the case even harder, but that didn't mean he would only work it from the office. He'd failed spectacularly and now he did need to pull out all the stops.

It was a dark and dangerous world he was about to step into, he recognised that. It was unknown. A path untested. The ground beneath his feet precarious. But it was one he had to tread.

Carefully. If this was to work.

As he hit the enter key, the screen before him changed from the banal-looking search engine page of dark net and morphed into the page of the address he'd keyed in. The address for Dedit.

Yes, he'd looked at the page before, but tonight he was going to properly step inside.

Ray clicked through to the section of the site for people who wanted to sell their organs. There were pages of information. Clean, sharp, clear information pages, as though this were a legitimate website and this was a legitimate and ordinary medical issue they were talking about. It spoke about the health and safety of their clients being of the first importance. It spoke of clean lines of transfer for funds. It spoke of the best in medical care and aftercare. Then it asked for your details if you were interested, including, if you knew it, your blood group, though not to worry if not, as they could test you with ease and speed.

The beer felt cool as it slid down his throat. Ray tipped his head back, necking the bottle, eyes on the ceiling. His mouth was dry so he drank the lot.

This was a huge step he was about to take.

He slammed the empty bottle down at the side of the laptop. His fingers hovered over the keys.

A car horn blared outside, breaking the silence inside the apartment. Breaking his uncertainty, his … fear.

He clicked the mouse pad to wake the cursor over the first box and typed Neville Gordon in the name box.

Shit, he'd need to remember that, and it was such a random name. He jumped up and paced around looking for paper and pen.

Then paced some more before he returned to the now sleeping laptop.

He could do this. He had to do this.

Neville Gordon. 41. Interested in information only at this point.

No point coming across too eager. Didn't want to put a beacon on his head that he was a cop.

56

Elaine walked into the incident room the morning after their rare day off. She'd set her alarm half an hour earlier than normal, showered herself before getting the kids up ten minutes earlier than she normally did, and still managed to find herself rushing through the door to get into work on time. The children seemed to sense that they had longer to mess about, and no matter how much she jollied them along they shuffled and moaned and griped at each other, and it turned into a day like any other.

Standing, she watched Ray from her desk. She could see he was reading from his computer monitor and making notes in his book. Catching up on the skeleton staff that were here yesterday no doubt, those continuing with the ongoing inquiries that could still be done. There was no way he would close the investigation for a day off, but he did take care of his staff and had noticed they needed a break. Elaine couldn't argue that she felt better for having yesterday at home with her family.

But how this kindness contrasted with the niggling feeling she was harbouring about him.

Ray lifted his head. Caught her watching, raised his hand to her. She removed her coat, slung it on the back of her chair and walked over to speak to him.

'Get you a coffee, guv?'

He looked at her. Studied her intently. Did he suspect her of knowing something? 'That'd be great, Elaine. Thank you. Good day with Paul and the kids yesterday?'

If he did suspect her of something, why would he bring her family up? She shook her head. This was ridiculous. She wasn't in the middle of some crazy movie. Ray might be hiding something, but she was letting her imagination run away with her.

'It was blissful, if I'm honest. It was needed.'

Ray smiled.

'You?'

His eyebrows lifted. A pause. 'Yes, actually. Also a necessary day.'

With coffees made and emails checked, the incident room had filled up. There was chatter about how well everyone felt after a day off. The room wasn't quite as busy, as yesterday's skeleton staff were now taking their day off. But there was an energetic hum which, Elaine realised, was what Ray wanted after the results of the day before. Everyone back, refreshed and raring to go. He more than anyone needed to get his equilibrium back.

Didn't he?

He stood at the front of the room. Coffee, which would now be nearly cold, she imagined, in his hand.

He talked about how events hadn't gone their way but how they needed to collect themselves and continue to work the case. That it wasn't the end, that there were still lines of inquiry to make and that they would work it like any other. Just because they didn't have an ID didn't mean they didn't have a case. They'd put away plenty of killers with evidence alone, without identification evidence, and that's what they would do with this one. This killer.

The speech was rousing and passionate. She had to give him that. She felt renewed enthusiasm for her work as he spoke. Unsure how she could have doubted him, she drained the last of her own cold coffee.

'The ballistic results came back on the bullet that killed Billy.' His face had dropped. She could see it was painful for him. 'It was a Glock and it comes back as having been used in an offence in Moldova, and there's intelligence linking it back to Russia.'

'So the link to Russia that was mentioned in the interviews appears to be true,' commented Paula.

'Looks that way. But just because we have this information, don't let it send you running down any rabbit holes. This still occurred on London soil. Our offender is here and we need to catch him. If we find him and we find the gun, it can be matched to the bullet and casing and then the intelligence. But we want him for the murder of Billy.'

Elaine made a note in her incident workbook.

'Isn't Rusnac from Romania?' asked Paula.

'Yes, but Borta is from Moldova and they're neighbours, and we know how weapons can move about.'

Paula gave a quick nod.

Ray continued: 'Those of you making inquiries on the medical side of the investigation, keep on with those and keep me up to date with them.' He paused. Put his mug down on the table to one side of him. Paced a few steps out, then moved back again before speaking. His voice with a slight edge to it.

'Okay, going back to the ID issue.' He looked around the room.

Elaine dropped her head, not wanting to catch his eye.

'I didn't pick Vova Rusnac out because I didn't get a real look at the person who killed Billy. That is not to say that Rusnac is not that person. We had enough grounds to bring him in and I think we need to take a proper look at him. So we look at him and we look at him hard. Find out everything you can about him. Turn over every stone. Find out what he does – really. Where he spends his days, and nights. Who his associates are, what vehicles he has access to, what properties he's associated with and what he brushes his bloody teeth with.'

She didn't expect that. Elaine closed her mouth when she realised it was hanging open. What was happening with him? She'd found a link that made her question him: the guy at the memorial, the failed ID; and now he was targeting the ID suspect and targeting him hard. This had thrown her. It was the last thing she expected him to do. The only move she had left was to ask him outright.

What would he say? Was she about to risk their friendship and her career?

57

It hadn't been easy for Ray to admit his failure to identify Rusnac. But the team had seemed to take it in their stride. He'd made the right decision when he gave them a day off. Not to make them forget what he'd done or to bribe his way back into their good books, but so that they would come back with the renewed enthusiasm that they clearly had done.

He felt jittery when he told the team that he wanted them to go after Rusnac on the back of his failed ID. To his own ears it had sounded like a sensible argument: he hadn't seen the killer, therefore he wouldn't be able to identify him, but evidence had pointed to Rusnac so it was worth pursuing.

It was good.

'Guv?'

Ray looked up. Squinted into the face. No curls. Not a Scottish accent, none of the other markers he had for the other female staff in the incident room. He hated to have to look for the scar. It was so damned personal. A sharp reminder.

'Guv?'

'Yes, Elaine, come on in. Grab a seat.'

She tugged at a chair until it was where she wanted to be. Her eyes looking anywhere but in his direction. If he didn't know any different he would say that something was wrong, but he'd spoken to her not an hour ago and she was fine then. He hoped all was okay at home. It was difficult, the demands of bringing up a family and this job, and he was the male in the relationship; he'd been lucky in that Helen had done most of the heavy lifting where their children were concerned, but he knew that Elaine's husband was a teacher and she had to do as much as any mother, whereas he could focus on his job.

A fact that had broken his marriage.

Once Elaine was settled in the chair Ray lifted his chin for her to go ahead and let him know why she was here.

She rubbed her face.

Then sat on her hands.

This didn't bode well.

'Everything okay?' he asked.

'How long have we worked together, sir?'

That was unexpected.

'Well, erm, let's see.' Ray tipped his head back, looked at the ceiling as he tried to work it out. 'I came to this job ...' His head bobbed as he counted back the years in his head. Then counted again to clarify by assessing his previous role.

Elaine waited.

'... from the Sapphire team a little over six years ago and you were already here.' He looked back at Elaine. 'Wow, has it been that long already? It only feels like a couple of years.'

Elaine was thoughtful. Where was this headed? 'Are you considering applying for another department, Elaine?' It was the only thing that made any sense.

She dragged her hand from under a leg and scrubbed it through her hair causing strands to stick out at unruly angles, for it to move away from her scar, for it to stand out more. 'No. No, it's not that.'

The sliver of pink glowed under the fluorescent strip-light in the ceiling. Ray pulled his eyes away. Down to the paperwork on his desk. Damn. Why could he not look her in the eyes?

'What, then?' He pulled his attention back up. Forced himself to appear normal. His stomach clawing in frustration at his ineptitude.

Elaine looked behind her at the incident room beyond the door. 'Can I close the door?'

He furrowed his brows. 'Of course.'

She stood, closed the door, then paced a couple of steps before she returned to her seat, and then jumped back up again. 'Sir, you'll have to forgive me, but I'm a little confused about some things and I need you to clear them up, and the reason I ask you how long we've known each other is because I believe we trust each other and that you know I would never be malicious and …' She was speaking at speed, not pausing for breath, with no coherent sentence structure, and now starting to stumble over her words.

'Slow down, Elaine. What is it?' Ray kept his tone even, calm, although he was starting to feel the way Elaine was behaving. She was rubbing off on him. He didn't like the way this conversation was going.

At that she sat back in the chair and put her head in her hands.

'I'm worried you're hiding things from the investigation team, sir,' she mumbled.

58

'Hiding things from the investigation team?' Ray looked out of the window at the team in the incident room. His voice no higher than a whisper. How had she got here? She was a bloody good copper. He was about to lose his entire career. He had to be very careful.

'I'm sorry, guv.' Her voice wasn't much louder than his own now. There seemed to be a heaviness blanketing them that their voices had to fight through.

'Don't be sorry. Explain it to me. Let me clear it up for you … if I can.' How could he?

She lifted her head. Eyes full of hope.

She talked about the memorial service. About how she had been suspicious of the male who had run away from him and how he hadn't seemed too fazed, but she had taken the partial VRM she could manage to get, and done the checks, followed them up, including through ANPR and it had come through with an ANPR hit, even if she hadn't got the registered keeper – it didn't have one right now, but the ANPR hit had been close to the garage that was burnt down and on the day it was burnt down. Then – and this was where there was a lengthy pause – she struggled to get through this bit, but she was a strong detective and she was adamant she wanted to talk it through, this was what she had come in for: then, the guy, Vova Rusnac, his back and semi-side profile, what she had seen of him, which, she had to admit, wasn't much – and Ray breathed a silent sigh of relief at this – looked like those of the guy at the memorial service, and yet he, Ray, her guv, hadn't identified him. Was it possible it wasn't the same person? She needed to know.

She stopped her pacing, her breathless monologue, and looked at him. Waited for an answer, or an axe to fall maybe.

But on whose head did she expect it to fall? he wondered.

Did she expect him to yell at her, to tell her that she had it all wrong and that instead of these flights of fancy and side inquiries she should have done the job he had told her to do?

Or was she suspicious enough of him to think the axe might be hovering over his own head, waiting to drop? Both of them holding their breath as the head of the axe hovered motionless, waiting for the moment to drop and shed blood.

Ray's head started to pound. He leaned back in his chair and rubbed his temples, playing for time.

What did she have exactly? She had what the inquiry team had – but she had the extra information of the vehicle from the memorial service. Which could be coincidence if he wanted to swing it that way. And she hadn't seen the male at the memorial herself. Not properly. She'd admitted that.

'Why didn't you come to me with the registration from the memorial service?' he asked, playing for time as he worked out his options in his head.

This was the only other piece of information she had that was different to everyone else. But she was querying him. Her trust in him, questioned. He wanted to own up, to tell her she was right, but he couldn't put her in the position where she had to keep his secret.

Because right now he was not prepared to walk away from the job before they had locked up Billy's killer.

Maybe afterwards.

But not before.

Elaine looked sheepish. 'I don't know, sir. You'd said it was nothing but my hackles were raised by the whole situation and I couldn't ignore it.'

She was tenacious. He admired her for that. Always had.

'I can't answer why his vehicle came up near our scene, Elaine. I really can't. Maybe he's linked. But for the life of me I can't remember his name. Like I said, he was involved in an old job of mine years ago and didn't like the fact that he'd seen me there, so legged it. He was already talking to Billy's friends when I walked over to them. If what you say is true, then we need to link up that vehicle on HOLMES and make it a part of our inquiry.'

Elaine finally sat down on her chair in front of him again.

'You think he went to the memorial on purpose rather than it being a coincidence, then? And maybe this is the friend that Rusnac mentioned? After all, we do know that it's an organisation that we were originally after, rather than one individual.'

He'd done it, but he didn't feel good. He felt far from good. He knew that Rusnac must be the person who burnt the garage down, who killed Billy, and who he had been face to face with at the memorial service.

59

Elaine pushed the door to the police station open and walked out into the busy street. It was cool and her breath floated up in front of her face as she breathed. 'Thanks for coming, Tamsin. I know it's a bit early for lunch but I needed a breather.'

'Hey, any time. I love this market, and as you're buying, I'm in.'

Elaine smiled and shoved her hands into her pockets. Stoke Newington farmers' market was right across the road from the station and was a great place to grab a bite to eat if you were in at the weekend, which they often were.

After a couple of minutes waiting for the traffic to thin they both trotted across the road, Tamsin eager to see what delight she could eat and Elaine anxious to put some distance between her and the office for ten minutes.

The market was fringed by a black metal fence. They walked through, into the bustling space. People wrapped in coats, strolling around the stalls. Stopping and chatting with familiar faces. It was a community. A place where people gathered once a week.

Elaine and Tamsin walked further in past the fish stall, the smell of fresh fish clinging to them as they walked.

'I know it's early but I love the organic burgers.' Tamsin knew where she was going.

Elaine followed. Soon Tamsin slowed, turned and looked at her friend. 'What is it that pulled you out here, Elaine?'

Elaine was about to shake her head that it didn't matter, but wasn't the reason she'd asked Tamsin out here to talk to her about it? Or was it simply to give herself some room to think? If that was the reason, she could have come alone. 'Remember that night in the White Hart?' she asked.

Tamsin came to a stop in front of the stall she wanted. There was a young couple in front of her getting served. 'Yes, it was a great night. Poor Will had the piss ripped out of him big time. He really does leave himself open for it though. After you left he approached those women, did I tell you?'

Elaine laughed, she couldn't help herself. 'No, no, you didn't. Did he get blown off?'

'Would you believe he came away with a phone number?'

Elaine shook her head. 'He really does have the gift of the gab, that one.'

'I don't know how he gets away with it.'

The couple paid and moved away. Tamsin looked at Elaine. 'You having one?'

'Okay, get me the same as you.'

Tamsin ordered two organic burgers with beetroot. 'So – what about that night?'

Elaine handed her the money from her pocket.

'Oh. Shit. The guv? Something else?' Tamsin handed the cash over.

Elaine waited for her to finish before she answered, giving only a silent nod. 'Let's sit, shall we.' Indicating with her head the wooden tables and benches, taking the burger that Tamsin proffered. The smoky scent of the griddle wafted up her nose. She was hungrier than she realised. The burger was warm in her hand. They moved to the bench and sat.

'So what is it?' Tamsin asked again.

'Shit.' Elaine shook her head.

'What?' Tamsin took a bite of the burger and wiped her chin, unable now to utter another word.

'I don't think I can.'

Tamsin raised her eyebrows in question as she chewed.

'I don't think I can tell you what's worrying me.'

Tamsin's brow furrowed. She chewed harder, then swallowed. 'You can't pull me out here and then say you won't tell me what's going on. Is it something I need to be aware of?'

Elaine let out a long sigh. What was she doing? She didn't know. She was concerned. She had wanted to discuss it with someone but now she was out here she was worried about inciting problems that maybe she had imagined. He'd provided an explanation. She needed to consider it more.

'I think I need to mull it over a bit more. I'm sorry, but until I'm sure of what I'm saying I shouldn't really pull you into it.'

Tamsin wolfed down more of the burger. 'Are you sure about that, Elaine? You know I'm here if you need to talk. And that you can trust me.'

'I know. I'm sorry. Getting out of the office for five minutes has helped.' They shared a look. 'Honestly. If I need to, I'll come to you and we'll sort it out.'

Tamsin shoved the last piece of burger into her mouth. Wiped away any visible signs that she'd eaten. 'If you're sure?'

'Yes. I'm sorry I dragged you out on a cold day like today.'

'Don't be. It was a perfect excuse to have one of those.' She nodded at the uneaten burger in Elaine's hands.

60

'I'm not staying,' Celeste said as she stood on Ray's front steps.

'Why did you knock, not come straight in?' Ray turned and walked back into the apartment expecting her to follow him. When he didn't hear footsteps behind him, he paused, turned and saw her looking at him, framed by the doorway. Light from the streetlamps bouncing a halo around her head. He couldn't decipher whatever it was she was attempting to say to him with her expression. He furrowed his brows.

Celeste stepped into the warmth and closed the door with a click. Ray continued into the kitchen, pulled two long-stemmed glasses down from the cupboard and the wine bottle from the fridge and half-filled each glass. Handing Celeste hers when she reached him.

'What is it?' he asked. Then remembered the phone call when he'd been with Helen and the kids. Kicked himself. Took a slug of the wine and waited for her to berate him. He leaned against the kitchen worktop.

'Things were going really well before your accident, you agree?' Her eyes were intense.

'I do. They were great. They still are.'

'Ray.' She dropped her bag onto the worktop next to her. Slipped off her jacket and folded it over the bag. 'Let's not do that.' She looked good. She'd obviously been home and showered and changed from work. She was wearing slim-fit jeans with a cream jumper that clung to her curves. Highlighted her natural colouring.

Her cheeks had a slight blush to them from the cold outside. She was beautiful.

Ray rubbed at his face.

'I was starting to feel for you. Really –' there was emphasis on that really '– feel for you.'

'I know, I –'

'Let me finish.'

He nodded. Took another gulp of the wine. Noticed Celeste was cradling hers but not drinking it. The difference between them.

'I was even beginning to get ideas in my head. Of the future. Just what ifs. Nothing to scare you away. They were just mine. For me to play with in my mind. But I noticed that it all changed after the accident. And what I want to know is, if it is something to do with the accident and I should hold on, or if it's something else and I should walk away. So tell me. Which is it, Ray, what should I do?'

61

Rusnac was happy with what he knew. The man had two addresses. Not technically two, but he had his own address and then he had a family at another.

Popa had done well when he'd tailed him. He hadn't been satisfied when he'd placed him in one address, he'd waited him out to check some of his haunts and they'd fallen lucky and found this other address in Harlow. A detached family home on a corner plot. It might come in useful if events didn't go the way he planned. Rusnac was taking a risk, after all.

He had no real idea why the cop had failed to pick him out, and to approach him to ask was maybe one of the dumbest moves he'd ever made; but seriously, to not pick him out of the line-up – the only logical explanation was that the cop was bent and wanted something from Rusnac and was waiting for the approach. Too proud or vain to do it himself.

Maybe even afraid.

Rusnac liked the idea that the cop was afraid. It made sense to him. After all, he'd seen him kill the kid in cold blood so he could walk away from a police sting operation.

After his night outside the police station, Rusnac knew the cop worked late. It was a cliché that murder cops worked late on the job but it seemed to be true – clichés were such for a reason. So he left it late to make his call. He didn't want to waste his time or be left waiting about in the cold again. The end of March had some mild days, but it was not a time of year he wanted to be left waiting around in the evening, even if he had a vehicle and heating this time. The temperature dropped. Work like that was for his men, not for him. He wanted to roll up and get on with the job at hand.

Ten-thirty p.m. He walked up the steps to the door, knocked, and waited.

62

The beer was cold, the only light came from the laptop and the standard lamp in the corner. The conversation with Celeste had been difficult. She'd been open with him. Laid herself bare. It was as honest as they'd been since he'd got out of the hospital. He'd asked her to bear with him. Told her things would get better. He hoped he hadn't lied to her. Hoped that he could resolve this case and then focus more on their relationship and link his feeling for her with the unknown face he saw every time they met up, as he did with the children. She was right in that they had been good before the accident. And Helen, she had this new guy, Lewis, Lonnie, something. Liam. He needed to make it work with Celeste. And he would.

Ray checked his Dedit account for the fifth time. Surprised when he had a response in the inbox.

Dear Mr Gordon

Thank you for your contact. The initial step you need to take is very small. It is in fact only a blood test so that we can see who you may potentially be compatible with.

It is a kind-hearted undertaking you are considering and for that you will be generously compensated.

Please let us know if you require any further information.

Ray leaned back in the chair. Still shocked that they'd replied, that they'd believed him. He felt as though he stood out like a lighthouse on stormy night. But there was no reason he should, at this stage. They had a website and he'd put in a query. Like any of the desperate people looking for what they thought would be quick and relatively easy funds for the difficulties in their lives.

He had to compose a response now. Consider how far along he was willing to go with this. A lot depended on the inquiry at work. If he thought they could get Rusnac through that route, he would back away from his off-books line of inquiry; but if, as it currently stood, they weren't getting anywhere, he saw no real option but to continue to push forward.

He might talk to Helen about a lot of his issues, but he hadn't informed her that he had made this move on the website. A stab of guilt caught him unawares as he opened the reply box. She'd been so supportive recently. He understood that it was because she wanted their children to be safe and secure and unafraid of the issues facing him and his life, but he still detected an underlying current of feeling between them. What was once talking and getting along for the sake of the children now had a warmth to it. And that was what made him feel deceitful in the actions he was taking and was about to take.

The doorbell chimed before he had chance to type a word. He was actually saved by the bell. He smiled. Then realised it was his door. And it would either be someone he knew or someone he'd never met, and either way he wouldn't know. It was rare that he received unannounced visitors and he couldn't remember one since he'd been out of hospital. How do you answer the door and know the person, without saying their name? Easy enough, he imagined: say hello in a bright voice, sound pleased to see them, but … That would be weird if they were here to talk about his religious beliefs or the state of his fascias and soffits. He looked at his watch; it was a little late for cold callers, so the odds were good that it would be someone he knew. He would have to pretend until it became clear.

He slugged back the remains of his beer and headed to the door. A bright hello ready on his lips, a hopeful expression that they'd jump straight in to ease his pain. He'd do the quick rundown of the people he knew, but it could take a while, and standing on a doorstep at this hour wouldn't serve him well.

There was a wall light at the side of the door that cast light and shadow on the visitor who was standing on the second to top step of the half dozen that led to Ray's front door from the street. A male of Eastern European origin, wearing jeans and a dark blue bomber jacket. A bright and breezy hello died on Ray's lips as the implications dawned on him. A bomber jacket that seemed familiar. He gripped the door, fingers white, as he waited for the visitor to speak, to alleviate his fear of who this was. At this hour.

'I want to know what the bent copper needs from me.'

63

'What?' A sudden chill scored through Ray. His hand cramped as it gripped the wooden door frame. Fingers bent and tight. Rigid. White.

This male at his door. Could it really be Billy's killer? He had to concentrate. 'What did you say? I think I misheard you. I'm sorry, my mind was elsewhere when I answered.' Concentrate.

'You know you didn't mishear me. Playing for time, maybe? Didn't expect me to make my approach at your home? Where did you think I would approach you?' His hands were shoved in his jacket pockets. Relaxed. At ease with the conversation.

'I don't know.' Dark hair. Tidy. Dark brows. Heavy and low on his forehead.

No connection.

Concentrate.

The street was quiet. Muted sounds of a car engine further down the street registered in Ray's consciousness, but other than that they were alone out here.

'We doing this on the doorstep or you inviting me in?' The male nodded towards the door Ray was blocking.

Something was familiar. Something about him screamed out that this was Billy's killer. But it wasn't his face, his identity. 'What are you doing here?'

'We have things to discuss, don't we. You made that clear. You want something. I want to know what that is. What I can do for you.'

'I don't want anything from you.' Shit, he should have asked him what they needed to discuss.

The male turned away. One foot down on the next step below. 'It's too bad, copper, we would have made a beautiful partnership.'

A memory flashed in Ray's brain. It's too bad, copper. The phrase, the intonation. The speech pattern. It was an exact match. This was Billy's killer. These were the words Billy's killer had uttered before he shot Billy. He couldn't say if this was Vova Rusnac, the man arrested for the offence, but what he could say was that it was Billy's killer. He couldn't let him walk away.

'Wait!'

The male turned back to him.

'You're right. The front doorstep is not the right place to have the conversation and I didn't want to be seen with you here, which is why I said that. You need to get inside, and quickly.'

But what would he do with him once he had him inside?

64

It didn't feel right. Rusnac wasn't about to stroll into the cop's house, be contained in a small space by him. He'd been about to let him walk away. Why the sudden change?

'No. You want to talk, we talk here or we walk.'

'Okay, let me grab a coat.' The cop turned to go back inside his home.

'No. No grabbing of anything. I'm not giving you chance to call anyone.' What the hell was going on?

The cop stepped forward, out onto the top step. Rusnac moved back onto the tread he was half on. The cop had seemed bemused when Rusnac had turned up, but now he seemed hardened. His face set. He grew a couple of inches before him.

It happened too quickly and caught Rusnac off balance. He'd recognised it, that look, the one that said you were deciding whether to make a move or not. Men had tried to take him on plenty of times in Moldova, but this time he wasn't prepared. He was too busy fumbling over his confusion around what the cop wanted. It had slowed his reflexes.

The cop's right hand shot out and grabbed him before he could counter.

'I'm arresting you for the murder of –'

He wouldn't go back there again. He knew it would have a different outcome this time.

Rusnac shied away, pulled back. Hard. He wanted this guy off him. He clenched his fist and struck the cop's face before the cop could even consider what to do next.

It was quick. Swift. Dirty. The way he was used to fighting when he was back home. He'd had little use for it since the Russians had sent him here. It felt good. The feel of his fist against nose as it yielded.

Blood came freely. Bright red. Easily visible even in the half light of the doorway.

But this sudden shift in purpose had made his knees unsteady. He'd been taken by surprise. He needed to move. To put as much distance as he could between him and this cop.

But the cop didn't relent; he pushed forward, grabbed for him, blood smearing them both. Running from the cop's nose, down his face, onto his clothes and onto Rusnac.

He refused to go back to jail again. And it looked like this time the cop wanted to ID him. It would prove to be more permanent. His feet moved without much thought as he backed away, used the weight of his body, the momentum from pulling downwards, in his favour. He needed to get the cop off balance.

He had the gun in the back of his waistband. But shoot a cop? That would bring the entire police force down on his head, on his organisation. They would never stop until they had him and he wasn't that stupid. He needed to get out of this situation without using it, if he could.

'The fuck?' screamed Rusnac.

He punched again.

Hard.

The cop held on. Dogged. His knee came up and powered into the side of Rusnac's leg and completely destabilised him.

Rusnac's balance gave way, a grunt escaped the cop as his weight and size worked against him and he was pulled down towards Rusnac. They both stumbled. All feet, tumbling down the last two steps.

The ground came up to meet Rusnac, the air caressing him as the cold concrete of the pavement slammed into him hard. His lungs expelled all the breath that was in them with an 'Uumph'. And the cop crashed down on top of him. A gasp of his own escaping. An elbow smashed into Rusnac's chest. A knee into his thigh.

A car slid past quietly on the road. The driver oblivious to the trouble on his left.

'You didn't fucking ID me,' Rusnac shouted into the cop's face. Spittle flying. He could feel the Glock digging into his back. All he had to do was get to it. He wouldn't be taken. 'Why the fuck not? I thought you were bent.'

The cop leaned up, his knees digging into Rusnac, his arms pinning him down. They were at the bottom of the steps, Rusnac's head on the pavement now. He had to get out of this situation. He had to get away.

'I'm not bent and you're under arrest for the murder of Billy Collier.' He started to pull himself up, yanking at Rusnac's arm as he did so, but it was his left arm, which meant Rusnac's strong arm was free.

Rusnac knew he still had the opportunity to extricate himself from this.

He twisted to his right as though to lift himself, as the cop pulled his left arm up and around his back. Rusnac reached behind, felt the handle of the Glock, wrapped his hand around it and tugged.

'Recognise this?' he sneered as he shoved it into the cop's side.

The cop's eyes widened. He was panting. Rusnac thought he was going to brazen it out and wondered if he was actually going to have to shoot him to escape. Then, suddenly, his arm was free and the cop heaved himself up and stepped back.

Away from the gun.

Rusnac stretched his arm out. Still on the ground, Rusnac pointed the Glock at the cop. 'Now, let's try this again, shall we?'

65

It hadn't gone quite as Ray had planned. His evening hadn't gone as he'd expected at all. How was he going to get out of this? His phone was still in the house. His neighbours hadn't come out of their homes to see what the noise was about, and right now he was glad they hadn't. He'd hate for them to become further victims of this man.

The weapon looked dull in the light from his door. You always hear about a glint in books, but really, they're dull, matt weapons, guns. The barrel pointed steadily at his chest. Point-blank range. He wouldn't stand a chance if Rusnac fired. Why had he come here? He'd said something about him being bent. Suppose it must have been confusing being released if he had shot and killed Billy. Knowing that the cop in front of him had been there when it happened. Not much further away than they were now.

Rusnac pushed himself up from the ground and stood in front of him.

Christ, he'd made a damn mess of this. No one to blame but himself.

'You don't have to do this.' It sounded clichéd even to his own ears, but what was he expected to say? 'You know how much worse it will get if you shoot me, a cop.'

'Why didn't you pick me out of the line-up?'

That same question again. The confusion evident on his face. How could he answer him, honestly? It would throw any chance of conviction out at court. But …

'You were there. When I shot him.' The confusion in the man's voice was evident.

His voice was deep and sounded rusty, with drawn-out vowels and hard edges. Ray would be able to recognise it again in the future, quicker than he had this time. He studied the man in front of him. Forced himself to turn away from the weapon levelled at his chest and took in anything else he could about the man. Rusnac's height, build and stance and the clothing he wore. He'd have to wait until he moved more to examine his gait.

'Yes.' He'd give him as little as possible to work with.

Rusnac stepped back a pace. Onto the pavement. A couple more cars passed in the street, engines humming loudly through the silence that enveloped them as confused thoughts scrambled for purchase. Rusnac took another step back, looked left and right along the street but kept the gun trained on Ray. 'You're not bent?'

'No.'

'Let me tell you one thing, cop. You think I only do part job? Eh?'

Ray didn't understand and shook his head.

'You think I only checked you out here?'

A slow chill crept up Ray's spine, tiny claws digging in as it made its way up one vertebra at a time.

'I have your other home. The one with your children.'

Ray stepped forward. His face closed, eyes narrowed, jaw hard. 'Listen to me, you fucker –'

Rusnac waved the gun from side to side, laughing. 'No, no. You listen to me, copper. I'm in the, what do you call it … driving seat

... I'm in the driving seat here. I have your other home. You mess with me as I leave or later, then I mess with your other home.'

Ray stepped forward again, fists clenched and pulled up to his waist.

Rusnac laughed again, louder this time. 'What you going to do against this, eh? Tell me that, big man.'

Ray snarled, 'You leave my family out of this.'

'You – you leave me out of this. Hear me?' He continued as he stepped back, keeping the weapon on Ray until he got to the curb, where his vehicle was parked. 'You didn't pick me out. You're bent, musor. I don't know what game you play, but I don't play game. Stay out of my business now.' He reached for his car door, opened it. 'Or I play with your family.' He climbed in and Ray watched helplessly as he drove away.

66

The night was still, but Rusnac's mind whirled. What the hell had happened? How had it happened? His meetings never went this way. He was a meticulous planner. And if something was to go off-piste, then the person was usually scared of him. But this guy, this cop, he was different. How had he read the situation so badly?

He had failed to identify him in the video line-up. That, he hadn't got wrong. He'd been arrested on suspicion of murder. He had thought his days were numbered. They had the garage, the car, his DNA, and they had a cop who was there, right in front of him when he put the bullet in the kid. And yet … yet he had walked out of the police station. A free man. Technically on bail, but if he'd been identified he would never have walked away, he would have been locked in that tiny stinking cell until court and then moved to another cell and he'd never have seen the light of day for many, many years.

But he had walked.

What explanation was he supposed to come up with other than that the cop was bent and wanted something from him?

Traffic was light. London was still alive, but it wasn't the excessively clogged-up system that churned through the day. He preferred the night. You could move. London could breathe now.

Rusnac rubbed at the back of his head, realising he'd hit it on the ground as they'd gone down together at the house. It stung. He rubbed more gently. One hand still controlling the car. There was a small bump.

The cop had tried to arrest him. That's how they had ended up on the ground. It appeared there was a point when the cop realised who he was. Which was weird. He'd already been locked up in his cells. He'd already known who he was. He presumed the cop had done the video ID thing.

He slowed for the lights on Lea Bridge Road and stopped. Watched a cyclist with his head down to the chill night air ride hard across in front of him. Picked up his phone and quick-dialled Popa, who answered on the first ring.

'That cop, the one you followed. Can't remember the name you gave me. I want you to find out all you can about him and call me straight back.'

The lights started to change in his favour.

'Yes, tonight. Right now.' He dropped the phone onto the passenger seat and moved off. It wasn't even ten minutes until his phone started to ring. A loud and obnoxious ringtone blaring into the silent car. He answered it. Listened. Dropped the phone again without acknowledging the caller.

So the cop had been in an accident, had he. Good old Google. What this had to do with events tonight, though, Rusnac couldn't quite decide. The guy had sustained some pretty serious injuries and was lucky to return to the job. He'd been the driver of the vehicle and had a colleague in the car with him. A detective sergeant who had also been injured. They had been in pursuit of a man in a car who had killed several women and had run from them. The crash had kept him off work for about six months.

Still didn't tell him why he let him walk.

The injuries: leg, arm, ribs. A knock on the head. Concussion.

Maybe that was it. Something to do with the knock to his head, the concussion.

But still. Why? What? How?

Concussion, he thought, that was supposed to be a temporary problem that went away with time. Gave you a headache. Not much else.

Rusnac still couldn't fit the piece into the jigsaw he was trying to put together. He let his mind drift back to the doorstep. When he confronted the cop, when he answered the door. He'd looked cheerful. Happy. Even when he'd first looked at Rusnac his face didn't change. That had made Rusnac believe with greater certainty that he was right about his assumption. But then things changed. It was as if … as if the cop suddenly … what? Recognised him …

As he drove through the shops on the A112, past Drapers Field, Leyton, an old woman crossed the road. Bent over as though her spine were crooked. Like the top of a question mark. Wrapped in a large coat, with a woollen hat pulled low over her head. Oblivious to traffic on the road. Rusnac slammed on his brakes. His head snapped forward. In normal circumstances he'd have yelled and shouted through the window at the stupidity of the woman, but his mind was elsewhere. He couldn't afford to lose his train of thought.

The woman made it to the other side of the road. Heaved herself up onto the pavement and continued, unconcerned, on her way.

Could he really have only just considered that? The cop, he recognised him long after he first saw him? But what took so long? It wasn't normal. You see someone and you know who they are. What made the cop change from not knowing to suddenly knowing?

Damn it. He'd told the cop who he was in the course of what he'd said. About him being a bent cop and Rusnac owing him.

The cop hadn't recognised him. The cop's banged-up head had something wrong with it.

And no one else knew.

67

It was late but Ray didn't care.

He couldn't not go around to Helen's and make sure she and the children were okay. Safe. He needed to see them, but he had no idea what he would tell her.

Her voice through the glass as she asked who was there sounded fearful. Shaky. Then angry as he told her who it was.

'What the hell, Ray?' she asked as she swung the door open, allowing the freezing night air to sweep into the house. 'Do you have any concept of time or did that bang on the head damage that as well?'

The dark of the night shrouded him from her view as Ray ignored her irritation and pushed past her into the house. He turned, took the door from her hand, slammed it shut, locked it, and pushed the bolt into place.

'Ray?' She stepped back. Her face changed from where it had been when she was using her irritated voice to something else. A hint of worry was there now.

'You know what time it is?'

He hadn't said a word yet; his mind was still reeling. He hadn't slowed down for any traffic lights or junctions, that was for sure. It was the fastest he'd made it here. Ever. It was a good job it was late, otherwise he might have been involved in an accident and not made it at all, and who knew what danger that would have left his family in.

Ray looked at his watch to confirm.

Eleven-twenty p.m.

'I'm sorry, Helen.' He ran his hands through his hair. What did he tell her? How did he keep her safe without scaring the living crap out of her? Should he go with the truth, that Rusnac had threatened her and their children, or some version of the truth, that he'd threatened Ray and this had driven a need to see his family, or a lie of some description and do his best to resolve the entire problem before anything went wrong? After all, Rusnac said he would only resort to coming here if Ray himself went after him. But how could he trust a cold-blooded killer?

And of course he was going after Rusnac. He wasn't going to walk away and leave him on the streets; besides, he didn't have the command to close the investigation anyway, it would continue regardless, and Rusnac would see that as him going after them. Better he do a proper job of it and get him locked up sooner rather than later.

But what to tell Helen? This wasn't something he'd thought about as he'd raced out of the city to get to them. He'd quickly washed his face and changed his top. But his mind had been consumed with the single thought of getting here, not with what he'd say when he did.

Now he was stumped.

'Ray?' She looked at him. Sighed, and walked towards the kitchen. 'I'm putting the kettle on. Get your act together.' She wore pastel pink and blue striped pyjama bottoms that showed her long legs off, with a long-sleeved fitted ribbed blue top. Wrapped over it was a cream Argyle knitted cardigan that she liked to relax around the house in. As she moved away from him, Ray caught the citrusy scent of her shower gel, and noticed, as she moved, that the underside of her hair was still damp.

He followed her.

What the hell was he going to tell her? Which way would he jump?

The kettle whistled to a boil as Helen brought mugs out of the cupboard, poured milk and spooned coffee. All without a word being spoken. She poured the steaming water into both mugs as Ray watched from his chair at the breakfast bar. His nerves making him feel as though he had an army of ants crawling all over his body.

She stirred each mug slowly. Carefully.

Placed the spoon on the drainer.

Waited a beat.

Walked over to Ray. Placed his mug down in front of him. Collected her own. Then sat with it on the chair adjacent, on the corner. Then she looked at him. Really looked.

'Ray, is that a black eye forming under your right eye? What the hell is going on?'

Decision time.

'I'm sorry, Helen.'

'That's not an answer, Ray.' She pinned him to his seat with her deep brown eyes. He wanted to squirm like a five-year-old boy, but he didn't move.

Okay, this was it.

'There's a problem at work and it boiled over and came to the house.'

The dark brown eyes surveyed him a minute. Digesting. 'What do you mean, came to the house?'

As he spoke, Ray still didn't know what he was going with. The truth or partial truth. It was obvious he was not going with a lie. Helen's hands were wrapped around her mug as though she were cold, and it was now that Ray noticed that there was a chill in the room. The heating had clicked off: she would have been in bed. 'A guy turned up at my door. He made some threats …'

Her mouth opened. She started to speak, but Ray put his hand up. She closed her mouth.

'Nothing I'm worried about.' He knew he couldn't mention the gun now. Or the threats towards her or the children. 'I got a bit agitated with him and we got into it.' He bent his head. Hoped she would think this was the problem.

'Oh, Ray.' She'd taken it. He hadn't realised where he was going until it happened, but then he realised: a fight with anyone involved with the investigation wouldn't be good for him.

She reached out a hand and rested it on his arm. Her touch gentle. Any anger or irritation she had felt had abated.

'Why did he threaten you in the first place, why was he at your place?' She moved her hand, and a look he couldn't decipher crossed her face. He felt a cool spot where her hand had been.

'Honestly?'

'Yes, Ray.' Sharp. Blunt.

Could he be that honest with her? He'd been honest about everything else.

'It was someone we arrested due to some evidence that meant he could potentially have been our victim's killer –'

A sharp intake of breath.

'But Prabhat needed me to do the ID for him, as you know. And I failed.' He looked her square in the eye. 'Obviously.'

'Okay.'

'The guy thinks I must be bent because I should have picked him out, and wants to talk about how we work together –'

'That means …'

'Yes …'

'The man who threatened you, who you got into it with, is a killer?'

He could read her face now. It was wide-open horror.

68

It was one a.m. by the time he closed the door on the world again back in his own home. Helen had taken some calming down once he had told her about Rusnac – though not by name, obviously. And not the whole story. She had become afraid for him and wanted him to come and stay with her, which had led nicely to him saying that he was afraid for her. She wasn't a stupid woman though. She could read him a hell of a lot better than he could read her – particularly since the accident. She had known he was keeping something back from her at that point, and he'd been forced to tell her that Rusnac knew her address; but he held off the information about the specific threats there. Helen inferred the threat from the knowledge of him having her address, and shouted at Ray for a good ten minutes in a hushed, blunt voice so as not to wake Alice and Matthew, but he could see she was furious with him for even contemplating not telling her.

How could he consider putting his children's lives at risk this way? She could choose to take whatever risk she wanted, but they – they needed their parents' protection, and she was livid.

When she calmed down she told him that he needed to get the bastard. That no one was going to threaten their family and stay on the streets.

They'd decided that the children would go to their grandparents' and Helen would go to her sister's. It wasn't unusual for Helen's parents to take care of the children for a couple of days if Ray was working and Helen also had something on. Although if Helen went to stay with them along with the children, her parents would get suspicious and concerned. So she'd go to her sister's. Give her a little information, but not enough to scare the shit out of her.

Ray woke his laptop up. He didn't have a plan formulated yet. Rusnac knew who he was. He was way too tired to figure it out. But he sent a message back on the Dedit site that said he was desperate to do this. His finances were burying him. What did he need to do?

69

The corridor this time was different. Ray was gripped by fear the minute he set foot inside it. He was aware it was a dream and knew there was a word for knowing this while he was in it, but it wouldn't come to him at the time.

He had other things on his mind.

Like the blood that ran down the walls.

That was the same.

So what was it that was different?

There was screaming. A screaming from a distant door that he felt he would never be able to get to in time. A screaming that ripped through your gut and tore you open, it was so afraid.

That was all the same.

But it was different. Something had changed.

Ray tried the first door on his right and to his surprise the handle turned with ease.

It was open.

The door was open.

Again, this had happened before.

Should he look or move forward to the screaming at the end of the corridor?

He pushed on the door. Last time the door had opened, someone had stood there, shook their head at him; but this time there was no one here. He peered into the space beyond. It was dark. Difficult to see. Difficult to make out the objects in the room – because there were objects. Something was moving. Moving towards him.

His stomach tightened. His fist balled at his side. He moved his left foot and stood square on to the door frame. Readied himself for whatever it was that was moving in his direction.

It moved closer. The darkness, a cloak.

The screaming tore through the corridor and ripped up the air. The pain and suffering shredding his nerve endings. Rattling his resolve. He willed the moving figure to go faster, but it was in no hurry.

How long could he stand here and wait while the screams rang out?

A string of blood dripped from the door casing. The figure was close to breaking through the darkness that enveloped it.

And then it was there.

In front of him.

A human form. Faceless but with a weird wide mouth that practically split the face in half. It started to laugh. At first slow and deep, and then louder and faster until it was hysterically laughing at a pitch that competed with the screams.

Ray turned and ran towards the screams. Away from the laughing figure.

He ran and ran and ran.

Sleep was a bodily state in the past tense that Ray had nearly forgotten the recuperative powers of. And when he did slip into some kind of unconscious sleep state, he was plagued by the corridor dream.

He escaped the frustration of feeling unsettled by being in his office at an early hour he rarely saw. His mind was wired from the previous night's visit from Rusnac. He was still spinning, reeling, furious. Lack of sleep was to be expected. Today they had to follow Helen's advice and find a way to identify Rusnac with good old-fashioned coppering, evidence. They would work their way through everything again, chase up information and documentation they were waiting on, and work on leads they hadn't yet managed to get to.

He'd push the team, but he knew they could cope. They'd had big jobs before. Jobs that had a lot riding on them. Jobs that had pressures from different places pushing down on them. Press and public pushing for quick answers. Higher-ups needing results for political reasons. Or simply because a connection had been made with a family member and the job had taken a particularly personal turn.

Tamsin – curls – was the first through the door.

'We need the results from Rusnac's phone,' Ray said as soon as she entered.

'Morning to you too, guv.' She slipped out of her jacket and hung it on the back of her chair.

'Morning, Tamsin. Can you get on to the phone today please? See where they are with it and if it hasn't been done yet, find out why not and kick some arses. I want it doing. I want it prioritising. I want it done. Now.'

'Coffee?'

'Did you hear me?'

'Yes, guv.' She looked at him. He couldn't decipher it. 'Is everything okay? It's only seven-thirty. They'll be no one in yet.' She walked towards the door. 'But I'll be straight on it as soon as.' She hadn't mentioned his black eye. It had become more pronounced overnight.

Ray stalked out of the incident room into his office. Damn working hours. Damn the snail's pace of the investigation. He slammed his door.

By eight-thirty everyone was in and Ray was standing in front of them wanting results.

'We're not getting very far with this investigation,' he started. 'It's been running too long and we need to start to pull it together.'

The room was quiet. All eyes were on him. It was clear they'd seen his eye. The thought passed through his mind: who would be the person to ask him about it? But it was fleeting. He was less worried about his looks and more interested in finding Rusnac.

'I've asked Tamsin to chase up the phone we seized from Rusnac, see what we can retrieve from that. Where are we on locating patients who have stopped turning up for dialysis?' he asked.

'We have to go on a hospital-by-hospital basis, guv, because with the transplant list, they leave the responsibility to the patient to make sure all records are kept up to date, but with dialysis being a

298

regular occurrence, hospitals will have more up-to-date records,' answered Paula.

'And?' he asked somewhat impatiently.

'Well, so far the local hospitals haven't found any patients who have failed to turn up for treatment. But just because the transplants happen in London doesn't mean the patients are London-based. Anyone with the funds will travel. They could be anywhere in the country. It's a long-winded inquiry, I'm afraid.'

'Goddamnit!' he spat out, and paced across the front of the incident room and back again. 'So we don't have a single patient to help us with this?'

'No, sir,' said Paula, quietly. 'Not yet anyway. It's a line of inquiry that will pan out, but a lead we haven't come across yet.'

Ray scrubbed his hand through his hair. 'What about the garage the BMW was burnt out in? Do we know who it was registered to?'

Elaine looked across at Tamsin before she spoke. 'Yes, guv –'

'Great! At last. Why aren't we doing anything with this?'

'We traced the owner. One guy owns the whole block of garages and lets them out. That particular garage was paid for up front in cash for a year. He can't remember much about the person who paid as it was about eight months ago, other than to say he was an Eastern European male. We had him in to do an ID procedure to see if he could pick anyone out, and we put Rusnac in the options, but he didn't ID anyone. It's possible one of his associates paid for it?'

'Seriously, this is where we are? I want more and I want it now. Get me something we can work with.' And with that he left the incident room for his office. Leaving his staff with their mouths agape.

'Wrong side of the bed, anyone?' muttered Will.

He logged on to his laptop as soon as he walked in from work. It had been an awful day. The investigation felt as though it had stalled and he had taken it out on his team. He never did that. Because of his mood not one person had felt able to ask him about his face. It was unusual for them not to be able to approach him like that. His role was to keep their morale up so they could continue to move forward, and all he had succeeded in doing today had been to force them to see the failure in the job. The reality was that the failure was all his, and he needed to rectify it.

First he closed the blinds to the world. Shut the darkness out. Grabbed a can of beer out of the fridge, which held little else other than beer. Some ready-made stuffed pasta that would take him ten minutes to heat up in a pan with some added sauce, and a block of cheese. He wasn't good at taking care of himself. Quick and easy was how it worked with him.

Celeste had fed him properly. She liked to throw things around the kitchen; but they had barely spoken in the last couple of weeks. Ray had been pushing her away and she'd picked up on it. She wasn't stupid. Though she thought there was a problem with his mental health that he was hiding from her. His behaviour had been off since the accident, she had told him constantly. How close she was. But his mental health was fine. There were no cures, no medication, no therapy for what was wrong, and that was the problem. How could they continue to build on what they had when he flinched every time he looked her in the face? And how do you tell someone you don't see them anymore? But Helen was right, it wasn't fair to her.

He'd sort it. He'd talk to her.

Maybe.

Because there was Helen. He couldn't figure out if how he felt about her was real or if it was simply because she had been supporting him. And she had that other guy anyway. His life felt such a mess. Once they cleared up this job, he needed to clear up his head.

When the laptop had woken up, he navigated to the Dedit site and found a message in his inbox.

The response was short.

They were more than prepared to help him. He needed the blood test and, at the same time as the test, Mr Bateman would meet him to explain the next steps.

Could he provide a few dates of availability?

Ray leaned back in his chair. He was stepping over a line now. Really stepping over. No going back. But not only did he have to get justice for Billy, for failing in his job, he now also had to take Rusnac off the street because he knew where Helen and his children lived, and he couldn't have an individual out there who had made those threats and trust that he would keep his word about not going after them if Ray left him alone.

He looked at the photograph on the wall of Alice and Matthew when they were smaller and he still lived at home with them, a time when they were a family. The photo showed them with their heads thrown back, giggling as sand surrounded them, after Ray had half buried them on the beach during a family holiday.

He leaned forward to the laptop and replied that he was available as soon as possible, anytime. Showed he was desperate. Not the obvious calm of a police operation.

A neat ding let him know there was a message in his inbox almost immediately. Someone was working the website right now. Lunch time tomorrow at Cottenham Park Road, Wimbledon. Directions were provided. A small map attached.

Now he needed to figure out how he would play this. Rusnac knew who he was. The minute he turned up he would recognise him even if Ray didn't know Rusnac immediately.

Did he go in alone or did he let his colleagues know he had lied to them all along? It would end his career. He'd be up on disciplinary charges for his failure to disclose the prosopagnosia and the events that occurred after his return: the farce that was the failed ID procedure, and the failure to notify at the point of Billy's murder that he'd been face to face with the killer. If he brought his colleagues into this rather than doing it alone, then all he had ever worked for, all he had worked for in keeping the prosopagnosia a secret – because he had managed and managed well – would all have been for nothing. But the alternative was him failing again, and that didn't bear thinking about. His failure was what had got him into the place he was in now. His failure to disclose from the start had him in a situation where he was unable to identify a killer, and if, he finally realised, if he had disclosed and been medically retired, then the op would still have gone ahead, but it would have

303

been someone else in the spot where he'd been concealed and it would have been someone else face to face with the killer, and that someone would have been able to ID the killer from the start.

He really did have to resolve this.

Ray wandered to the fridge, looked at the beer, thought again and closed the door without picking one out. Instead he collected his phone from the arm of the chair and dialled Helen.

She sounded upbeat enough when she answered.

'How are the kids?' he asked.

'Mum says they're good. Having a blast by all accounts. Treating it like a holiday.'

'And you?'

'Yeah, holiday as well.'

'Helen.' He wanted her to talk to him.

'I'm okay. Spending most of my time wondering what you're doing and if you're still safe or whether you've had any more run-ins with out-of-control killers.'

He laughed. How else was anyone supposed to deal with a sentence like that?

'It's not funny,' she scolded.

'I know.' He made his tone conciliatory. 'But you don't have to worry. It's quiet here. He's going to be fine unless he thinks I'm coming after him, and so far I haven't.'

'So far?'

'Yeah.'

There was silence.

Ray pushed the blinds apart with his spare hand and looked out of the window into the dark beyond. In the glow of the streetlights he could see that it had started to rain again. He waited for her. The silence a huge invisible barrier between them. Filled with unsaid words.

'You'll be careful.'

'I'll be careful.'

'I want the children back, Ray.'

'I know how you feel,' he said before he thought about it.

The silence was so heavy, Ray was sure he could feel the pressure in his ear.

'It's just ...' he started.

'It's okay.'

He said goodnight. His mind in turmoil. One thing was certain, he had to end this. One way or another. He'd do it his way, but deep down, in his gut, he knew he was going to have to throw away his career and his friendships within the job: he had spent so long deceiving people, they wouldn't be happy. He would have to come clean about the prosopagnosia. It was the only way to bring Rusnac in. Once he identified him, by voice, it was the only way to tell the investigation team that this was their man and that he had identified him. He would have to tell them he'd been lying to them all this time. He'd put the investigation at risk, and he'd betrayed their trust.

But if losing his career, his friendships, brought an end to the risk he had now put his family in and brought Billy's killer down, then he'd do what was needed.

He wanted his family back.

71

The run into work on the roads had been smooth and Elaine felt positively relaxed and ready for the day ahead rather than the scrabbling-to-catch-up feeling she usually started the work day with.

The children had got out of bed without complaint. They'd eaten their breakfasts without shouting at each other and had dressed without challenging any item that had been laid out for them.

Instead of enjoying it, she had been perturbed by the feeling. Feeling rushed, anxious and stressed were her daily norms and how she functioned. Working under any other conditions threw her off kilter.

Tamsin laughed at her when she explained why she was so put out that morning.

'You're not happy because you feel so relaxed?'

She slurped at her coffee, eyed Tamsin over the rim of the mug. Aware of the ridiculousness of the explanation.

'And this is why I don't have children.' Tamsin laughed again.

'Why don't you have children?' Will strolled up behind her.

'Elaine is feeling relaxed this morning,' Tamsin explained.

'Stop the presses.'

'See my point?'

'I'm never having sex again if this is what happens.' He threw on his most horrified expression.

Tamsin tipped back her head as she laughed this time. Her curls springing out around her.

'What?' He was indignant.

'From what I know of your love life, that would be difficult to believe.'

'If you two have had quite enough …' Elaine put her mug down, a smile across her face. 'Have either of you seen the guv yet?'

'Nope.'

'Not yet.'

'Strange. He's usually in by now.'

'Or at least he's always in by the time you come dashing through the door.' Will smirked at her.

'Okay, but he is usually in, isn't he?'

'Yes,' Tamsin agreed. And as she spoke, Elaine's phone vibrated with an alert that a message had come through. She picked it up and read the text.

'It seems he has an inquiry out of the office and he won't be in until later.'

'Do we know what it is?' asked Tamsin, opening HOLMES.

'He doesn't say.' Elaine looked across at Tamsin. 'Anything on the system?'

Tamsin shook her head. 'Looks like your kids were right.'

Elaine was puzzled. 'In what way?'

'Today is not going to be a good day.'

Any smile on Elaine's face was now gone. 'We need to locate the guv.'

72

The office Ray had been directed to was a temporary structure, although one that had a permanent appearance. Solid and substantial. Long, with cream walls, and windows that had a slightly darkened tint to them so you couldn't see in. It was clean and sleek.

The car park it stood in was a different matter. Uneven ground, with random patches of gravel thrown down as though someone had started a job but couldn't be bothered to finish it. Ray wasn't familiar with this part of Wimbledon but the whole set-up had a transitory feel to it. Vacant ground on a main road, now made use of.

He turned the car engine off and waited. Around him the air was still. He was alone. No back-up. He felt his pocket for his mobile phone and was relieved when he patted the rigid patch in his jeans. He'd already saved Jain's number, and Elaine's, and at a push, if really needed, he had the control room in his favourites to speed up any call.

There was a twisting in his stomach, but a determination in his head. Ray took a breath and got out of the car.

The rain had finally stopped and the sky was bright, the air, light, warm. He could hear birds singing. Spring was breaking through. His footsteps crackled on the ground beneath him as gravel slid beneath his feet. It was an enclosed area, off the main road. The trees of Wimbledon Hill Park towered behind them.

He'd made an attempt to change his appearance. To look like a man in desperate straits, willing to sell a body part to make ends meet. He wore the jeans that he did the decorating in and an old sweater that had worn thin at the elbows. He wasn't even sure why he still held on to it. He'd left his hair without running a brush through it when he woke, so there were clumps sticking out at odd angles. He'd also failed to shave and a salt-and-pepper stubble grazed his chin and cheeks.

There was something he needed to do before he went inside. He should have done it last night but he'd been thinking of Helen and it didn't feel right. Ray pulled his phone out of his pocket and dialled. Celeste picked up on the third ring.

'Ray? Are you okay? You don't normally call in the day. What's happened?' She sounded worried.

'I'm fine. I'm sorry, I didn't mean to worry you.'

'Where are you?' She wasn't having it.

'I'm out on a job at the minute so I haven't got long. I wanted to call you before it got going.'

He heard her muffled voice speak to someone where she was. A hand covered the handset, and then she was back.

'You know I'm worried about you.' A statement, not a question.

He answered anyway. 'I do and I'm sorry. I didn't mean to worry you. I want you to know I'm going to sort this job out at work today and then we can talk. I'll talk.'

'Ray?'

'It's okay. I promise.' He wasn't sure but he didn't want to scare her. He couldn't be certain she wouldn't walk away when he told her about the prosopagnosia, or that he even wanted her to stick around. What he did know was that she deserved his honesty. She'd deserved it from day one. 'I'll see you later and we'll sort it all out.'

There was more muffled talking. 'Okay. I have to go, Ray. You sure you're okay though?'

He told her he was, and ended the call.

With a deft rap on the door, he waited for it to be answered. He spun on the spot, taking in the desolate plot of ground he was standing in, and wondered what events would have transpired by the time he saw it again.

A woman answered. She was dressed in a blue nurse's uniform, sensible black loafers on her feet. Her almost totally grey hair was pinned on top of her head, with wisps escaping and falling about her face, giving her a pallid look. Bright green eyes shone out from her face though, at complete odds to the rest of her. They shone with intelligence.

He introduced himself as Mr Gordon and she stepped aside to let him in. She moved with ease, clearly comfortable in her surroundings.

The room was filled with a couple of sofas, a table with magazines littered haphazardly across the top, and a water cooler in the corner. She introduced herself as Lisa Adams. Said she would take a few drops of blood from him today, and then smiled. This was not a woman who Ray feared was here under any duress. What made people come and work for a man like Rusnac? Come and do such dangerous procedures as these underground transplants?

311

Maybe Adams only took the blood and didn't know what went on after the fact.

'That's an understatement, yes?' Ray asked.

Lisa smiled again. 'It's not that bad,' she answered, without providing an actual answer.

He nodded, expecting as much.

'Can I get you a drink, Mr Gordon? And then I'll sit and explain what I'm going to do today.' It was the coming conversation that would tell Ray if Adams knew how much was going on here.

'Coffee, black, no sugar, thank you.' Not that he needed caffeine right now, but he'd keep up appearances.

The nurse drifted out of the room, leaving him alone. He was the only one here. There were no other waiting 'patients'.

Confidentiality.

Keep everyone separate. Minimise the risk of information leaking out.

He looked around, there was nothing else in the room. It was an average-looking waiting area. Nothing to be used as a weapon, by him or by Rusnac. Ray knew this would happen quickly: Rusnac would recognise him a hell of a lot faster than he would recognise Rusnac. And if Rusnac didn't speak, then, damn, he wouldn't recognise him at all. That was, if Mr Bateman was Rusnac, which he presumed he was. The MIT hadn't got the impression that the organisation was that large a concern. They imagined he would do the sales pitch, the 'you're in safe hands' speech, and this was where Ray wanted to find him.

Ray pulled his phone from his pocket. Checked the battery life. It was fully loaded. He pushed it back into his jeans. Picked up a magazine.

Country Life.

How did every waiting room he'd ever been in have this magazine? Even the fake ones.

Adams pushed the door into the waiting room open with her bottom, holding a steaming mug of coffee in each hand, a clipboard stacked with paper held to the side of her ribcage by an arm. Ray stood, crossed the room and took the milk-free drink from her hand. She thanked him and moved to the sofa at right-angles to the one he'd vacated.

Ray looked at the door she'd come through. Waited for it to open again.

It wasn't until Adams spoke, nudged him with a name he didn't recognise, that he realised he was still standing, staring at the door with the coffee in his hand.

'I know it's daunting, but we're here to make the process as simple as possible for you.'

Ray looked at her face. Tried to work out her motivation. Her thought processes as she talked. Her empathy level for the people she was about to put through an underground, illegal and dangerous donor procedure; but his condition had built a solid brick wall around him and all he saw was a woman. One who smiled in the right places.

He closed his eyes. He could gain more information from her voice. That's what he could do. Rely on his other senses more. He dipped his head. Closed his eyes.

'I'm going to go through some questions with you, health questions. Screening questions. If at any point you want to jump in with a question of your own, jump away.'

He felt a smile in her voice. She was relaxed.

'It's a pretty long questionnaire, but don't get put off by it, we want to make sure we do everything correctly. For your safety.'

What was that he heard in her voice? Concern? For what?

'Mr Gordon? Are you okay?'

Ray lifted his head. 'Yes, yes, I'm fine. Trying to take it all in, you know?'

She smiled at him. 'It is a lot. But, don't worry, we'll take care of you.'

The easiest thing had been for Ray to be mostly honest about his health and family history, but he made the answers up to the questions that he felt gave too much away about himself; after all, he might be here now, but he wasn't going to go ahead and give up part of his body to catch Rusnac and clear up this organisation.

Had he travelled abroad in the past three months and if so, where? Did he have a heart condition, did any members of his family have any problems with their heart? Was he prone to fainting, palpitations, irregular heartbeat? Asthma, bronchitis or emphysema? Excessive bleeding, bruising, clotting disorder or anaemia? And on and on it went.

'I know it's a lot,' Adams agreed as they got to the end of the questionnaire. 'But better to be safe than sorry.'

Ray didn't know how he would or should respond, and thought he would probably be overwhelmed if he was really going to sell his kidney, so he forced a smile and she seemed happy enough with this.

He was then ushered through the door Adams had walked through to get his coffee, into a corridor where several other doors branched off. She led him into the nearest room, which was small but sterile-looking. It had a smell of antiseptic. Clean. It was whitewashed, with a pale blue linoleum floor, a desk in the corner that held a blood pressure pump, a laptop, a thermometer, several notepads and various other bits of paperwork. Alongside it was a table with vials and boxes holding needles of varying sizes. A metal kidney bowl, cotton pads and sticking plasters. A medical bed split the room in its centred position, a roll of paper covered the length of it. A chair at the end of it.

The strip-light in the ceiling provided a bleached-out feel.

Adams directed Ray to the chair at the end of the bed, filled the kidney bowl with the items she needed, and placed it on the end of the bed to one side of him, directing him to either roll up the sleeve of his sweater or take it off if it wasn't possible.

Ray pulled it over his head and laid it over the back of the chair, glad he wore a T-shirt underneath.

Adams continued to chat, attempting to keep it light, probably because people were worried about injections, needles, giving blood, he thought as she prattled on about the weather, how changeable it was, how she never knew what to wear and how frustrating it was when she had to get dressed in the morning.

Ray looked at her nurse's uniform and wondered if she had a job other than carrying out blood tests for illegal transplants. Had this uniform been bought especially for this role, or was it one she already possessed?

Then he pressed down on the cotton wool swab she had provided as she wrote his name, the one he'd given, onto the labels of the vials.

He liked this woman, who was still chatting away to him as she scribbled on the four blood-filled vials. But he knew she would have to be arrested, when Rusnac was. You couldn't be involved in this and walk away from it.

'So what next?' he asked.

Adams looked up from the last label. 'I'll finish this, get you another coffee if you'd like one, then take you through to see Mr Bateman, who will talk to you properly about the process. The ins and outs. Everything you need to know. Not just the medical stuff. The entire process as a whole. Make sure you understand it all and that your mind is at ease.'

So she was aware that this was an illegal procedure, if there was a part of the process that wasn't medical. The exchange of money. Ray felt disappointed. He hadn't known her long, but he wanted her to not have been so aware.

Declining the coffee, because he needed to be on his game now, to not have any distractions, to be focused, he stepped back with her into the corridor. Adams told Ray how lovely it had been to meet him, and wished him well. Ray tuned her out. If Bateman was Rusnac he would recognise him instantly whereas Ray wouldn't. How would Rusnac react? He'd already made threats, to both him and his family.

Ray stood to his full height. He was ready for whatever would happen. He was here. He'd shown up.

Adams reached a door close to the end of the corridor. He'd no idea what she'd been saying as they walked, but now she turned to him, with her hand on the handle, her face open in a smile. 'This is a good thing you're doing, Mr Gordon.'

And she opened the door.

74

It looked like a living room. That was the first thing Ray noticed.

Meant to make him feel welcomed and at home. Which was at odds with the office vibe that was given off by the exterior.

The second thing he noticed was the male relaxing on one of the sofas.

An Eastern European male.

Adams was chattering. Introducing him as Mr Gordon. Talking about his medical history. About his general good health. About how well he'd done during the drawing of his blood as though he were a five-year-old child that needed encouragement.

And all the time the male on the sofa smiled at her. Relaxed.

There'd been a minor twitch. When he'd first walked through the door. Ray had picked up on it. The male's leg, the one he had crossed over the other, had twitched as the man had laid eyes on Mr Gordon, but then he'd relaxed again.

Leaned back even more into the sofa, if that was possible.

With a look about him that reminded Ray of the proverbial cat with the cream.

Ray shoved his hand in his pocket. Felt the phone. Tried to go for the relaxed look himself. Reminded himself that it was okay to appear nervous; after all, he was here to sell a part of his body. Surely the people who did this looked anxious? He withdrew his hand.

'So, Mr Gordon, I'll leave you in the more than capable hands of Mr Bateman.'

'Thank you, you've been very kind.' She had. It was a shame.

'Are you sure I can't get you another coffee?'

He needed to make sure she wasn't going to leave the premises straight away. He needed her to still be here when he called in the troops. If anyone was going to talk in interview it was going to be Lisa Adams. 'I'm sorry – actually, I think a coffee would be a good idea.' He pulled what he hoped was an apologetic face, looked at Bateman, who was watching the interaction, then back at Adams. 'I think it must be the nerves. I don't know what I want.' He forced a laugh. Looked back at Bateman.

Or whoever he was.

The male smiled.

Relaxed.

'Don't you worry about it. Leave it with me. You stay right there.' And with that she left.

Ray looked at Mr Bateman.

He had no idea if he'd seen him before.

75

Rusnac hadn't expected the cop to walk through the door today. He'd thought he'd warned him off properly. Threatening a person usually did the trick. Yes, this cop may well think he was above Rusnac's threats, but threatening family members usually got the message across. After the disastrous meeting on the cop's doorstep, Rusnac figured he was safe to continue his business. Get it up and running again. He'd been cautious after the incident with Billy and then the cops being at the meet, but he'd felt safer after he'd been released by police and the face-to-face with the cop. He knew his guys in the hands of the cops wouldn't talk, otherwise, again, he wouldn't have still been free. And yet here he was, face to face with the cop again.

Only this time the cop had been brazen enough to come into his turf. His ground. And by the looks of things, alone. But it was a fact he wouldn't take at face value.

It was an issue he needed to assess.

It had thrown him when he'd first walked through the door with Lisa. Who was talking incessantly as she always did. He'd punch her in the face to keep her quiet if he could, but it wasn't how business was run here. It wasn't how you treated women here. He needed her, her skills. He had to smile and put up with the stupidity that came out of her mouth so that she would do her job; after all, it wasn't easy to find people who could draw blood and who were in debt up to their eyeballs and who would turn a blind eye to what he was doing, for extra money. As long as he sold it to them as he sold it to the customers. He doubted she believed that shit deep down, she just needed to be told that they were saving lives. Lives that were otherwise on a losing streak on the waiting lists. And the people helping them were no different to the living donors in the system, they were simply being recompensed, as she was. Which, as he told her, was a much fairer system, if you asked him.

Which, of course, she was. Asking him.

To salve her conscience.

And now here she stood, blathering, with the cop standing by her, calling him by some weird name that wasn't his own.

And he was asking for coffee.

Rusnac relaxed into his seat. He knew the cop didn't recognise him, it was obvious from the fact that he hadn't spoken or leapt towards him the minute they'd come through the door.

Why, then, would he come here?

All Rusnac needed to do was assess a couple of things before he made a decision.

A couple of questions.

How did the cop find them?

And was he alone?

Then the decision.

What was he going to do about it? About him, Mr Gordon, or, as he knew full well, Detective Inspector Ray Patrick.

76

The door closed behind Ray. Adams left. The sound of her voice, the constant voice, leaving with it. An echo stayed in his brain as a small click closed her out and the handle locked into place.

Ray surveyed his surroundings; he needed to know where he was, what risks the room held, if this man in front of him was indeed Vova Rusnac. It was compact, but warm, inviting. Made to give visitors a feeling of home, he imagined. Comfort and peace.

There were real flowers in a large glass vase on the floor in one corner. Beautiful flowers in reds, oranges, whites and pinks. Interspersed with the darkest green foliage. Their scent strong. The hard scent of cut flowers that invades your nose, rather than the natural, light smell of flowers growing outside.

A side cabinet held a small flat-screen television. Two sofas and a chair were arranged in the centre, with a coffee table between them. The wallpaper floral but pale and discreet.

Ray looked to the male again, who was smiling at him. His face holding the smile in place. Frustration grabbed at his stomach that not a single feature stood out and helped form an identity. He didn't move, there was nothing he could hold on to that would match him to the male he knew as Vova Rusnac. And the man's relaxed stance threw him.

Could Rusnac really have another male here doing this? Would he have to go through this and then try and move further through the donor process? But would Rusnac go anywhere near the process? Maybe he organised it without getting his hands dirty at all. And how far was Ray willing to go to find out? Would he turn up to have an organ removed? It would be one way to identify the doctors and nursing staff involved. Unless he involved SCD10, the undercover team, he knew he would be in a world of pain owning up to his deception, his failure, without anything to show for it. But he was prepared for that. By turning up here today, he had made the decision that catching Billy's killer was more important than his job, so any further steps he needed to take were irrelevant: he was in for the long haul.

The male indicated with his hand for him to take a seat on the opposite sofa.

Ray looked long and hard at the face. Focused on the eyes. The smile of the mouth. It wouldn't register as familiar. The dark hair tidy, neat. That rang a bell. But men's hair – it wasn't like women, who could style their hair any way they liked. If a man wore his hair short, it pretty much looked the same as every other man's.

He took his seat where indicated.

'So, Mr Gordon, you want to donate your kidney to someone in need?' Still with the smile, but Ray nearly jumped out of his chair. It took all his strength to stay where he was. To not flinch or react. This was Rusnac. There was no doubt about it, now that he had spoken. But why was Rusnac pretending he hadn't recognised him? It made no sense.

'I'm kind of in real financial straits,' Ray responded. He pushed his hand into his pocket, felt the phone, but realised that with the flat touch screen there was no way he could pocket-dial anyone without seeing where on the screen the buttons were.

Rusnac leaned forward a little. 'We can of course help with that. We wouldn't want you to go to all this trouble without giving you what you deserved.'

How could he make this call? And what game was Rusnac playing?

Rusnac leaned forward even further, elbows resting on his knees. 'We like our donors, as well as our recipients, to be well supported. But I see that you are alone today. Have you come here alone, Mr Gordon?'

77

Before Ray could answer, Adams came bustling in. She carried a tray with a coffee pot, cream jug, sugar bowl and two coffee cups. Not mugs this time. It looked a much nicer set-up now that she was supplying the boss.

'Here we are, this will make you feel more at home.' She looked at Ray. 'I can feel those nerves radiating off you. Don't worry, you're in safe hands here.' A natural smile lit up her face. It travelled to her eyes and Ray felt a sliver of guilt for what he was about to do to her life, but reminded himself of Billy's brother, and of Mrs Kayani's dead husband.

He jumped up. 'Thank you, Lisa. That last cup you gave me has gone through me.' He paused, tried for a sheepish look. His acting skills being put to the test. SCD10 wouldn't be taking him on any time soon. 'And the nerves, probably, so I need a men's room. Do you have one close by I can use?'

Rusnac tipped his head to the side. Still relaxed. This didn't fill Ray with any level of ease. Why was he so comfortable having him here, knowing who he was? He obviously had a plan. Ray needed to keep his wits about him.

'Of course.' Adams placed the tray on the coffee table and walked towards the door. 'This way, I'll take you.' She gave Rusnac a smile. He returned it. Ray followed her to a small cubicle toilet a couple of doors down. Adams left with a breezy wave of a hand.

He had to work fast. And quietly.

Ray strained an ear for footsteps having followed from the room he had vacated. He heard none. He yanked the phone out his pocket and dialled Jain. It rang and rang and rang. Come on, come on. Ray's nerves were frayed but there was no response. He had no time to leave a message because he had no idea when Jain would pick it up. He needed support here and he needed it now.

He dialled Elaine.

She picked up on the second ring.

'Guv? I thought you were –'

He cut her off. 'Elaine, listen to me. Don't interrupt, this is important. Whatever you feel, we'll deal with it later, I promise.' His voice was low. Urgent. 'But you have to listen and pay attention.'

'Okay, I'm worried, but I'm listening.'

'Grab a pen and paper while I talk,' he started, and heard shuffling and a drawer opening. 'I'm at a temporary office building off Cottenham Park Road, just before Cranford Close …' There was a huff of air as Elaine was about to jump in with, he knew, the obvious statement about it not being the place he said he was going, but she stuck to the plan to not interrupt. 'I need you to organise back-up here right now. Everyone.' He paused; this would be difficult, telling her, opening up.

He listened again, out into the office space he was in. It was quiet. He took a chance and opened the door a crack; the corridor was empty. He closed the door and pushed the bolt across. He had to be quick or Rusnac would come and search for him.

'SCO19, dogs, forensics, we might even need the Air Support Unit, depending on what happens. I'm with Rusnac. He's the guy who killed Billy.'

Elaine couldn't contain the silence any longer. 'You didn't pick him out, how can he be? What are you talking about?'

'Elaine.' His voice was sharp. He had to do this quick, he only had a few more seconds. He had to tear that sticking plaster off and he'd check the wound underneath later. For now, he needed the back-up and he needed Rusnac in custody. 'After our accident, I was diagnosed with, the simple word is "face blindness". I can't recognise people. I'll explain more on it later as well. But I can recognise this guy by his voice because he spoke to me before he shot Billy and I'm telling you this is him. I'm in a meeting with him and I don't know what he plans to do with me because he knows who I am, so please, get on with it.'

There was a quiet gasp at the other end. Ray couldn't wait any longer. He closed the call, peered out of the door again, quickly deleted the one-call log entry and walked out of the men's room and back towards Rusnac.

78

Rusnac was about to go and find the cop when he quite calmly walked back into the room. As though he didn't have a care in the world. Or rather, as though the only care he had in the world was the fictitious concern to sell his kidney. What Rusnac wanted to know was, why he would come here if he couldn't identify him? It seemed such a fruitless act.

But who was he to agonise over the decisions of others when he was in possession of facts that the cop didn't even realise he knew.

It was called having the upper hand.

A position he liked to be in.

What did he do with him now? So far, he'd played along with his little game. Maybe he was waiting for him to admit to who he was, to jump down his throat again and threaten his family. But where was the fun in that when he knew what he knew now?

Rusnac still needed answers before he acted. The decision before him was a large one. Not one he would take lightly. The outcome of today would have repercussions. Rusnac needed to work out what he was willing to put up with, deal with, out of those repercussions.

'Tell me, Mr Gordon –' he leaned forward '– how did you find us?'

'It wasn't difficult.' The cop stayed in role. 'I'd heard about this kind of thing. I'm quite technically aware, so I knew the first place to search was the dark net. Once in there I was given the address I needed. And boy, I'm glad I was. It couldn't have come at a better time.' He picked up his coffee. Eyed Rusnac over his drink. What was he thinking?

'And you never answered my question about support. As I said, it's a difficult journey, this one; do you have support or are you in this alone?'

Ray smiled. 'Oh, I have support. In the background, you understand.' He paused, drew in his eyebrows. 'I hope it's still there.'

79

Ray felt weirdly hemmed in, sitting there in front of Rusnac. He was free to stand and roam as he wished, but he had no idea if Elaine had understood or believed his message. He hoped she would deal with the problem at hand and speak to him about his deceit afterwards. But what she had to do first was explain it all to Jain and get all the troops on board, to get them all tripping out on the say-so of his voice identification. Especially after he had already officially failed to ID Rusnac once.

He had no idea if help was on its way.

'It's quite good for me,' Rusnac spoke again, 'that you did come alone today, though I'm sorry to hear you may have troubles.'

Ray looked out of the window at the still empty parking lot.

Rusnac shifted in his seat. Pushed himself up and stood. 'You see, it gives us a chance to talk, because I think you need to know all the facts yourself today.' He walked to the sideboard that the television was sitting on and pulled open a drawer. 'Isn't that right, Mr Gordon?'

'Yes. Yes, of course,' Ray answered to Rusnac's back.

'And I want you to have all the answers today,' Rusnac turned. In his hand was a Glock.

This was now the third time Ray had seen it in his hand, and the second time it had been pointed directly at him. He rose from his seat.

'Sit back down ...' Rusnac waved the gun, indicating the sofa. '... Mr Gordon,' he said, curling his upper lip, 'I think we need to have a chat, don't you?'

Ray did as he was told. He was confused: he'd identified Rusnac, he'd known it was him, but why the games from Rusnac, why hadn't he been aggressive from the start?

Rusnac perched himself on the arm of the sofa, his left leg planted firmly on the floor, his right leg bent and swinging, relaxed, as though talking to a friend.

With a gun in his hand.

'So,' he started, 'What brings you here, all alone?'

'You do,' Ray answered.

'And how do you know who I am?'

Ray was confused.

Rusnac laughed. 'You think I'm stupid, cop? That I couldn't figure out what happened? You couldn't recognise me in that line-up, that's why I was released.' He laughed again. 'Something wrong with cop's head.'

The idea that he'd figured this out shocked Ray. He'd underestimated the man in front of him. 'There's nothing wrong with my hearing though.'

Rusnac stood. Gun firmly pointed at Ray. 'What do you mean?'

'You're so smart, you figure it out.' He needed to keep him talking. He wasn't sure how much of a good idea it was to antagonise him though, as he was the one holding the gun.

Rusnac paced across the room, keeping the Glock in the general direction of Ray. He paced back again. Then across and back. Ray watched. And waited.

'Empty your pockets.' Rusnac waved the gun lower, towards Ray's jeans pockets.

Ray stood, pulled out his wallet from the right pocket, minus his warrant card, dropped it on the sofa. Stared at Rusnac.

'And the other one.'

With a sigh he pulled out the phone and dropped that on the sofa.

'No. No. Hand that to me. I didn't think I had to worry about you after I threatened your family, but you've been stupid, cop. Now I worry.'

80

Ray picked up the phone and handed it to Rusnac, who poked the screen with a stubby finger.

'Pin code.' Rusnac pushed the phone back to Ray, who took it and put his thumb on the home button, bringing the phone to life.

Rusnac yanked the phone back and tapped through to the call log. The last had been made four hours ago.

Ray smiled to himself.

Rusnac checked the text messages. There were no new messages. Rusnac dropped the phone to the floor and stamped on the screen. A web of fractures spun out. The glass crunching like splintering ice as it broke underfoot.

'What did you mean, there's nothing wrong with your hearing? And what have you done?' His voice was raised now, but he wasn't shouting. Ray suspected Adams was still in the building.

'Exactly what I said. I came to find you. I can recognise you by your voice. Now you've confirmed the identification by pointing a gun at me. Are we going to do this all again?' He sounded way surer of himself than he felt, which gave him hope that Elaine had listened and assistance was on its way.

'I told you that you'd pay if you didn't leave this alone, and yet you come. You really are stupid.' The gun bobbed in his hand. He was nervous. 'Come, we walk.'

Shit. 'What? Where?'

'Where I tell you is where. Move.' Again the gun was a pointer, and this time it was to the door.

Damn, the back-up was on its way here. They needed to stay here. Ray sat down. 'You want to talk, we'll talk.'

The metal was cool against his temple. Rusnac's breath smelled of shellfish and rosemary. An undercurrent of rot. It drifted across his face. Invasive as it permeated his olfactory senses. Ray held his breath.

'I said move. Now get up and move, unless you would prefer to resolve our issue here and now.' His voice was barely above a whisper.

Ray stood. There were no options. He had to move and hope they didn't go far, or that his team and any other support en route knew what they were doing.

They filed out of the room and turned right, towards the end of the corridor, where a fire-exit door was located. An exit where Adams wouldn't be able to see them and therefore wouldn't be able to inform attending cops where they'd gone.

'Through.' Rusnac indicated with the gun again.

Ray pushed on the bar handle and opened the door. There was no screeching alarm, just a pregnant howling silence from beyond. He felt the muzzle of the gun push into the small of his back. Rusnac wanted him to walk. He walked.

The day was still bright and warm, blue was the colour palette that lay over them.

'Keep walking.' He was a man of few words now that they had the reintroductions out of the way.

Ray looked around; it was a closed in area. 'Where to?'

'Ahead, push through the bush.'

There was an evergreen bush that partitioned the wasteland area they were parked in – the area that the office building was set up in – and the woods beyond. It was about waist height, and thin. Though evergreen, it had still lost some of its life through the winter months. It wouldn't be difficult to get through. Ray needed to engage with Rusnac. 'What are your plans?'

'I'll let you know when we get there. Just walk.' Another prod.

Ray moved. Gravel crunched.

'You know, killing a cop will bring a lot more pressure to bear on you than it did when you killed Billy. Bad as that sounds, it's true. We turn up to protect people and we don't like it when one of ours is killed doing that job.'

'You don't leave me with a lot of choice.' Another push in the back with the muzzle.

So that was what he planned. 'You do have a choice. You've already threatened me once –'

'Look how that paid off.'

Ray twisted sideways, pushed with his hip through the woody bush. Felt it snag on his clothes. Try to grab hold of him, detain him. He wished it would. He wished it had the power to stop this.

'Yeah, but I think I get the message this time. You're serious, yeah.'

'Oh, I'm serious.'

He was through, into knee-high grass and uneven ground that ran out in front of him towards the woods of Wimbledon Hill Park. Rusnac pushed his way through the bush behind him. 'Well, now you know I can't identify you. All we have to do is keep out of each other's way.' Ray turned. Looked Rusnac in the face. He didn't even register as the person he'd been talking to in the building not five minutes ago. Damn – if the guy even realised how bad it was.

'We're past that. You're in my way. Like a bad … what do you guys call it? … coin. Like a bad coin.'

'Penny.'

'What'

'I'm like a bad penny.'

The area started to thicken, trees grouping together. They pushed on. They trudged for about ten, maybe fifteen minutes. Ray tried to talk to Rusnac but he had made his decision and was silent. He threatened to put a bullet in Ray's head then and there if he didn't stop talking.

Ray stopped.

His thoughts went to Helen. To Alice and Matthew. How his children would grow up without a father. How he hoped Helen would tell them great things about him, but encourage them to grow and flourish without him, not shrink and fall.

Then he thought of Celeste. How he'd let her down. How their relationship hadn't been strong enough to weather his condition.

But then his mind was back with Helen and the children. He couldn't summon up images of them, but the warmth of feeling flooded his heart.

'Stop here,' Rusnac said behind him.

Ray stopped and turned. Again, the picture in front of him brought back no memory of anyone he had ever spoken with. He'd never be able, as he'd proven, to pick this guy out in an ID procedure.

'This is where we sort it out.' He levelled the gun at Ray's chest.

81

The cop yammered on like an old woman. Rusnac was fed up of hearing it. He'd ordered him to stop. Had to threaten to shoot him on the spot if he didn't keep quiet. Not that he was one to make such rash decisions.

His brain was running at a speed he could barely keep up with. A damn mess. What the hell would he tell the Russians? They would find out about the murder of a cop. But could he let this guy run roughshod over his organisation and everything he had created? He'd already threatened his life and that of his family once, and the guy had still turned up here, posing as a patient. The man must have a death wish.

Well, he'd grant him his wish if it would produce the better outcome.

The cop didn't care about himself. He obviously didn't care about the lives of his family either. He'd proved reckless.

Rusnac couldn't wrap his head around that. He'd come to this godforsaken country because of his Mama. He would do anything to keep her alive. He'd done everything he could in Moldova and he'd pushed himself to make the operation work here so he could send money back for her to have the anti-rejection drugs she needed. He spoke to her every week. Made sure they kept their side of the bargain. Which they were. She was well, thriving. Worried about him, as any Mama was. Nagged him about what he was up to, what he had got himself involved in to keep her well. Told him off nearly every time she spoke to him, but he didn't care, hearing her voice was enough for him. Kept him focused.

And yet, this guy, he'd willingly put his family at risk, and for what? What did this matter to him on a personal level? Nothing. It was a job. Why did they insist on pushing all the boundaries for a job? He would never understand that. These Brits, they didn't understand family, hardship, honour, duty, and, behind it all, real fear. Their lives were so easy and this made them stupid. Docile.

What an idiot.

As Rusnac placed one large foot in front of the other, going deeper into the wood, out of the sunshine, into the darkness, away from people, civilisation, he had no idea what he would do. On the one hand the cop was right. He wouldn't be able to pick him out of a line-up, he'd proved that. But he'd also proved he was incapable of letting this lie.

And he didn't need the interference.

He pulled him up. Levelled the gun at him.

82

His stomach twisted. Ray looked around. He couldn't hear sirens or see blue lights slicing up the day. His time was up and there was no one here to prevent it. No one here to witness his time. No one here to say a final goodbye to, apologise to, give his heart to. This was how he was going out. Alone in the woods.

He only had himself to blame. He hadn't shared any of what he had known or what he was about to do.

Under his foot a twig cracked in the quiet. The sound loud in his head, like a firecracker, it broke through the blood that pounded in his ears.

The woods had darkened. The daylight blocked by the overhead tree canopies. The blue of the spring day, now a haze of green, black and grey. It felt damp. Ray's vision tunnelled. The edges greying out, the gun, the hand, the finger on the trigger, the face he didn't know.

'You don't have to do this,' he said again.

Rusnac took a step closer. The barrel of the gun so close it blurred. 'Oh, but you've left me little choice. You couldn't leave well enough alone and I don't trust that you would leave it if I left you here now.'

He was going to do it. Pull the trigger. The option of talking his way out of this was slipping away. Like water through his fingers. There was no assistance coming. He was on his own.

It was over and only he could decide how it would go. The man he would be.

Ray stepped forward, swung his right hand up and grabbed hold of the gun by the muzzle, pushing upwards as he did, using all his body weight and momentum. He wouldn't go down without a fight. He wouldn't stand there and wait for it to happen.

Rusnac's mouth opened in an Oh. A grunt escaped. He stumbled.

Ray continued to push. His hand tight on the Glock. His heart thundering in his chest. He forced it up and back. Hoping to take it out of Rusnac's hand or at least remove himself from its aim.

They lurched backwards.

Rusnac fought to keep his grip on the weapon. His free hand went up. He pulled down on the trigger and it exploded, crashing through the quiet of the wood. Birds scattered from the tops of the trees in a mass of beating fright. The Glock recoiled, neither Ray nor Rusnac had a proper grip on it now, and they fell to the damp dark ground.

Ray's ears rang. The shot echoed through his skull. Bouncing against the surface like a ping-pong ball. It made him dizzy. Disorientated. But he couldn't give up. He shook his head to clear the noise and static. Fought to orientate himself.

He'd landed on top of Rusnac, who was on his side. He'd been here before. He couldn't allow the same outcome, because this time Rusnac wasn't going to walk away and leave him standing there.

The Glock had slipped from the grasp of both men as they tumbled and fought to retain their hold. It had flown free, and was just out of reach on the ground.

Ray dug his elbow deep into Rusnac's clavicle. Forced it into a sharp point and leaned in. He had to keep him down. Rusnac howled. Ray knew from his training that this was a sensitive area of the body and that the amount of pressure he was applying would be causing the man below him some serious pain.

But before he could consider his next move, what to do about the weapon, how to restrain Rusnac, there were stars, and a searing pain jackhammered into the already saturated space in his skull as Rusnac smashed his head up into Ray's nose. Yet again blood erupted, spattering over Rusnac. In the shock Ray was forced onto his back by the strength of the blow.

Rusnac rolled over, reached out, clawed forward on hands and knees, fingers tearing up the woodland floor. Ray reached out for his ankle. He had to stop him reaching the gun. Rusnac looked back, shook his leg free of the fragile grasp Ray had, lifted himself up onto all fours, and forced a foot out at Ray's head, his boot connecting with his cheek and temple. White-hot pain starburst up into Ray's eye, blinding him. This was a fight for his life but the energy was being stripped from him second by slow second. He collapsed back down onto the soft damp ground.

And now there was no fight to be had. Rusnac turned to face him, sat up, and with the Glock clasped firmly between two hands, pointed the gun straight at him.

Ray lay there. Blood smeared over his face, his clothes. His cheek already twice the size it should be and his head containing a poorly orchestrated brass band.

It was over for him. This was where it would end. With him as a mess on the ground. But he'd put up a fight. They'd see that. They'd be able to tell Helen that, at least. He was filthy and bloodied.

Rusnac was grunting as heavily as Ray was. They sounded like a couple of pigs on the floor of the wood. Ray's nose was stuffed up with blood; he turned his head to the side and spat. Blood and spittle dropped to the ground in thick heavy globs.

'You think you can beat me?' asked Rusnac, heaving with the effort of getting his breath back. 'You stupid?'

'Obviously.' Ray spat again. 'But c'mon, I don't recognise you. There's no need to do this. I think I take you seriously now.' This was his one chance. To persuade Rusnac of the truth of the matter. Walk away with his life and maybe figure out how the team could take him down another way.

'Now. Now is too late. You cause trouble. I don't need trouble.' Rusnac used one hand to push himself to a standing position. He stepped back from Ray.

Ray lifted his chin to see him. To see the barrel of the gun looking down at him. Boy, he never imagined it would be like this.

'You have to go. You cause too much trouble for me. I gave you chance. You screw it up.' Rusnac's decision was made. Ray could hear it in his voice. Flat and determined. His arm shifted to point the Glock at his head.

Then it exploded.

83

It was as though the world had exploded in slow motion. So much so that at first Ray didn't know what had happened.

There was a loud crack that tore through the surrounding woodland, rupturing the quiet part of Ray's brain that was succumbing to his imminent demise and scattering the brass band that had taken up residence.

Rusnac's eyes widened in shock as the sound echoed around and through them both as if it was part of them. Invading the space they had carved out in the world for this moment to themselves.

Another piercing crack. And another.

The sound shattered the silence of the woods.

Then Rusnac's mouth dropped. His hand quivered in mid-air before he split open and blood sprayed out. His arm dropped, and all at once he was falling. Down onto the mulchy ground. It was sudden. Ungainly. Ugly. Bloody.

Ray felt damp.

Shocked.

He'd been about to die at the hands of Rusnac in the woods without talking to his family, his friends.

And now – now the world had turned upside down.

He coughed, his throat felt clogged and irritated. He spat and bloody mucus with slices of hell knew what in it were expelled from his mouth. He spat again and cleared some more. He pushed his hands against the ground to heave himself upwards; they were red, speckled with the palest white he had ever seen. That was his hand. The rest was red. Bloody. Rusnac.

He looked across at the man who had been about to kill him, who was now in a heap on the floor, unmoving.

Never to move again.

Ray looked around him, confused.

He was being approached by men in black combats tucked into black boots, with black jackets and black helmets, carrying guns still aimed at the prone figure on the ground. They reached him and kicked the Glock away. Checked him, and nodded.

Two came up to Ray and he was hoisted up from under his arms.

'Sir? You okay?'

'I'm good. Thank you,' he said as he regained his balance, standing in a puddle of dark fluid. He stepped away, moved around the mess that was once Vova Rusnac and made his way towards the waiting group behind the black-clad officers. He recognised a bundle of curls. Next to the curls was a male, wide but short, and a female wagging a finger at him, and another, who stood, one arm across her chest, the other hand up to her mouth, biting her nails. And striding out to meet him was a slim, smartly dressed Asian male. Ray took a deep breath.

Things were about to change.

84

Watching from a distance was painful for Elaine. Being held back by the armed guys when all she wanted to do was run to him and punch him in his stupid unrecognising face was unbearable. Hearing the shots ring out and not being able to see what had happened nearly broke her in two. Her nails were taking the brunt of the stress. How could he not have said anything to her? He had the perfect opportunity at the hospital. Did he think she would have ratted him out? After what they'd been through together? The guy had a block for a head.

And he'd well and truly gone and proved it now.

Telling Jain had been one of the most difficult things she had ever had to do. She felt as though she was letting him down, but she had needed to do it and needed to do it with speed.

Jain had remained dispassionate. Not a flicker of emotion crossed his face. She imagined what Ray must feel like on a daily basis. Once she finished her quick run-through of what Ray had told her, he picked up his phone and barked commands and requests through to the relevant departments and told them all to get their gear and get moving.

They hadn't needed to be told twice.

And now she stood here.

Ray half walked, half stumbled out of the woods. He was covered in blood and Elaine's stomach jumped into her throat. But he was walking, and walking unaided.

As he got closer, she could see that his cheek was swollen and bruised under the blood. He'd been in a battle. The punch she owed him would have to wait.

Jain walked towards him. She wanted to turn away, but couldn't stop watching.

85

'Ray.' Jain reached out a hand. Ray clasped it. It kept him steady. Upright.

Jain pulled him towards him and threw an arm around his shoulders, patting him hard on his back. Three solid slaps. 'I'm glad you're okay.' There was a rasp to his voice that wasn't usually there. If Ray had been trying to identify Prabhat by voice it would have made him hard to identify. But Ray knew it was him. The scent of his cinnamon-undertoned aftershave wafted up his nose.

'I'm damn glad you turned up.' Ray returned the hug. Grateful for the contact, the warm human contact, the life-saving.

'I'm glad we turned up in time too. It looked like it was a close call. We nearly lost you, mate.'

'I'm acutely aware of that.' A strangled laugh that turned into a cough. He bent over, hands on knees, and spat onto the ground. Still blood and bits of solid matter evacuating his mouth. Bits he didn't want to think about. 'There was a nurse here. Lisa Adams?'

'Yeah, we got her. Uniform have taken her back to the station.'

'Great, I was worried she might have already left.'

Jain stepped back and studied Ray. 'You know we need to talk about how it got to this point, don't you?'

Ray nodded. Too exhausted to do much else. His head was killing. His mouth – well, he didn't want to think about that too much. And his ribs were sore as well. His old injuries didn't take much of a knock to flare up and cause him pain.

'We need to talk about it, me and you. As friends.'

'I know.' He nodded again.

'But also, I need to talk to you as your supervisor. I'm going to have to refer you to occupational health for an assessment, Ray.'

He nodded again. Words wouldn't come right now. They walked towards his colleagues. Prabhat's arm hanging around Ray's shoulder.

86

Ray looked up from his desk. Studied the woman in the doorway. No curls. No ring. He went to her face. It was Elaine. 'Come on in, Elaine.'

'How do you do that?' she asked as she walked into his office and closed the door behind her.

It had been a week since she'd found out about his prosopagnosia, since that awful day, and this was the first time she had come to speak to him. He hadn't wanted to force the issue with her. He'd left the ball in her court.

'They're called identifiers,' he told her as dread crept over him. 'Every person I know has something about them that I store in my memory to identify them by. It might take me a while, as I have to cycle through the identifier box, but it's quite effective.'

Elaine dropped into the seat in front of his desk and Ray closed down the computer.

'You knew I would come and see you?'

'Yes.'

'So – why didn't you tell me? I get that you didn't want to tell everyone, that you were trying to deal with it and not tell the job, but after what we went through together once already …'

There was a heavy silence. It expanded in the small office. Filling the space. Suffocating.

Ray broke through it, his voice quiet. 'That was why I couldn't tell you, Elaine.'

She looked at him. Cocked her head to one side. Drew her eyes together. 'I don't understand.'

'Your identifier ...'

She looked puzzled for a moment, then said, 'My scar.'

Ray felt as though someone had punched him in the guts. 'Yes.'

And then she smiled at him and he could see the smile travel right up to her eyes. 'I don't mind my scar, guv, I'm confident in my own body. This scar doesn't detract from who I am, it simply shows where I've been. My husband doesn't love me any less, I don't love me any less, and my friends don't love me any less. And I certainly don't blame you.'

Ray's face had paled.

Elaine continued, 'There was not one single action you could have taken differently that would have changed the outcome of that day. How could I blame you? You need to stop blaming yourself. And if that's the way you identify me, then that's the way you identify me.' Her smile widened.

Ray couldn't speak. It wasn't that he was choked. He admired the strength of this woman in front of him.

'Anyway,' she carried on, 'how's life desk-surfing?' She was positively relaxed now she had her answers.

'Ah.' He was on firmer ground now too. 'I love it.' He grumbled, 'The occ health appointment isn't for another month so I'll be stuck inside, unable to interact with real people for all that time, and then longer while they decide what to do with me.'

'You brought down the whole trading in human organs ring though.' Elaine leaned forward in her chair. 'Adams provided the names of those she knew, and those in turn gave any extra names of those they knew. None of them were scared once they heard Rusnac was dead. Providing helpful information was in their best interest.' She paused. 'That has to count for something, right?'

'It counts as policing, Elaine. I can't see faces.' He scrubbed his own face with his hands. 'Who knows if they'll let me stay on as a copper.'

'What will you do?'

'First I'll wait and see what happens. If the job decides I have to be medically retired, I'll have to go. I've had a good run.'

Elaine looked aghast. 'But you've done so well, none of us knew.'

'But I did put the investigation at risk.'

She leaned back in her chair again. Deflated.

'I've figured out so many things this past couple of months, Elaine. Priorities. Life. When I was in the woods with Rusnac, well, let's just say I saw a lot more then than I've been able to see for a while.'

If you enjoyed Dead Blind but haven't yet received your FREE copy of Three Weeks Dead which is the prequel to the DI Hannah Robbins series, then you can claim it on Rebecca's website at rebeccabradleycrime.com

Acknowledgements

This book means a lot to me and I couldn't have written without the help of some very generous people who gave their time to help me.

My thanks go to Sharon Bolton for her help and support in researching the transplant process. To Marina Sofia for spending time talking to me about Moldova. Lisa Cutts for homicide team supervisor cover procedure. (Yes, I still have to check some things myself.) Rosie Claverton for advice on Ray's injuries after his accident.

Elaine Aldred for being early reader. Jane Isaac and David Jackson for their encouragement from the start, before I had even written a word of this book. I told them the idea and they pushed me on and read an early draft.

Huge thanks go to Sarah Manning for bashing it into shape and being an ongoing supporter. Even if it at times felt like an uphill battle.

Thank you to Anne O'Hara for checking my continuity

Thank you to Martin Ouvry and Julia Gibbs for their editing expertise.

To all my early readers and book bloggers, I thank you, for your time and your continued enthusiasm. Readers make the book world go around.

To my family, without whom I can never create any book, because they give me the space and time and love to do this. I love you.

And finally I have to thank Dr Brad Duchaine, Jo Livingston and Bob Cockshott for their invaluable time, help and experience with prosopagnosia. I really could not have created this book without them.

Books in the DI Hannah Robbins series;

Three Weeks Dead (Prequel novella)
Shallow Waters
Made to be Broken
Fighting Monsters

About the Author

Rebecca Bradley is a retired police detective who lives in the UK with her family and two Cockapoo's Alfie and Lola, who both keep her company while she writes. She needs to drink copious amounts of tea to function throughout the day and if she could, she would survive on a diet of tea and cake.

If you enjoyed Dead Blind and would be happy to leave a review online that would be much appreciated, as word of mouth is often how other readers find new books.

Have you claimed your FREE prequel novella, Three Weeks Dead, yet? A young DC, Sally Poynter, has to get through to a desperate husband before he commits a crime that will have far-reaching consequences. You can claim it at Rebeccabradleycrime.com

When you Sign up to the Readers Club mailing list you not only receive a FREE novella, but you will also receive early previews, exclusive extracts and regular giveaways. As well as keeping up to date with new releases.

37350844R00209

Printed in Great Britain
by Amazon